Praise for Cleo Coyle's
New York Times Bestselling Coffeehouse Mysteries

"As bracing as a great cup of espresso and as flavorful as one of the delicious recipes she includes."

—*RT Book Reviews* (top pick)

"Coyle's Coffeehouse books are superb . . . Highly recommended for all mystery collections."

—*Library Journal* (starred review)

"Fun and gripping."　　　　　　　　　—*The Huffington Post*

"A delicious mystery!"　　　　　　　　　—*Woman's World*

"Clever style . . . Delicious-sounding recipes . . . Action and energy."　　　　　　　　　—*Booklist*

"A tasty tale of multigenerational crime and punishment lightened by the Blend's frothy cast of lovable eccentrics."

—*Publishers Weekly*

"Clare and company are some of the most vibrant characters I've ever read."　　　　　　　　　—*Mystery Scene*

"A realistic depiction of New York City high and low life . . . Recipes, romance, and caffeine-fueled detection add up to a lively tale."　　　　　　　　　—*Kirkus Reviews*

"What a pleasure to read a book by this author."

—*Portland Book Review*

continued . . .

BILLIONAIRE BLEND

CLEO COYLE

BERKLEY PRIME CRIME, NEW YORK

THE BERKLEY PUBLISHING GROUP
Published by the Penguin Group
Penguin Group (USA) LLC
375 Hudson Street, New York, New York 10014

USA • Canada • UK • Ireland • Australia • New Zealand • India • South Africa • China

penguin.com

A Penguin Random House Company

BILLIONAIRE BLEND

A Berkley Prime Crime Book / published by arrangement with the author

For information, address: The Berkley Publishing Group,
a division of Penguin Group (USA) LLC,
375 Hudson Street, New York, New York 10014.

ISBN: 978-0-425-25551-3

PUBLISHING HISTORY
Berkley Prime Crime hardcover edition / December 2013
Berkley Prime Crime mass-market edition / August 2014

PRINTED IN THE UNITED STATES OF AMERICA

10 9 8 7 6 5 4 3 2

Cover illustration by Cathy Gendron.
Cover design and logo by Rita Frangie.
Interior text design by Kristin del Rosario.

To Antonio A. Alfonsi—
A daughter may outgrow your lap, but she
will never outgrow your heart. I love you, Dad.
Rest now, and I will see you again.

Money often costs too much.

—Ralph Waldo Emerson

PROLOGUE

~~~~~~~~~~~~~~~~~~~~~~~~~~~~~~~~

> *Should I kill myself, or have a cup of coffee?*
> —ALBERT CAMUS

"**ABOUT** *time!*"

The words were not spoken, they were screeched. Bianca Hyde's shrill echo traveled down the quiet hallway of the Beverly Palms Hotel in an octave seldom heard outside of nursery school playgrounds or tween soccer matches.

Another potential scene, *thought the Visitor.* How charming.

At one o'clock in the afternoon, Bianca's puce lipstick was smeared, her platinum hair sleep-mussed, her designer halter stained and wrinkled. Clearly, she'd been drinking (again) . . .

"So come in already!" Wheeling backward, Bianca released the self-closing door.

The Visitor lurched to catch the edge and wedge it back open. The slab of northwest maple was heavy and thick. Thick enough to absorb a scream? *The Visitor began to wonder . . .*

Inside the posh space, words were exchanged, bottles shoved over, caffeine ordered and delivered. Only after the room service waitress had come and gone did the real conversation begin—

"You're making things far too complicated," the Visitor argued. "The solution is simple: Occam's Razor."

"You want me to shave?"

"Occam's Razor is a scientific rule of thumb, a heuristic."

"A what?"

"Just go to rehab, Binky. All things being equal, it's the only way to repair this relationship. If you fix what's broken, all will be well . . ."

But Bianca didn't agree. She wanted her freedom. And she wanted more money; lots more. The demands came after the whining and cajoling; then tears dried up and demands became threats.

"I'll ruin you!" she promised. "I have the proof; you know it. I can ruin you for good!"

"Then you'll ruin us both . . ."

The Visitor's tone remained reasonable, but Ms. Hyde never had much use for reason. Despite her refined surroundings, the spoiled little plaything had cultivated a savage soul.

When her own threats were returned in kind, she lunged for a bottle. Not a room service baby but its grown-up sister. Strangling the neck, she swung it like a club.

The Visitor dodged the blow, simultaneously shoving and tripping the girl, perhaps a tad too violently.

On the way down, Bianca met the coffee table—or rather, her forehead did. The flow of red stained everything—the white blond hair and porcelain skin; the perfect breasts in the halter top; the cream-colored carpet; even the long-stemmed Blue Velvets, once stunning and rare, now a spilled tangle of petals among thorns . . .

The Visitor had become a slayer. For a moment, sheer panic set in. The impulse to dial 911. Then Occam's Razor came sharply to mind. All things being equal, the coffee table had done what the coffee could not—

Shut her up.

Risks were considered, of course, loose ends and evidence. The Slayer could handle these. This mess could be tidied quickly, a new strategy devised, and in a few short hours, all would be well, for the best solution to this problem was to leave it exactly where it fell.

One

As long as there was coffee in the world, how bad could things be?

—JUDITH RUMELT

"Guess where I am? You can't imagine . . ."

Pressing the phone to my ear, I waited for Mike Quinn's gravelly voice to ride a cellular wave up the Eastern Seaboard.

"Given the choice," he said, "I'd rather imagine . . ."

That shouldn't have surprised me. After all, Michael Ryan Francis Quinn was a decorated narcotics detective, and if there was one thing the NYPD looked for when recruiting from their uniformed force, it was imagination—that and "inquisitiveness, insight, and an eye for detail." (According to Quinn, the New York brass referred to these as "the four *I*'s," although I had pointed out the last one started with an *E*.)

For the past six months, Quinn had been working in Washington, DC, where a U.S. Attorney had drafted him for a special assignment. He wasn't permitted to tell me much about his Justice Department job, although I did deduce his Federal Triangle desk phone had caller ID because he always answered my rings with a husky hello reserved only for me.

Just the sound of his voice relieved the tension I'd been feeling about the night ahead. Of course, I didn't have a clue what was *really* ahead. If I had, I might have gone straight home and pulled the covers over my eyes.

In a short space of time, I'd be bribing a Bomb Squad lieutenant, cracking a mathematician's seventeen-digit password, and conjuring culinary ideas for a billionaires' potluck. That I could handle. But battling a giant octopus; raiding a forbidden coffee plantation; defusing a nitro-packed knapsack; stopping a Slayer (while working with one); and fixing my daughter's love life? I think even 007 would have flinched.

At this point in my story, however, my life was manageable, even pretty nice. I was sitting on hand-rubbed leather in a private limo, and a good cop was purring in my ear.

"Let's see now . . ." Quinn continued. "I'm imagining you in your duplex above the coffeehouse. You just stepped out of the shower, and I'm holding your robe. I've got a nice blaze going in the bedroom, the champagne's poured, and I'm about to—"

"Mike!"

"Yes?"

I glanced at the glass partition separating me from the male chauffeur. It wasn't raised all the way.

Okay, phone sex in front of an audience (even an audience of one) might have been acceptable for your average world-weary urbanite—and, yes, after living in the Big, Bad Apple for years, I was weary enough for any middle-aged single mom. But I was still my nonna's granddaughter. (Not that my dear daughter would agree. I could just hear her now: "That's why my generation does *sexting*, Mom! Type it out and it's totally private!" *Right, honey. And nobody shares stored data in cyberspace.*)

"I'm not at home," I explained to Quinn. "I'm on my way to dinner. You'll never guess where—"

"You better just tell me, Clare. I have a conference call in twenty."

The "boyfriend voice" was gone, the warmth chilling into a tone I knew far too well—stoic, emotionless cop.

I should have replied with something generally reassuring, like: *"I miss you"* (which I did); *"I wish you were here"* (ditto); or even . . . *"On your next visit, I'm baking you up a Triple-Chocolate Italian Cheesecake like the one you inhaled on New Year's Eve"* (which I planned to).

But I didn't say any of those things. My excitement level was so high that I simply blurted the news—

"I'm riding in a chauffeured limo, on my way to dinner at the Source Club!"

The silence stretched on so long I was sure our connection was lost.

"Mike?"

"You're pulling my leg."

"I'm not pulling anything."

I couldn't blame the man for doubting my words. Even I had trouble believing it. The Source Club was one of the most elite enclaves in Manhattan. With my anemic bank account, I was lucky to get into Sam's Club, let alone a zillionaires' club.

"So what's the story? Did your former mother-in-law give up and sell the Village Blend to a national chain?"

"Bite your tongue."

"You inherited a fortune from a lost relative?" He grunted. "Maybe I'd better get you to the altar already—in handcuffs, if necessary."

"It's nothing like that, and I'd rather you kept those handcuffs on your belt, if you don't mind. The last time you used them on me, I needed an ice pack."

"Are you fishing for another apology, or another bunch of flowers?"

"Neither . . . although I did love the daffodils and white tulips."

"I'm glad," he said. And I was, too, because the warm tone was back, and on that blustery evening in late January, I needed all the warmth I could get.

Outside, frosty flurries were beginning to fall, and the inviting lights of my coffeehouse were no longer in sight; neither were the cozy pubs and intimate bistros of Greenwich Village. The golden glow of the historic district had been replaced with the silver glare of downtown skyscrapers.

"You would love the limo he sent for me, Mike. It's an antique Rolls-Royce—or is it a Bentley?"

"A Bentley *is* a Rolls, and who is he?"

"It's so British, like something the late Princess Diana would have ridden around in, but he's modernized the inside with all these gadgets—"

"I repeat, who is *he*? And how did you end up in his limousine?"

"That's kind of a long story."

"Give me the short version."

"You know part of it already. Remember that poor guy I helped out the other day?"

"The billionaire? I wouldn't call him poor, Clare."

"You know what I mean. This special dinner is his way of saying thanks."

Suddenly I was listening to a whole new dead zone. The cellular waves kept rolling up from DC, but Quinn's voice wasn't riding them.

"Maybe you'd better give me the long version," he finally said. "And start at the beginning."

"I thought you had a conference call in twenty?"

"The Los Angeles District Attorney can wait."

Uh-oh. "It's completely innocent, Mike. Why do you think I'm telling you?"

"Go on."

"You remember, don't you? This all started with a coffee drink order."

"A coffee drink order?"

"Actually, more like two dozen coffee drink orders . . ."

Two

≈≈≈≈≈≈≈≈≈≈≈≈≈≈≈≈≈≈≈≈≈≈

"He's early . . ."

With my crack-of-dawn shift over, I was about to head upstairs for a long, hot (hopefully) rejuvenating shower when Esther Best sounded her alarm—

"Like the aftertaste from a bad sidewalk hot dog, I knew he'd come back!"

"He" was the eccentric customer I'd been hearing about for going on two weeks now, and this was my first chance to see him in action.

Like clockwork, the man came in every afternoon and proceeded to drill my baristas on the prep steps of some obscure coffee drink. It's no wonder they'd labeled him the "Quiz Master."

With the coffeehouse still packed from the lunchtime crush, Esther pointed him out in our long line. At first glance, I was surprised by his appearance. Given the accounts of his perplexing behavior, I was expecting a middle-aged malcontent with Einstein hair and a shopping bag. Not so.

Nearly as tall as Quinn, the "Quiz Master" had boyishly

handsome features complete with dimpled chin, yet his expression looked determined and mature, and he carried himself like my police detective boyfriend, with confident authority.

His age was closer to thirty than twenty, so I doubted that he was an undergrad. With the intelligent look about his gaze (cold-fused to his smartphone like most of my customers his age and younger), he could have been a Ph.D. candidate, except Esther didn't recognize him from campus.

His physique appeared quite solid, not street-tough pumped, but the kind of athletic body that came with a personal trainer—well-developed swimmer's shoulders, trim waist, and a lean pair of hips clad in what appeared to be artfully faded designer denims.

He wore a common Yankees baseball cap slouched over surfer-shaggy golden locks, his bangs pushed to one side. But his shearling-collared bomber was far from common—I'd bet real money the jacket's gorgeously distressed leather was stitched together in Florence.

Finally, this guy's skin had a healthy, sun-kissed glow while most New Yorkers—from subway-trekking office workers to academics toiling in cramped college cubicles—displayed complexions with less color than the walking dead, especially in the dead of winter.

Add it all up and the sum spelled *rat*.

"Calm down," I told my staff, who were already buzzing about the man's approach. "Handle him just as you would any other difficult customer."

"You don't plan to wait on him?" Esther asked, her tone almost pleading.

"I plan to *watch* him."

Over the last six months, two major West Coast coffee chains had tried to reverse the Gold Rush by coming East to dig for consumer treasure. One of their major hurdles had been finding well-trained baristas.

This "dude" had California written all over him. Combine that with the "coffee quiz" act he'd been performing going on two weeks now, and his intentions seemed clear: he was coming here to evaluate and poach my employees.

Well, I wasn't going to stand for it, and the way I was going to accomplish that (whether Esther understood or not) was to *sit*.

Gritting my teeth, I grabbed a newly vacated stool at my own crowded espresso bar. With a sound between a huff and a grunt, Esther pushed up her black-framed glasses and set a freshly pulled espresso in front of me before her ample hips carried her off again.

"What's bugging Esther?" the man beside me asked.

When I failed to reply, Matteo Allegro's long thumbs paused over his smartphone. His espresso dark eyes studied me from under a head of bushy, black hair.

"Okay," he said, "forget Esther. What's bugging *you*?"

"Me?"

"You've got that stressed look again."

Matt was my partner in this coffee business (and former partner in the business of marriage). His great-grandfather had started this century-old concern, and over the past few years he and I had found a way to make our "new normal" work—i.e., our divorce, his remarriage, and my move from Jersey back to Manhattan to manage the family business again, this time for a piece of the equity.

No matter our past difficulties, I couldn't deny that my ex-husband was one of the most accomplished coffee hunters in the trade, and this shop was lucky to have him as its buyer.

Last night, he'd arrived from a sourcing trip looking like the subject of a documentary on South American refugees, yet he'd spent the better part of this morning using state-of-the-art software to move thousands of pounds of green coffee beans to clients around the planet.

But then Matteo Allegro always had been a collection of contrasts, and today was no exception. Stubbly and unshaven in his natty New York style, he displayed a deep, East African tan all winter. Between his hands, he worked a top-of-the-line communications device, while around his neck the open collar of his Egyptian cotton shirt revealed a worn leather cord with a tiny charm vial from the Ayacucho region of Peru. The overall effect was an undeniably attractive cross between a counterculture hipster and an Ivy League anthropology professor (who'd gone slightly native).

"Are you really interested in why I'm upset?" I asked him. "Or is this your way of changing the subject?"

(And, yes, I admit, I was the one now changing the subject, primarily to prevent Matt's typically hot head from causing a scene. If he knew what this golden-haired poacher was up to, he'd lose it. And with all the cell phone cameras in this place, I could just imagine the Facebook fallout: "Rumble in the Village! Coffee Hunter Takes Swing at West Coast Customer!")

Matt's brow wrinkled. "What are we talking about? Not all that DIY stuff you brought up this morning?"

"More like all the *major repairs* I brought up this morning . . ."

The wiring on the second floor was going glitchy, the building's wood-plank floor and brick exterior needed repairs, our espresso machine was becoming a nightmare to calibrate, and my roaster's exhaust system was begging for an overhaul.

"Given our landmark status, this is much more than a 'do-it-yourself' project," I said. "I wish it could be fixed by magic, but it can't, and I don't want to see you treat this place like you did our marriage."

"What's that supposed to mean?"

"Worthwhile things require *maintenance*."

"I told you, Clare, I'm overextended. Until my international clients pay up on this quarter's shipments, the cupboard is bare; and are we forgetting the major hit I took with the hurricane damage to my Red Hook warehouse?"

"Excuses won't fix a leaky roof. How about a short-term loan?"

"Don't you have a credit line at the bank?"

"That line is in place to support the shop's cash flow for stock and payroll. There's not enough for capital improvements."

"My mother's still the owner. Talk to her."

"I did . . ."

Unfortunately, Matt's elegant mother was on a fixed income. Oh, sure, the annuity she collected, courtesy of her late second husband, was generous, but her real assets were tied up in property, and she wasn't about to sell the Fifth Avenue penthouse she'd inherited or the artworks she'd collected over a lifetime of running this café—and I wouldn't let her, anyway. Cashing those works in for maintenance was akin to selling your baby's bronzed booties to get your toilet fixed.

A small-business loan seemed logical, but the bank officer suggested a mortgage instead, using this landmark town house as collateral.

Madame's response was a visible shudder.

"Neither a borrower nor a lender be, dear, and do you know why? Because in borrowing, you give the lender power to control you. The Village Blend is my life's legacy. I am resolved to bequeath it to you and Matteo, just as you both are resolved to leave it to your lovely daughter—my dear granddaughter. One does not cart a precious family heirloom to the pawn shop!"

"I tried talking sense into her," I assured Matt. "I told her that she was being overly cautious, but you know her history . . ."

He grunted. (Matt-speak for: *You don't have to tell me.*)

As a young Parisian girl, Matt's mother never expected German tanks to roll past the Arc de Triomphe. But they had, and in a short, brutal window of time, Madame had lost her mother, her sister, and everything she recognized as home.

Somehow she'd found the courage to survive and the spirit to build a new life in America. Like flowers in a ravaged garden, she even found the optimism to cultivate love and happiness again. But those shockingly sudden losses had altered her. Never again would she trust the wind not to sweep in and tear up everything she'd grown. As a result, she met nearly every transaction, business and personal, with a slightly skeptical eye.

On the other hand, I needed cash on the barrelhead now, and (as I'd told her) last I checked, panzers weren't blowing by the Washington Square arch.

"What did she say to that?" Matt asked.

"She told me to talk to you."

THREE

~~~~~~~~~~~~~~~~~~~~~~~~~~~~~~~~~~~~

"WELL?"

Matt said nothing, and simply refocused on his smartphone screen. He might as well have slammed down a gavel and declared, "Subject closed."

Maybe for *him*.

I was about to try again when Esther approached us.

"The Quiz Master's getting closer to the counter," she said in a whisper that wasn't. "What humiliation does he have in store for us today, I wonder?"

"Who are we talking about?" Matt asked, swinging on his stool.

"That dude in the Yank-me cap," Esther replied.

"Stop staring, both of you," I whispered (in an actual whisper).

Matt made a strange face then turned to me. "Come on, Clare, you don't know this guy?"

"No. Do you?"

Matt didn't affirm or deny it, just asked: "What's his game?"

Esther leaned in. "He started showing up two weeks ago,

armed with a mean game of Stump the Barista. Every day, he asks us if we know how to prepare a collection of obscure, off-the-menu coffee drinks—then he orders a double espresso."

"Why would he do that?" Matt asked.

"To make fools of us, but . . ." Esther snapped her fingers. "I pity the tool / who thinks he's cool—"

"Without the rap, please."

"The dude's got mental health issues, IMO, a chronic need to feel superior."

I could see why Esther held that opinion, but in my "O," the Quiz Master had stumped her the previous afternoon, and she was still smarting from the encounter. She wasn't the only one, either, judging by the speed at which Nancy Kelly, my youngest barista, scurried off to scour the bathroom.

Esther jerked her thumb in the wake of the girl's flying wheat-colored braids. "You can't blame Nancy for running. The Quiz Master took her down on his very first visit."

"What did he ask her?" Matt asked.

"If she knew how to make Norwegian Egg Coffee."

Matt glanced at me. "You've heard of it?"

"Of course. It's just Cowboy Coffee with an egg broken into it."

Esther gawked. "Why break an egg into a perfectly good pot of coffee?"

"If you do it correctly, the proteins in the egg help the grounds to flocculate—"

"To *what*?"

"Clump together," Matt supplied.

"Yes, but *why* would you do that to good coffee?" Esther pressed.

"You wouldn't," I assured her. "That method should only be used for less expensive coffees that are brewed in large quantities. The egg removes bitterness by binding to the polyphenols—"

"Ex-squeeze me!" Esther pointed to her Edgar Allan Poe tattoo. "But do I look like a chemistry major?"

"Ladies," Tuck excitedly interrupted, "he's getting *closer*!"

Lanky Louisiana-born Tucker Burton was my assistant manager—by day, anyway. When moonlight came, he was a cabaret director, playwright, veteran of off-off-Broadway, and occasional PSA announcer. With showbiz on the brain, Tuck was convinced the Quiz Master was an undercover talent scout hunting for a new reality show cast—that, or he was a Food Network producer. Either way, our resident thespian was determined to pass the audition.

Esther waved a finger at him. "You are *waay* too confident."

"He can't stump me."

"The dude who thinks he knows it all / is doomed to take the hardest fall."

"Oh, stow it, DJ Jane!"

Matt elbowed me. "Come on, Clare, you *must* know something about this guy?"

I studied him. "You say that like I should."

Before Matt could explain, Tuck waved for my attention. "How do I look, CC?" He flipped back his floppy brown mop and smoothed his apron. "He could be recording me with a hidden micro camera."

Esther rolled her eyes.

By the time the Quiz Master reached the front of the line, our coffeehouse was the picture of normalcy (as normal as we could get, anyway). Esther quietly stacked demitasse cups. Matt was hunched over his glowing smartphone screen, and a beaming Tuck greeted the ball-capped mystery man.

"Welcome back to the Village Blend, sir!" With a lilt sweeter than a pecan praline, he began rattling off some of the obscure drinks the Quiz Master had requested.

"How'd you like a Chocolate Dalmatian today? Or maybe a Lillylou? Perhaps you'd prefer a Green Eye or a *Café Noisette*? I pour a mean Peppermint *Affogato* . . ."

The Quiz Master's response was a dispassionate smile and a completely different request. "I'll tell you what I'd like—*if* you know how to make it."

"I'm sure I can. Hit me!"

"One *Yuanyang*, please."

Tucker's confident expression fell, and his narrow shoulders sank. The Quiz Master had scored another victory. He'd finally stumped my assistant manager.

Looking suddenly helpless, Tucker glanced in my direction. Matt nudged me.

"It's all right," I whispered, rising from the stool. "I've got this."

"I know you do," Matt replied, looking strangely amused.

I ignored him, threw Tuck a nod, and approached our so-called challenging customer.

It was time the Quiz Master met his match.

Four

$\infty\infty\infty\infty\infty\infty\infty\infty\infty\infty\infty\infty\infty\infty$

"Excuse me," I said in my best customer-friendly tone. "If you'll step out of the line, I'll assist you." Gritting my teeth, I motioned for him to follow me to the other end of the shop—far away from Matt.

"*Yuanyang* is a coffee drink," I explained to the man, "but it doesn't happen to be on our menu."

Though I'd judged the Quiz Master's age as thirty-something, the superior grin he flashed looked more like the smirk of an adolescent boy—and, brother, did I want to slap it off.

It took me three months (at least!) to train a rookie barista. Factor in the years of knowledge I'd shared with my people about what a Manhattan clientele loved (from music to muffins) and what they loathed, and you had an extremely valuable employee crop, ripe for the picking.

Stealing that human investment out from under me would be a blow, but it wasn't what boiled my soup. I had great affection for my staff. I cared for them like my own kids, and I didn't want to lose them.

"How about a *Ying Yong*?" the Quiz Master countered with a look that said, *You're stumped, admit it.*

"Sorry," I said, "but we both know it's the same drink."

"You think so?"

"I know so. Three parts coffee; seven parts Hong Kong–Style Milk Tea, and to save you the effort, we don't serve CoffTea or Tea Espress, either, since they're also the same beverage." I shrugged.

He laughed. "I'm Eric."

"Clare."

The shake was firm. The cold superiority in his expression had tempered into something warmer, yet far from warm.

"So, Clare," he said after a pause. "If you don't serve coffee-tea mixes, does that mean you won't make me a Zebra Mocha? Unless"—the challenging smirk was back—"you've never heard of it?"

I met his gaze. *So you're officially quizzing me now? Well, bring it on. When I'm done with you, you're going to make me a job offer—and I'll have the grounds to kick your designer denim–clad derrière out of my shop for good!*

"The Zebra is a simple mixed mocha," I told him flatly. "You start with quality dark chocolate and blend it with white chocolate."

"Fun drink," he replied. "Like those old deli counter black-and-white milkshakes—but with an espresso kick."

"Some customers call it a Penguin Mocha or a Marble Mocha. Add raspberry syrup and you've got a Red Tux."

"Thanks, Clare, but I think a Bombón might be worth a try. Do you know how to make it?"

"It's an espresso served with sweetened condensed milk."

"An *Antoccino*?"

"A single shot with an equal amount of steamed milk—the drink will give you the taste and texture of a double-shot latte without the high caffeine level."

"Really?"

"Really."

His smile was real now, too, displaying openly amused interest, but the quizzing didn't stop. We covered the Gibraltar, Cortado, and Shakerato. Then we came to the Guillermo.

"The drink consists of an espresso shot or two poured over slices of lime. It's very good sweetened; it can also be served on ice and with a touch of milk."

He made a face. "Coffee with lime? Who likes that?"

"You never heard of *Aguapanela?*"

He shook his head.

"It's practically the Colombian national drink—a hard, brown sugarcane is grated into boiling water. It's delicious cold or as a base for coffee or hot chocolate, and sometimes lime is added. In the summer, I do a chilled version. Or I'll use lime sherbet and do it as an *eiskaffee.*"

"You mean ice coffee?"

"I mean *eiskaffee.*"

His confident expression faltered. "I'm not familiar with—"

"It's a popular coffee drink in Germany that includes ice cream."

"Oh? Germans aren't tea drinkers, like the English?"

"Per capita, Germans consume more coffee than Americans. But they're not number one in world coffee consumption. Do you know who is?"

Eric blinked.

"Scandinavians," I informed him.

For a prolonged moment, he stared intensely at me with an almost rude fascination, like a little boy pinning a new butterfly to his board. "Do you do that a lot?" he finally asked.

"What?"

"Invent new drinks based on existing ones?"

"It's a standard technique for recipe development."

One eyebrow rose. "A barista heuristic?" he said, almost to himself. "Intriguing . . ."

Oh, please, I thought. *Make me an offer already. Better yet, beg me. Beg me to work for you, Eric. Then I'll pin you—right to the wall.*

But he didn't make me an offer. He reached for his smartphone. "Excuse me a moment . . ."

Forcing a smile, I waited. One minute . . . two . . .

"How about I make you that *doppio* now?" I offered.

"What's that?"

"Isn't that one of the things you always order here? A double espresso . . ." (*To test the most basic abilities of my baristas? That seemed the obvious reason.*)

"Just a sec . . ."

"Our machine's a bit temperamental today," I went on, trying to provoke a reaction. "Of course, if I had a Slayer, I wouldn't mind . . ."

His head jerked up. "What did you say?"

"Just thinking out loud—when it comes to a Slayer, more like wishing out loud."

He gawked, looking less than pleased. "You're wishing for a *killer*?"

"A killer *espresso*. That's what comes out of a handmade espresso machine." *What kind of coffee pro has never heard of the Slayer?*

"Oh, I see . . ." he said, looking almost relieved. "The Slayer is a brand of espresso machine."

"More like a dream machine."

"Why is that?"

"A barista can adjust it on so many levels that it can make the same handful of coffee beans taste completely different with every espresso pull."

He began staring again. "I wonder, Clare, have you heard of a rare, single-origin coffee called Ambrosia?"

Was he kidding? I was the one who'd coined the name— after Matt had sourced the exquisite cherries and became the exclusive world supplier. Unfortunately . . .

"*Ambrosia* was a once-in-a-lifetime experience. Sorry, Eric, but you missed it. The farm that produced it is on lockdown, courtesy of the Brazilian authorities and the DEA."

Rather than looking disappointed, he seemed pleased.

"Clare, I want to thank you for your patience with me. The truth is . . . I had very good reasons for asking my questions."

Finally! Here it comes.

"I'd like to make you an offer . . ."

I knew it! This jerk was out to steal my staff! Well, now I'll make him an offer—

But I never got the chance. A pounding shock wave rattled my frame. The blast vibrated through my muscles a microsecond before the noise hit my ears. Tables rocked, chairs toppled, and the windows facing Hudson Street blew inward bringing freezing winter air and deadly sharp shards of glass.

My body reacted faster than my brain. My torso doubled over, my arms flying up to shield my face and head. As vibrations shook our wood-plank floor, I was gripped with a horrible thought. Was my basement roaster responsible for this? Had our own aging gas main finally blown?

It was Matt's shout that set me straight. "That was a car bomb!"

My partner had seen his share of violent acts in his travels, which was why he knew what it was—and what more it could be. A secondary blast was possible now, an explosion as dangerous as the primary.

"Everyone on the floor!" Matt shouted. "Drop and stay there!"

This was one time I didn't argue with my ex.

I hit our plank deck.

Five

My staff obeyed Matt's command. The customers did, too. All except one.

In disbelief, I realized Eric was milling around, mumbling to himself.

"Hey, get down!" I shouted up at him. "Get down on the floor!"

Ignoring me, he stumbled toward the shattered front window.

Oh, man! I got up fast and went to him. "Get away from the street, you idiot! Don't you understand? It's still dangerous out there—"

As I gripped his shoulder, something warm and wet sprayed my face. I touched my cheek and my fingers came away sticky with blood. But it wasn't mine.

Eric's face was suddenly pale, his slate gray eyes wide. "My Charley . . . My Charley is in the car—"

I didn't reply. I was too busy staring at the ragged strip of broken glass sticking out of Eric's body. The shining shard, less than an inch from his carotid artery, went right through a flap of skin at the base of his neck. The slightest jarring could move the glass and sever the vein.

Good Lord. "Listen to me, Eric, you're badly injured. You have to stop moving and remain perfectly still."

Eric's hands moved to the area of pain. "Oh no . . ." Realizing the danger he was in, he wavered, weak at the knees.

If he falls, he'll die. "Stay calm, okay? Lean on me . . ." I draped his heavy arm over my shoulder. Straining under his not-yet-dead weight, Eric and I sank to the floor together.

His skin felt cool, and I was sure he was going into shock. But when I carefully slipped out from under his weight, my first concern was that second explosion, and how I was going to protect this wounded man from the blast.

As I looked around for help, Nancy stumbled out of the restroom, dripping wet, her hands over her ears.

"Holy smokin' rockets, what the heck blew up?"

"My car," Eric murmured.

Matt dragged my youngest barista to our floor—just in time.

The second, fiery blast was more light and heat than sound and fury, but was no less dangerous. It came so fast I had no choice but to shield Eric with my own body.

Splinters of glass and pieces of wood and metal filled the air. As the shrapnel bit into my flesh, I bit my cheek. If I shouted or screamed in pain, this man could move suddenly and die, so I squeezed my eyes shut and swallowed the dozen bee stings. Then black, sooty smoke flowed through the empty window frames, filling the shop with choking smog.

Still on my knees, I turned to look at the burning pyre, now visible through my beveled-glass front door, which hung crookedly by a single hinge. Eric's vehicle was nothing more than a silhouette inside a red-hot inferno. My shell-shocked ears began to detect other sounds: the moans and cries of my customers, the shouting and screaming in the street, the car alarms howling up and down the block.

"Charley, Charley," Eric kept moaning. "What about Charley?"

"Stay still," I warned. "Help is coming, but you have to *keep still . . .*"

I cast about for help and saw Matt, Esther, and Nancy busy giving aid to other injured customers, so I worked alone, carefully lifting Eric's long legs and elevating his feet on an overturned chair.

The blood flow seemed to be increasing, and I grabbed a wad of folded towels from behind the counter. I tucked a few under Eric's head and saved one to use as a compress. Taking a deep breath, I pressed the clean cloth to the wound, praying I wouldn't cause more damage by applying pressure.

"Clare . . ." Eric's intense, little-boy stare was back, but much different now. I could see it in his eyes: *I'm scared.*

I took his right hand and squeezed. "I'm going to get you through this. I promise. It's going to be all right . . ."

His eyes filled and he squeezed my hand back. Then his muted voice mumbled something. His left hand rose weakly, as if he wanted me to take the smartphone still in his grip.

"Nine ones squared," he said.

That's when Tuck appeared next to me, describing the scene—and Eric's injuries—to an emergency operator.

"Nine ones squared," Eric repeated.

I leaned close. "We've already called 911. Hang on now, help is on the way."

"No . . ." Eric shook his head, like I'd missed something. "Nine ones . . ." Then the smartphone tumbled from his hand and he slumped back, his breathing shallow. His hands felt like ice, and I knew he'd gone into shock.

The next thing I heard was the wail of approaching sirens. Within minutes, paramedics were pushing through the broken door, coughing from their brush with the burning car at the curb.

I moved aside as the medical technicians took over Eric's care. They immediately staunched the bleeding, started an

IV, and strapped him down on a stretcher a fourth man had wheeled in.

As quickly as they arrived, the first group of medics were gone, even as a second ambulance team began to check out the rest of my customers.

I took a step toward Matt, but a paramedic stopped me.

"Whoa, where are you going?" she said. Flipping her short pageboy, the woman laid a gloved hand on my back. I felt a sting and yelped. Her hand came away bloody, and this time the red stuff was mine.

"Oh, hell."

The medic swept debris off a chair and sat me down. Dizzy and queasy, I didn't argue. Seconds later, I was clutching my blouse, sweater, and bra to cover my naked form while she gently probed lacerations on my bare back.

"No deep punctures, so that's good," she said. "Do you remember when you had your last tetanus shot?"

"Last summer—ouch!"

"I'm sterilizing the wounds, so this is going to sting," she explained, too late. Finally, the paramedic applied several small bandages across parts of my back, and a bigger one behind my right shoulder.

"You're going to need help changing those—"

"I'll take care of it."

"You don't want to go to the ER?"

"No, absolutely not . . ." Gritting my teeth, I scanned the chaos. "I'm staying."

"I need help over here!" Esther cried as she examined a tear in Nancy's pants. "This girl has cut her knee on broken glass."

"I need a towel, too," Nancy called. "When I heard the boom, the toilet kind of blew up in my face."

"Oh, yuck," Esther cried, jumping backward.

"It's okay. There was nothing in it but water."

Still, Esther eyed me. "All of us deal with crap at retail, but that's above and beyond."

"You're right," I said, tugging my clothes back over my

injuries. "Nancy, you're getting a big bonus in your next paycheck."

"Wow, thanks! That kind of makes it worth it . . ."

Tuck handed Nancy a wad of paper towels. "Miracle of miracles," he said, "except for cuts and bruises, everyone seems okay."

Not everyone. One poor soul had been in that car, someone Eric knew and cared about.

But Tuck was right about the rest of our customers. Most had come through with minor scrapes. A group of them had moved to the front of the shop, where they began talking and tweeting, cell phone cameras snapping the scene as firemen doused the blazing car with smothering white foam.

Our coffeehouse had been lucky (if you could call it that). Eric's car had been double-parked at the time of the explosion, so an SUV sitting by the curb had absorbed much of the blast coming our way.

As the flames were extinguished, smoke began drifting into the shop. Working together, Matt, Tuck, and Esther herded the customers out. When the Village Blend emptied of everyone but staff, Matt approached me, expression serious.

"Are you okay? I saw that paramedic working on you."

"Just a few cuts, no danger of rabies," I said, ignoring the pain.

"So, what did he say to you, Clare?"

"What did who say?"

"Your Quiz Master."

"Excuse me?"

Matt scooped up the fallen baseball cap. "The guy who owns this hat."

"Eric?"

"Yes. What did he say to you?"

"Not much. I stopped him from going outside, that's all. He went into shock after that and didn't say much of anything, except that his Charley was in the car."

A thin ribbon of blood trickled from a cut above Matt's hairline. Frowning, his eyes scanned the shop's shattered interior. "Whoever blew up the billionaire's car sure did a number on our Village Blend."

"Wait. Who are you talking about? What billionaire?"

"Clare, the man they took away in the ambulance is Eric *Thorner*, founder and CEO of THORN, Inc."

It felt like a second bomb.

Apple, Google, Facebook, Thorn; *everyone*, including me, knew those names.

"Your Quiz Master is an Internet wunderkind, Clare, a *billionaire*. And you just saved his life."

"What?"

There was no time to say more, not with the *crash* that ensued.

Three burly guys, axes in hand, burst through what remained of our door. For a crazy moment, I thought some wild barbarian horde had invaded Manhattan, but the helmeted men weren't Vikings. They were members of our city fire department.

"This area is being evacuated!" announced one of them. "Everyone out, now!"

Six

~~~~~~

With our door off its hinges, Matt stayed behind to keep an eye on our place while I herded our staff into a nearby pub. Huddling our group together, I treated them to a few rounds of warm apple cider until we were allowed to return to the coffeehouse. Then we crunched across the broken glass and went to work cleaning the mess.

By now, the boxy, blue and white trucks of the New York City Bomb Squad had joined the knot of emergency vehicles. With the fire out, these specialized detectives were gathering evidence.

For a time, all of us were silent, unnerved by the violent explosion that had occurred just steps from our front door. Finally, Esther hugged herself against the tiny snowflakes drifting through our broken windows and cried—

"It looks like *The Hurt Locker* out there!"

I couldn't argue. Outside, a bomb technician in a padded suit and space helmet examined the smoldering wreckage of Eric Thorner's luxury limo; inside, my shop exemplified the word *trashed*.

The French doors were shattered, leaving glass everywhere, along with a lot of broken crockery. Tables and chairs were overturned, the shop's shutters were scorched, and so was the woodwork on the façade facing Hudson—which did look somewhat like Kandahar, but with a fairy dusting of snow over the debris.

Even more distressing, Con Edison had cut off our electricity because of damage to the lines. While insurance would cover many of the repairs, my head spun thinking about all the red tape, the cash-flow problems, the construction, and the fact that I lived upstairs—now without electricity for lights or even my refrigerator.

I tried hard to think of a silver lining, but . . .

Nope. Nothing.

As Matt set the front door back on its hinges, he continued the discussion we'd begun earlier. "Clare, I can't believe you didn't know who Thorner was."

"Honestly, Matt, I doubt I would have recognized Bill Gates or Mark Zuckerman if they'd come into the Blend arm in arm."

"Gates isn't a boy wunderkind anymore," Matt said. "And *Zuckerberg* isn't one of *Money and Finance* magazine's Most Eligible Bachelors of the Year. That honor went to Eric Thorner."

"Sorry, that issue of *Money and Finance* eluded me."

"Yeah, I missed that one, too," Esther added. "Along with *Investor's Daily*, *Hedge Fund Fun*, and *Fat Cats 'r' Us.*"

Suddenly Nancy stopped sweeping. "Holy smokin' rockets! Are all of you forgetting about *Pigeon Droppings*?!"

Pigeon droppings? I frowned. "We're going to board up the broken windows, Nancy. No birds will get in—"

"Not *real* pigeons! I'm talking about the app game!"

Esther knocked her own head. "Of course! I should have remembered! I see that stupid ThornE barbed-wire logo every time Boris plays *Pigeon Droppings*, which is constantly, by the way, because my boyfriend is absolutely obsessed with that game."

Nancy's head bobbed up and down. "So are a million, billion other people. It's like the number-one entertainment app."

"How did I never hear of this?" I asked no one in particular. "What's the point of a pigeon dropping game, anyhow? I mean, how do you even win?"

"You get points when your pigeons drop all over people," Nancy explained. "Sometimes you miss. Sometimes the person opens an umbrella, splats your dropping, and you lose points. It's really fun, and in the premium version you can add phone photos of yourself or your friends, and have the birds drop all over them, too."

Esther snorted. "Talk about a photobomb."

Photobombs? Crap-loaded entertainment apps? Wow, was I out of touch.

"Come on, boss," Tuck said, "don't you remember that mess at the Clothing Corral stores last summer? They made a whole line of *Pigeon Droppings* kids' T-shirts with vaguely vulgar slogans printed on them."

I blinked. "Define 'vaguely vulgar.'"

"Let's see . . ." Tuck tapped his chin. "'My teacher is full of *drop.*' 'This is bull *drop.*' And my favorite, 'I used to give a *drop.*'"

"That's not *vaguely* vulgar, that *is* vulgar."

"Parent groups agreed," Tuck said, emptying a dustbin into a plastic bag. "Teachers were outraged, too—"

"And ThornE made a fortune," Esther noted.

Matt finally finished fixing the door while I'd closed the shutters against the draft. I had yet to find the chiming bell that had hung over the entrance for the past five decades, and asked everyone to keep an eye out for it.

Together Matt and I began to right the overturned café tables. When he realized the legs were bent and wobbly on one of them, he grabbed our toolbox from the pantry and set to work adjusting the ancient bolts.

"What were you and Thorner talking about before the blast?" Matt asked.

"Coffee. He quizzed me, like everyone else. I thought he was a competitor out to steal our staff."

Tucker perked up. "Really?"

"Forget about it. I would never have let Eric Thorner poach you."

"Well, not for nothing, CC, but there are worse fates than pulling shots at a billionaire's espresso bar. Imagine the tips!"

"I don't know," Nancy said. "His games are fun, but that guy was a royal pain at our counter. Every day, another weird drink order! Why? What for?"

"I wouldn't worry about it," Matt replied. "Given the fireworks outside, I doubt you'll be seeing the Quiz Master back here anytime soon."

"Coffee's ready," Esther called from the counter.

Miraculously (or more like ironically), the century-old gas lines I was most concerned about had held fast against the blast, which meant we had boiling-hot water for a French-pressed pot.

While Esther poured, I dug out every last treat in the pastry case. (Why not? We weren't going to sell them anytime soon.) And Matt coaxed our fireplace into giving up more heat. Then we all huddled up.

Hungry hands reached for cookies, muffins, and tarts. After a few quiet minutes of famished chewing and swallowing, my curiosity got the better of me.

"So how do you know so much about Eric Thorner?" I asked Matt around a mouthful of happiness—a Cinnamon-Glazed French Apple Cake Square (a new addition to the pastry case thanks to a recipe from my aspiring-chef daughter).

"I went to one of his product launch parties last fall," he replied between bites of Pumpkin Spice Latte Bar.

"Really? You never mentioned it."

Matt shrugged.

"Why didn't he recognize you?"

"The party was held at Versailles, Clare. I was there with fourteen hundred of the man's closest friends."

"But if you were invited, he must have known your name."

"My wife's name—and her European trends editor's. Bree and her employee were really the invitees. I went as Guest."

"So what exactly was this lavish party for? Not another bird-poo game."

"No . . ." Matt touched the screen of his smartphone and handed it over. "This is Thorner's latest product."

I looked at the logo. "*App-itite?*"

"Enter the zip code on the right. Use those three dropdown menus to pick a cuisine, a specific dish, and distance you're willing to travel, and you get the details about every eatery that serves what you want."

"So it's just a restaurant guide?"

"More than a guide. You can make reservations, read reviews, write reviews, link to the eatery's website, get directions from a Google map link, and ask the app questions about the menu. Don't recognize an exotic dish, an oddball cocktail, or fine wine? Thorner's app makes you an expert on it in seconds."

"Didn't I read something about THORN, Inc., buying some prominent guidebook company?" Tuck asked.

Matt nodded. "*Marquess Guides*—a French-based food and travel guide for all of Europe. He rolled the content into his European app. There's an *App-itite Asia*, and an *App-itite Latin America*, too."

"But it's still just a restaurant guide!"

"You said that, Clare. What's your point?"

"Thorner's not a defense contractor, or even a computer designer. He makes foodie apps, for goodness' sake—"

"And gaming apps and learning apps," Matt added. "His company and its subsidiaries are the largest independent app creator on the planet."

"So why would anyone want to blow him up?!"

My question hung in the air.

Tucker, our resident curator of celebrity gossip, offered a theory, his own smartphone now in hand. "TMZ has archived stories. I'm skimming the history . . . it says he's a recluse. He has a rep for being a geekish tech nerd, but Thorner does have a dark spot. His former girlfriend, Bianca Hyde, was a bikini model turned indie film actress. Now, she had a *much* higher profile—"

"Wasn't she the one who killed herself at the Beverly Palms?" Matt asked.

Tuck's finger swept across the tiny screen. "According to these e-tabloid headlines, it was ruled an accident."

"An accident?" I asked, hairs prickling. "Did it add up?"

"What do you mean?" Tuck asked.

"I mean, were there any suspects who may have contributed to her death?"

"Suspects? Sure—two pints of vodka, three-quarters of a mini bar, one coffee table, and gravity," Matt added.

"But how long ago did this happen?" I asked Tuck.

"About a year ago—"

"And did Bianca Hyde have any friends or family? Someone who might have blamed Eric for her death?"

"Don't answer her," Matt commanded Tuck. Then he eyeballed me. "I don't want you getting involved with this."

"Involved with what? I'm only asking a question."

"I'm curious, too," Esther said in my defense. "After all, I've heard of violent rappers, but never violent *appers*."

"I don't know . . ." Tuck arched an eyebrow. "That Facebook founder does wear a hoodie."

"Rich and powerful people are targets; I get that," Nancy said. "What I don't get is the car bomb. I mean, why not just shoot the guy and avoid hurting innocent bystanders?"

Matt shook his head. "You're expecting compassionate consideration from a madman bent on murder? I think the words *mad* and *murder* answer that. Don't you agree, Clare? You're the one with the cop boyfriend . . ."

I didn't reply. For the first time since the explosion, I wasn't thinking about Eric Thorner, or bombs, because I'd spied a familiar face through one of our still-intact windows, a formerly loyal customer, one who hadn't stopped by our shop since late December. And I wanted to know why.

I set my empty cup down and grabbed my coat.

"Where are you going?" Matt asked.

"The bank," I lied. "I want to make sure my line of credit is long enough to cover repairs until the insurance company reimburses us."

Matt nodded and went for another pastry, obviously relieved that I'd given up on Thorner's case. Good thing, too, because if my ex-husband knew who I was going to speak with and why, I'd have another explosion on my hands.

SEVEN

∿∿∿∿∿∿∿∿∿∿∿∿∿∿∿

◆IGHTENING my scarf, I stepped onto the cold sidewalk.

The cops had closed Hudson Street, creating a snarl so bad it would have made the news even without a car bomb. A wall of waiting vehicles idled beyond the sawhorse barricades, their drivers curiously watching the NYPD load Eric Thorner's (practically) cremated limo onto a flatbed truck.

The frosty air reeked of burned rubber and scorched metal, and I crunched through the snow, skirting yards and yards of crime scene tape before reaching the man I'd come out here to see.

Emmanuel Franco was stationed on the next block. In his lemon yellow vest, the young police sergeant was hard to miss. Loitering in front of a French bistro, he'd attracted a fan base—a pair of stylish females. This was no surprise. No other cop at the Sixth Precinct could fill out a traffic vest quite like Manny Franco.

"Can't you tell us what's going on?" asked the brunette, sprucing her hair with a leather-gloved hand. "It'll be on TV tonight, anyway. We won't tell anybody before those news reporters do."

The blonde was bolder. "They closed the office, so we've got the afternoon off, and we don't even know why! If we buy you a drink, will you tell us about it?"

Franco shook his head. "Girls, what makes you think I know anything?"

The blonde narrowed her eyes. "You look like someone who knows plenty."

"I'm just a guy in uniform."

"I'd like to see what you look like *out* of uniform," the brunette purred.

Franco took a step backward, palms up. "You know what? This has been lovely, and you ladies are charming, but I'm going to have to ask you to move on."

Reluctantly, the girls headed off toward the subway. I waited until they were out of sight before I caught Franco's attention.

"Hey, Coffee Lady." His smile was sincere—yet a little nervous.

Well, he has good reason to be. "I thought you worked undercover, Detective?"

"Those were the days," Franco said wistfully. "Things have been quiet in the OD Squad lately. Too quiet."

"That's hard to believe . . ."

The OD Squad was Mike Quinn's NYPD task force, and Franco was a handpicked member. The team was responsible for following up on drug-related deaths throughout the five boroughs. Before Mike took over, the squad had had a low profile. After he was put in charge, they were making major cases and national news. That's what brought Mike to the attention of the U.S. Attorney who'd drafted him.

"Mighty Quinn kicked ass when it came to pursuing leads. He was gung-ho on cutting through red tape, too. But our interim leader, Detective Sullivan . . ." Franco paused to tug his hat against the wind. "Let's just say he lacks initiative."

"That's pretty vague for you, Sergeant."

"Don't get me wrong, Sully's a good cop, but for him the squad is just a job, not an adventure."

A horn blasted nearby, and Franco gave the driver the fish-eye. "Anyway, given the lack of action on the squad, I'm grabbing odd jobs at the Sixth. Like today, when the fit hit the shan, the captain needed manpower so I'm back in the bag."

"Are you telling me that Mike is completely out of the picture? And you're in uniform again?"

"Quinn's been AWOL for over a month."

"Define AWOL."

Franco shrugged. "When your boyfriend first started in DC, he checked in almost daily. But the Federal Triangle is starting to look like the Bermuda Triangle—a place where people mysteriously disappear . . ."

This was news to me. And not good news.

Quinn had put his second-in-command in charge of the daily operations. But if his squad was flagging, and Quinn was neglecting it, the NYPD brass could replace him. Then what? Would my boyfriend stay in DC when his year's assignment with the Justice Department was done? What would that mean for our future?

"Sorry for the crap news, Coffee Lady, but I should be disappearing, too." Franco gestured to the blocked street. "Any minute now, this traffic's going to start rolling again."

"Not so fast, Sergeant." I poked his hard chest. "First, you're going to tell me why you haven't come to my coffee-house since your trip to visit my daughter in Paris."

"Well, uh . . ." He shifted, clearly uncomfortable. "I've been meaning to drop in . . ."

"Haven't you at least needed a caffeine fix?"

"Actually, I sort of got hooked on these." He pulled out a shiny brown bag and flashed the logo.

"Perky Jerky?"

"Turkey Perky Jerky," Franco said with an enthusiastic nod. "Traditional meat jerky laced with the pep of an energy drink. They make beef with a buzz, too, but I like turkey best."

"You and I both know your absence has nothing to do with your sudden addiction to Perky Jerky. What *happened* in France? Come clean. If you broke my daughter's heart, I swear—"

"Hey, hey! I would never hurt Joy, and that isn't what happened."

"So what did?"

Franco sighed, looked away. "Ask her."

I blinked. "What?"

"I'm not the one with the problem. Talk to your daughter."

My head was spinning. Last I'd heard, Joy was smitten with Franco, completely in love. She'd admitted as much—to her grandmother, of course. (Joy would never share such personal things with me. I'm only her mother.)

"Look, Sergeant, right now I'm talking to you. What happened?"

"Joy said she was 'conflicted,' that she wasn't sure she wanted to date a cop. She wasn't even sure she was coming back to New York. That *maybe* she'd rather stay in Paris . . ."

I suddenly felt Franco's pain.

Unlike Joy's disastrous past boyfriends, Emmanuel Franco was a good man. He wanted only to make her happy; and my daughter had been hooked on him, hinting at marriage and future plans, and suddenly she was pushing him away? Why?

Getting the truth out of my daughter wouldn't be easy. Over the last few months, most of our "conservations" had taken place via texting, cell phone photos, and social media updates.

I wanted to talk to my girl—really talk to her, see her body language, gauge the look in her eyes, and *not* let her cut me off until I got to the bottom of what was really going on. Gritting my teeth, I made a heartfelt *wish* in that moment. *I wish I had the money to charter a flight to Paris right now, this minute!* But the expense of such a trip and my responsibilities here made that impossible.

"I'd like to see her one more time, try again," Franco admitted, "but I have no idea when she's coming back for a visit, and booking another international flight is more than I can afford—that's another reason I'm back in this bag." He tugged his vest sadly. "My credit card is maxed out. I need the overtime to pay for the last trip."

A loud rumble interrupted us, and we both watched a police flatbed haul away Eric Thorner's burned-out car. Franco frowned down at me.

"So is everyone okay at your place? That blast was pretty close."

(At last, a subject we could both feel comfortable about getting to the bottom of . . .) I told him about the damage and mentioned the name of the intended target. Like me, Franco knew little about the young billionaire.

"The city's Bomb Squad is headquartered in your precinct," I noted. "Have you heard anything about the explosion?"

"I overheard two guys from the A-Team. They said no dynamite or TNT was used—"

"What? That can't be right! I heard the explosions myself. There were two, a big one and then—"

"It was a firebomb, Clare. The Bomb Squad recovered pieces of an aluminum can that contained the accelerant."

"Didn't you once tell me that fingerprints could be taken off bomb fragments?"

"Good memory. That's true."

"Well, if I know that, the bomber might, too, right?"

"A friend in the Bomb Squad doesn't think so."

"What does that mean?"

"If the perp had access to real explosives, he would have used them, which means he's an amateur. And if he's an amateur, then he probably doesn't know that his fingerprints could be had, so we may get lucky." Franco paused. "I heard something else, too."

"Give."

Franco glanced around and lowered his voice. "One of the Bomb Squad guys thinks the killer wanted to do more than just get Thorner out of the way. He must have had a real hate on for his victim, and I'd have to agree."

"Why is that?"

"Because the device wasn't designed to blow up the car so much as roast the occupants alive. And burning to death is one hell of a horrible way to die."

Eight

~~~~~~~~~~~~~~~~~~~~~~~~~~~~~~~~~~~~~~

HOURS later, I was gazing at flames again, but (thank goodness) this roaring fire didn't come from a bomb. This blaze emanated from my bedroom's comforting hearth. Unfortunately, my thoughts about today's violent act were far from a comfort. Most troubling of all were Franco's final words.

Who hated Eric Thorner enough to want him roasted alive? And what had sparked that animosity? Was it something in Eric's public life? Or was it more private?

I'll admit the young billionaire was a thoroughly smug individual. In the few minutes we spent together before the bomb went off, even I was dying to smack the smirk off his face. But such a superficial encounter, even a dozen of them, would not be a reasonable motive for murder.

Whatever the reason, the bomber was sure to be exasperated by tonight's news. After emergency surgery, Eric Thorner was expected to make a full recovery.

If the bomber knew he had failed, would he—or she—try again?

It was a dark thought, but it had been a dark day; and in

winter, night arrived early in Manhattan. The moment the sun dipped below the horizon, the towering steel-and-stone skyline speedily slipped from twilight blue to solid black. Now electricity was tasked with the sun's job and the city was illuminated by the golden glare of lightbulbs, millions of them shining in countless streetlamps and apartment windows. Unfortunately, not one of those bulbs was working in mine.

Along with my phone line, the power was out, and the only light in my duplex apartment came from my two fireplaces, a few battery-operated hurricane lamps, and a dozen votive candles.

Earlier, Matt had offered to stay with me, and his mother invited me to move into her penthouse, but I turned them both down. This was my home, and I didn't want to leave it. Besides, an NYPD patrol was posted on our block, and I had my cell for emergencies.

As the night wore on, however, having no heat or electricity made me feel vulnerable, and I *hated* feeling vulnerable, so I turned up the classical music on my battery-powered radio and cooked dinner (mercifully, the ancient gas lines had weathered the blast). After a few bites, I paced the floor. Several times, I crossed to the window and peered outside, watching for Quinn.

By eleven, I gave up and tucked myself into bed. Thirty minutes later, over the quavers and sways of a Beethoven piano sonata, I awoke with a start. Was someone on the back stairs? I bolted upright on the four-poster and threw the snuggly coverlet aside.

Animated by my own frantic movements, Java and Frothy bounded at my heels, furry cat tails high. I hurried down the carpeted steps and across the chilly parquet floor, cell phone in hand—911 on speed dial.

But there was no need to call the cops. One was at my door.

Peering through the peephole, I sighed at the sight of Mike Quinn's broad-shouldered silhouette filling the shadowy landing. I unlocked the door.

"I'm so glad you made it! Are you hungry?"

Quinn didn't reply, except to inhale sharply. His arctic blue eyes melted with sweet appreciation, and I remembered I was wearing my threadbare Pittsburgh Steelers shirt, a few bandages underneath, and little else.

On my next breath, his arms were around me; and while I badly wanted Quinn's embrace, its aggressiveness surprised me—the man not only squeezed the air out of me, he was stinging the lacerations on my back. But I didn't care. By the time he let me go, I was feeling no pain.

"Ready to take off your coat now?" I smiled. He returned it, and I began undoing his buttons.

I'd hardly had time to hang the thing up before he was cornering me again. When we broke our embrace, his tie was askew and his eyes were vibrant behind a veil of fatigue.

I touched his rough cheek. "Slow down, we have all night."

"I hope so," Quinn replied.

"What does that mean?"

"Nothing, don't worry about it . . ."

But I couldn't help myself. Quinn had been summoned back to DC on his last weekend visit, right in the middle of our Sunday-morning brunch—a "break in the case" that wasn't. The false alarm cost him an afternoon with his kids. I did my best to make up for it, but I was a poor substitute. While Molly had a fine time window-shopping along Fifth, Jeremy sulked. He missed his father.

"My boss has been putting on the pressure," Quinn admitted, checking his phone for messages.

"No personal life allowed?"

"I'm here, aren't I?"

"Don't you want to be?"

"Clare, when the Homeland Security alert crossed my desk, I nearly lost it until I heard your voice. *Of course* I want to be here—I want to be with you, wherever you are."

Now I felt guilty. This weekend had been my turn to travel, and I'd been ready to hop my usual Friday-afternoon train to DC, but not after the bomb. I refused to leave my ravaged coffeehouse, and I told him so over the phone. That's why he'd changed his own plans and caught a late flight.

"So how about dinner?" Hooking an arm around his waist, I steered him toward the kitchen. "I didn't have time to bake lasagna, but I did a shortcut skillet version for you, and it's pretty tasty, if I do say so. With no electricity, I couldn't use my mixer, so there's no Triple-Chocolate Italian Cheesecake, but I'm going to wow you with my Baileys Irish Cream and Caramel-Nut Fudge. I don't know about you, but I could use a little Irish comfort—"

"Good, because I'm ready to provide it—and not in the kitchen." Mike pulled me in the opposite direction, toward the bedroom. "Let's lie down by the fire . . ."

It was a genuine thrill to be desired, but there was a note of urgency in his manner that made me wonder if things were really all right.

Quinn's temperament was naturally circumspect. He felt things deeply and was rarely impatient. In fact, he told me that waiting was a detective's game—waiting for witnesses to tell their story, for suspects to incriminate themselves, for forensic labs to deliver the kind of results that could nail a case closed.

Mike's police academy instructor had driven that point home with a test for his class of eager, young cadets. "Go into your garage and sit alone in your car for twelve hours," he'd ordered them one Friday night. Those without cars were instructed to stay awake in their bedrooms. "Remain alert and respond immediately to a mock distress call from me, when and if one comes."

In the wee hours of the morning, that call came for Police Cadet Quinn, and he'd not only been ready, he'd beaten every other member of his class to the rendezvous point.

Likewise, his steady, determined nature helped him build a solid career in the NYPD. I'd watched him make his cases, painstakingly working them for weeks, months, even years. But that was before he'd gone to Washington.

At first, things had been fine—sometimes better than fine. I enjoyed my trips to see him, and we'd shared some lovely weekends, including romantic outings in Maryland and Virginia. But the last month had been trying; Quinn was drinking more and acting chronically impatient.

I'd been making excuses for him, but Franco's revelation made me realize something. A new supervisor had come on board for Quinn around a month ago, the same time he stopped regularly checking in with his squad. Were the two events related? It seemed to me they were.

While I was itching to discuss this with Mike, by now we'd reached the bed, and the last thing I wanted was for his work to come between us. He clearly felt the same.

Too bad his new boss didn't share our feelings.

As Mike's mouth began nuzzling my neck, his cell phone buzzed.

"Son of a—" He froze and closed his eyes.

"It's past midnight," I whispered.

Mike's expression was stoic, yet his jaw was clenched tight, and I knew he was warring with himself, part of him wanting to throw the phone through the window. In the end, Cadet Quinn and his lifetime in professional law enforcement won out.

"Quinn," he answered, half turning his back on me.

His shoulders slumped as he listened for a long moment.

"I'm in New York," he protested. "I'm sorry that Tom didn't place my weekly update in the case file, but I just got here, and I'm not doing a turnaround—"

Interrupted, Mike listened, his frown deepening.

Can this boss actually expect Mike to fly back to DC to retrieve a file? That's ridiculous . . .

Mike thought so, too. His shoulders squared and he pushed back.

"Look, the situation report is fairly routine. Call me again on a secure line and I'll summarize the salient points. *Or* you can get Tom on the horn and tell him to open his safe in the morning. *Or* you can wait until Monday morning, when I'll be back in Washington."

After impatiently enduring another long response, Mike's reply was icy.

"I'll speak with Tom to make sure this doesn't happen again. You'll have that report on your desk Monday, first thing."

He ended the call and slammed the phone on the dresser.

We sat in silence for a moment. "Your boss is calling you at midnight?" I whispered. "Over paperwork?"

He turned on the bed to fully face me. "Forget it, sweetheart. I'm going to." He touched my cheek. "We have all weekend now, and I'm going to make sure it stays that way."

This time Mike's hug caused me to yelp—he'd pressed too hard on one of my cuts.

"Clare, what is this?" He found the bandages on my shoulder.

"I caught a little shrapnel today. Flying glass."

Mike spun me around, pulled the tee up to my neck, and examined my naked back.

"There's fresh blood on one of these dressings!"

"Oh, right. The paramedic told me to change them—"

I hardly got the words out before Mike peeled off my shirt completely.

"Don't move."

He went to the bathroom and returned with my first aid kit. Soon the man's firm but gentle hands were stripping off the old bandages and applying new ones.

"That's it," he said with a sigh. "You'll take it easy tonight. No physical activity."

I felt a stab of disappointment and turned to face him. His eyes took in my naked curves, and the expression in them changed. Concern melted into something else, something that prompted me to meet his gaze and smile.

"You really mean it?" I pressed. "No physical activity?"

"Well, you can't lie on your back—"

"No I can't, but—" I grabbed the man's tie and rolled him onto the bed. "You can."

Mike's grin nearly outshined the glow of the fireplace.

NINE

~~~~~~~~~~~~~~~~~~~~~~~~~~~~~~~~~~~

"**ARE** you there? Can you hear me?"

A whisper in the dark.

With my back in its current crappy state, I was lying stomach down on the mattress, one arm dangling over the edge.

"Mike?" I yawned, rubbing my eyes. "Was that you?"

Silence.

The room felt cold; the hearth was barely glowing. I swung my arm back and connected with Mike's solid form. He lay still as a stone beside me, breathing with the regular rhythms of comatose sleep. But if Mike was sleeping, then who was whispering?

"Mom, pick up!"

That was no whisper. My daughter was shouting at me through the cell phone on my nightstand. *How did she manage this?* I didn't care. (Mother's Calculus: When your child is calling, you don't ask questions. You lunge for the phone.)

"Joy, honey? What's wrong? Where are you?"

"The airport."

"Charles de Gaulle?"

"I'm in New York. You have to come. There's a bomb."
"What?!"
"There's a bomb on my plane."

"Now boarding at Gate 91 . . ."
I must have dressed and hailed a cab, but I couldn't tell you how. Between a moment and an instant, my dark bedroom transformed into the bright bustle of JFK, and I was running through the crowded center aisle of Terminal One.
"Last call for Air France, Flight 911 . . ."
Joy's flight!
I careened down the corridor, counting gate numbers aloud, arms flailing like a *Sesame Street* Muppet.
"51 . . . 52 . . . 53 . . ."
I pushed through a knot of travelers, shoving aside backpacks, kicking over suitcases. People turned, stared, and cursed.
"There's a bomb!" I shouted. "A bomb on my daughter's plane!"
Then I was moving again, through the sixties, the seventies, and the eighties. At Gate 89, the phone in my hand vibrated again.
"Mom? Are you there?"
"I'm here, honey! Where are you?"
"On the plane. I'm buckled in. They want me to end my call—"
"Don't turn me off! Listen to me, Joy, please, listen . . ."
By now, I'd reached Gate 91, but the gangway door was locked. I ran to the terminal's picture window, and saw the jumbo jet pulling away.
I spotted Joy's face through a passenger window, the round glass receding like a collapsing telescope. Every yard the plane moved, her face grew smaller and (somehow) *younger* . . .
There she was at her high school graduation, laughing in cap and gown, handing out Diploma Fortune Cookies. Another yard and she was blowing out candles on a Sweet

Sixteen cake she'd insisted on baking herself, dancing with her father like she was all grown up. Another and she was fifteen, crying over a bully boy's hurtful remarks. Back she moved until she was winning the Tri-State Junior Gingerbread House Challenge; marshaling fellow Girl Scouts to stage a Thin Mint–palooza in front of the local supermarket. Finally, she was waving at me in her tomboy braids and braces, looking just like she did in my little Honda when we moved out to the suburbs; mom and daughter together, taking on the world——starting with New Jersey.

"Stop!" I pounded the glass with my fists. "Come back!"

But my daughter's flight seemed inevitable.

"Excuse me, ma'am, what's wrong?" A steward approached. The young man's shaggy, golden hair and winning smile looked oddly familiar——like Eric Thorner's.

I grabbed his arm, dragged him over. "You see that plane? We have to stop it!"

"I'm sorry, Clare, but you missed the plane. You're early."

"Early? What do you mean *early*?!"

Air-France-Eric shrugged and pointed. I followed his finger to the terminal wall. A huge clock hung there, hands moving counterclockwise, noisy ticking growing louder.

"Mom! What do I do?"

Tick, tick . . .

"Stop your flight, Joy. Come back to me!"

TICK, TICK, TICK . . .

Finally, it happened. The blast was massive, severing the jet, savagely breaking its solid, silver body in two. Flames erupted, igniting both halves of the plane, incinerating every helpless passenger.

"NOOOO!"

The destructive energy moved in almost visible waves across the tarmac, shaking the high window, and driving me to the floor. Then the glass splintered and a thousand brittle shards arrowed toward my back.

I squeezed my eyes shut and screamed.

Ten

~~~~~~

I opened my eyes.

Pain.

Sometime during the night, I'd shifted off Quinn's sturdy chest and rolled onto my ravaged back. Gritting my teeth, I sat up. The events of my nightmare may have been a grand illusion, but the pain was undeniably real.

I checked the glowing digits on my alarm: 3:55 AM. With a deep breath, I tried closing my eyes—

"I'm sorry, Clare, but you missed the plane. You're early."

"Early? What do you mean early?!"

Tick, tick, tick . . .

The images would not go away. Neither would the stark feeling of terror. It flooded my waking mind; dislodged bits of memory: the fear in Eric Thorner's eyes; the blood seeping from his wound; my landmark shop, wrecked and damaged; and the charred black body of that firebombed car, human remains trapped inside.

"Charley" was just a name to me, remote and unknowable. Like the subject of a TV news reports, he was just another casualty of war or random violence. Yet Eric's chauffeur was a person, a fellow soul, and his senseless murder *should* have mattered more to me. I was ashamed to say it didn't.

"Mom! What do I do?"

TICK, TICK, TICK, TICK!

Maybe that's why I dreamed of my daughter suffering the same fate. If *she'd* been in that car, the paramedics would have had to sedate me.

I glanced across the mattress. Quinn was still sleeping, so I slipped quietly out of bed.

I have to call Joy . . .

I knew my nightmare wasn't real, but my heart was still hammering, and I wasn't closing my eyes again until I made sure my daughter was safe. Tying on my robe, I stepped into slippers and shuffled down to the kitchen.

"MRRRoooOW . . ."

My little, furry raptors wasted no time circling my legs.

"No," I firmly told the pair. "It may be morning, but it is *not* time for breakfast."

Java and Frothy begged to differ—in stereo—and loudly enough to send me groping through the cupboard for a giant can of Savory Salmon.

Reading the label made my stomach rumble, and my mind conjured a brief, happy vision of Murray's pink-smoked salmon glistening on a toasted bagel with a snowy schmear of cream cheese. Despite knowing the difference between premium lox and Fancy Feast (really, I did), by the time I dished up their grub, I was salivating.

Ignoring my pangs of hunger, I sat down at the table and hit the first number on my mobile phone's speed dial. Joy's voice mail asked me to leave a message. Instead, I placed another call—to Joy's best friend.

"Bonjour!"

"Yvette?"

"*Oui?*"

Yvette's name might have been French but she was as American as mass-produced soft ice cream—a product that had made her family a small fortune. She and Joy had been friends since their first day of culinary school. Now they shared an apartment in Paris.

"You can speak English, Yvette, this is Joy's mother. I tried her cell, but she's not picking up—"

"Joy's at work, Ms. Cosi, and she never answers calls at work on pain of a Gallic tongue-lashing. Have you forgotten the time difference? You're six hours behind us in New York, and—"

"Joy is on the dinner brigade. Her shifts don't begin until two o'clock, your time."

"Her day starts earlier now."

"I see. But she's all right?"

"*Mais oui!* I just stopped by the restaurant to talk to her and she's perfectly fine—considering the incident."

I tensed. "Incident?"

"Last week the sous chef went a little *fou.*"

"Crazy? He went *crazy?*"

"The Bresse supplier shorted the restaurant on *poulardes* for, like, the third time in six weeks. So the chef drove all the way to Bourgogne, got into a shouting match with the chicken farmer, accused him of taking a bribe from a rival restaurant to sabotage their menu. They hurled insults at each other, then vegetables, then *poulardes*, then it really got ugly."

"Joy wasn't with him, was she?"

"No, but she totally heard all about it. They called in the gendarmes. It took, like, four to pull the two apart. So now the sous chef is stuck in the country, charged with assaulting an officer and cruelty to poultry, which in Bresse is a huge deal."

"What does all this have to do with my daughter?"

"After the executive chef had a meltdown, he revised half the brigade's duties. The saucier was promoted to sous chef, and Joy is now the restaurant's new saucier, at least until the sous chef gets out of jail for assaulting the policemen—and the farmer."

"And the chickens."

"Especially the chickens. Joy's thrilled, of course; it's a promotion, even if it is temporary. She's getting a bonus, too, but she has to start work much earlier in the day."

"Will you tell her to call her mother as soon as she's able?"

"Oh, sure, Ms. Cosi, no problem."

I was about to sign off, when I remembered the little talk I'd had on Hudson Street with Sergeant Franco. Since I couldn't be sure Joy would be forthcoming about her love life (and I didn't have the bank account to hire a private eye), I took a chance . . .

"Yvette," I said, "before I let you go, would you help me solve a little mystery? I understand things didn't go so well on Manny Franco's last visit. Do you have any idea what went wrong?"

Dead silence.

"Yvette? Are you there?"

"I'm sorry, Ms. Cosi, but . . . *um*, why do you care?"

"Excuse me?"

"I said, why do you—"

"I heard what you said. I just can't believe you asked a question like that. I *care* because Joy is my daughter. And I *like* Franco."

"Ooooh, that's right. *You're* dating a cop—so you would."

"What is that supposed to mean?"

"No offense. It's okay for you. I mean, you're divorced, you know? And of a certain age . . ."

Oh, for the love of—

". . . but Joy's got her whole life ahead of her. She doesn't want to make a mistake, you know?"

"No. I don't know. Why is Franco a 'mistake'?"

"Oh, come on. You have to admit the guy's salary is a joke."

"A joke?"

"Yes, and if Joy walked down the aisle with a man like Franco, the punch line would be a lifetime of sweating in kitchens like the ones she's in now. There's no way a young couple can make it in New York on a cop's wages."

"Your definition of 'making it' and mine are apparently different."

"Apparently."

"And my daughter has ambition. She has dreams. She *wants* to be in that kitchen because she wants to own and run her own restaurant one day."

"Exactly! A boyfriend with *real resources* could help her do that a lot faster. Franco's sweet, I'll give him that. He makes Joy laugh and he's got great abs, but he's not going anywhere. Like I said, she can do better."

"Well, I've had enough of this conversation."

"If you say so."

"Please tell my daughter to call me as soon as she's able."

"I will, Ms. C. *Au revoir!*"

I flipped my cell closed, but it failed to satisfy. *Oh, for the days when I could slam down a receiver!* Instead, I kicked the table leg. (Bad idea in fabric slippers.) Big toe throbbing, I frowned in fury at the tabletop, until a deep voice interrupted my mental tantrum—

"So? What's *the joke?*"

Quinn was leaning against the doorjamb, arms crossed. I had to admit, the sight of him standing there bare-chested, wearing nothing but a curious, slightly bemused expression and low-slung pair of panda bear pajama bottoms (a gift from his kids) did wonders for soothing some of my ire, but far from all of it.

"You heard the call?" I presumed.

"Only your end, something about a joke?"

"Franco's salary . . . *apparently.*"

"Joy said Franco's salary is a joke?"

"No. Her roommate did."

Yawning, Mike rubbed his newly stubbled jaw. "And this is something that couldn't wait till morning?"

"I had a bad dream. I wanted to make sure Joy was okay."

"Is she?"

"Yvette says she's fine."

"So what did you dream that upset you so much?"

"It doesn't matter—because that call upset me more."

"Go on."

"I will, but first I'm reheating that dinner we never ate." I pointed to Java and Frothy, still smacking their lips over the Savory Salmon. "They're not the only ones who need sustenance. I'm starving."

"Me, too . . ." Mike sauntered into the room and took a seat at the kitchen table. When Frothy curled her little white body around his leg, he picked her up and scratched her ears. "I don't have to meow, do I?"

"Not unless you want a cat toy."

ELEVEN

∞∞∞∞∞∞∞∞∞∞∞∞∞∞∞∞∞∞∞

SKILLET Lasagna turned out to be a great idea for a post-poned supper. For one thing, the dish tasted better reheated: just a splash more sauce and a fresh sprinkling of cheese. The mozzarella bubbled under the heat, becoming somewhat crusty as it cooled; but when you got below that crust, you were rewarded with a world of soft, gooey goodness (the culinary equivalent of my longtime relationship with Mike Quinn, when you got down to it).

"Smells fantastic," Mike declared, inhaling the tangy tomatoes and floral oregano. Then he picked up his fork and dug in.

Since my building was still without power, I'd cranked up the oven for warmth and lit a few candles for light. The little kitchen felt cozy, even romantic, and for a few minutes, I enjoyed our silent munching of ricotta-enriched noodles. Then I began to unload, filling Mike in on my talk with Franco and my call to Paris.

"It's obvious now. The problem between Franco and Joy is

Yvette. She's been talking trash about Franco, filling Joy's head with offensive ideas, and—"

"And why would Joy allow her roommate's opinion to sway her?"

"Because she's close to Yvette. They're like sisters."

Given Mike's twenty years as a detective, I shouldn't have been surprised when he asked, "Particulars please?"

"The two shared an apartment here in New York during culinary school. So, of course, they've been through ups and downs together, parties and Pilates, crushes, breakups, and—"

"And if you know that, why is the situation upsetting you? Has something changed?"

"Yes, Yvette's changed! She never talked like a brat before. Until that phone call, she's been gracious to me and generous to Joy."

"Sometimes 'generosity' comes at price."

I thought about that. "You're suggesting Joy feels obligated to her? That she'd dump Franco just to please her rich girlfriend?"

Mike gave a half shrug.

"Look, I know my daughter. I didn't raise her to judge people with such superficial yardsticks. She never cared if a friend—boy or girl—had money or not. And she's never been a gold digger."

"Maybe Yvette's not the only one who's changed."

My fork stilled in midair. I set it down. "Don't even *think* that."

Mike held my gaze. "Then how do you explain what Franco told you earlier today?"

I shifted on my chair, not liking the question. "Why are you so prickly? Is it that remark Yvette made about a cop's salary? Are you taking it personally? Because I don't feel that way."

"But it seems Joy does—or she's willing to consider it, based on her roommate's opinion."

"We're going in circles. I need to talk to Joy, find out—"

"Find out what, Clare?" His tone was sharp. "You found out. You just don't like what you found out."

I stared across the table. A shadow had crossed Mike's face. The room felt colder all of a sudden, and the candlelight didn't seem so romantic anymore.

"Whose side are you on?"

Mike exhaled tension. Then he leaned forward, out of the shadows. "I'm on your side, sweetheart. I'm always on your side. I've just run enough investigations to know we can't change facts—as much as we'd like to sometimes."

"I don't care. I'm still going to talk this out with my daughter."

"Of course you are . . ." He leaned back again, picked up his fork. "Just don't do some kind of hard sell on Franco. You shouldn't try to defend him."

"Why not? He's the best thing that's happened to my daughter in a long time—and she said so herself. Don't you like him?"

"It's because I like him that I'm saying this."

"Excuse me?"

"Police work is a worthy profession, but it's also a demanding one. Franco should have a woman in his life who understands that, one who's proud to stand by him. No man wants to hook up with a partner who looks down on his work—or his income."

"You *are* taking this personally," I said and he shot me a look that confirmed it.

Given what Mike had been through in his marriage, I shouldn't have been surprised. His ex-wife had never liked his profession—not its demands, its sacrifices, or its salary. But then, the two never should have married . . .

Leila had come to Manhattan as a privileged, out-of-town girl. Her family had pulled strings to help start her career in modeling. When she wasn't at photo shoots, she was partying in bars and clubs with such frequency that she attracted a stalker, a real creep who'd beaten and nearly raped her. Mike had been the street cop who saved her and put the rapist behind bars.

Rattled by the attack, Leila clung to him. They dated for a short time before tying the knot. At his wedding, Mike's precinct buddies made him feel as if he'd won the lottery; he had a gorgeous model for a wife, one who was completely infatuated with him—until the shine wore off.

In a short space of time, Leila had gone from glittering parties and Manhattan shopping sprees to changing diapers in the "wrong part" of Brooklyn. Gone were the designer clothes and exciting photo shoots, nightclub passes, and fawning men buying her overpriced drinks in trendy bars.

As the danger of that rapist became a distant memory, so did the reasons she'd married her husband. Mike the Blue Knight became a square-jawed bore. She didn't understand his dedication to police work and didn't want to hear his sordid stories of dealing with lowlifes. He couldn't afford lavish vacations or gourmet restaurants. She couldn't even depend on him to come home on time.

The way Leila saw it, Mike was cheating her; so she felt *zero* guilt when she began cheating on him.

Right from the start, Mike knew—he was a detective, after all. He'd tailed her a few times, saw the pattern: she would travel to Manhattan on some pretense or other, buy something sexy, wear it to a stockbroker bar, and relive those years when she was young and happy.

He once told me what it felt like, the first time she'd cheated—a nuclear explosion in his gut. The second, third, and fourth times had struck him with lesser impacts—a grenade, a gunshot, a firecracker.

Then came a fifth time, and a sixth . . .

When he stopped counting, he stopped feeling.

Confronting Leila hadn't helped. She lied to his face, claimed his job made him paranoid. He showed her the credit card bills, recounted her movements. She accused him of trying to control her.

Mike didn't want to face the mistake of his marriage so when Leila promised to stop, he looked the other way. If stepping out was something she needed to do, then he'd let her do it as a kind of therapy, a way to help her feel young, pretty, and special again. In Mike's mind, she deserved better than he could give her, anyway, and he was "fortunate" she chose to come back to him again and again.

Then he met me.

A case of homicide brought us together, and we got to know each other solving it. After that, he became a regular at my coffeehouse.

When he found out I'd navigated through a difficult marriage, he began to confide in me about Leila. For years, he'd kept his troubles private. He'd been ashamed to tell friends, family, or the guys on the job who continually told him how lucky he was.

I enjoyed pouring his coffee and listening to him talk, not just about personal things but also his cases. Given the NYPD's continual public scrutiny in the news from "stop and frisk" policies and traffic ticket quotas to frame jobs on suspects, Mike was surprised to find a civilian who admired his vocation—who actually *liked* hearing the particulars of police work.

I looked forward to our time together, and he did, too, until finally Mike realized that maybe *he* deserved better.

Still, Mike's venal wife and toxic marriage left him with more than literal debt. Leila had forever branded her husband with a deep-seated feeling that he wasn't good enough.

"Look . . ." Mike finally said after a long exhale, "if you want me to admit that my base salary is a sore spot, I'll admit it. Do you remember that crack your ex-husband made before I took this job in DC—that comment about my civil servant pay?"

I racked my brain. "I don't remember Matt saying anything about—"

"Allegro can be a class-A jerk, but that's not my point. The man wasn't wrong."

"I don't understand."

"As a Fed, I'm finally making good money, Clare, *very* good and it *feels* good."

"Wait. You're not saying . . ." I studied him. "Please tell me you're not considering staying in DC beyond your one-year commitment."

Mike leaned forward, reached out for my hand. I pulled it back.

"Answer the question."

"I can't answer it—because I don't know the answer. Not yet."

"I don't believe you."

"It's true. My new boss has changed the game plan. We've been directed to expand our case, cast a wider net."

I stared. "How long?"

"There's no set time frame. The sooner we close the case, the sooner I get the bonus."

"*Bonus?* What bonus?"

"Lacey, the new boss, struck a deal with me—if I agree to the wider net, which will help Lacey's career, then I'll get a bonus—a very big one—when the case is closed."

"Since when do you make decisions based on money?"

"Don't you think it's about time? Like I said, your ex-husband can be a jerk, but he was right about my base pay. I want to send my kids to college, Clare. I'm their father, and I want them to know that it's *me* writing the checks, not their new, investment banker stepdad. You can understand that, can't you?"

"To quote you, doesn't that money come 'at a price'?"

He fell silent a moment, gave me an expectant look. "Does it have to?"

Oh no, you don't! "You are not turning the tables on me!"

"When I started this assignment, you said you would stick by me—through thick and thin. Was that idle talk? Maybe you've changed your mind. Maybe these woods are getting too thick and you want to turn back, go AWOL."

That did it. I was on my feet. "I'm not the one going AWOL! Franco told me you haven't checked in with the OD Squad in weeks!"

Mike blinked, clearly taken aback. "I've called in. Sully's been assuring me everything is A-okay."

"Maybe for Sully they are. According to Franco, your cases are being poached by rival jurisdictions. Things are so slow that Franco's started volunteering for uniform duty just to earn overtime."

Mike frowned. "I admit I haven't been stopping by to review cases in person. I figured Sully would step up, handle any jurisdictional beefs. He's a trustworthy guy."

"Sure he is. Franco says he's a *real nice* guy, too. So nice that he's refusing to step on toes to keep new cases. Why should he stick his neck out? It's your team. He's just babysitting."

Mike blew out air, massaged his forehead. "I wasn't aware things were slipping."

"The squad, me, your kids . . . it's all starting to add up. All these problems started a month ago, when this Lacey person became your new boss and began pressuring you—and I know why."

"Oh, you do? I wasn't aware you worked for the Justice Department."

"Well, you're aware I'm a *boss*, aren't you? And as a boss, I know how important it is to keep good employees. This *bonus* you're being promised with no time frame is only part of the plan."

"There's a plan?"

"Of course! Open your eyes, Mike: If your life here in New York gets disrupted often enough, your boss knows you won't have a life to come back to. Your only alternative will be to stay in DC."

The room fell silent after that. Mike simply sat, studying me. Finally, I threw up my hands. "Don't you have anything to say?!"

"Yes."

"Well?"

He leaned forward, dropped his voice. "I think you're overwrought."

"Overwrought?!"

"Anyone who's been through what you have in the past eighteen hours would be a little emotional, even a little paranoid, and—"

"And so what? It doesn't make me wrong."

"Listen, sweetheart, it's like I said. Nothing is definite yet. Time will tell. And right now time is telling me to give this a rest, literally. Let's go back to bed."

He rose from his chair. I sunk into mine.

"You go. I can't sleep."

"Why not? What good will it do you to sit here stewing in the dark?"

"None—but that's not the reason I'm staying awake." (I hated to admit this, mostly because it bolstered the man's "overwrought" argument, but—) "When I close my eyes, I'm in that airport again."

"What airport?"

I filled Mike in on the delightful climax of my nightmare: the exploding jet with my daughter inside, the terminal's window shattering, glass shards raining down, and the pain in my back that was all too real.

In the flickering light of the votives, Mike pulled me out of the chair, pressed earnest kisses to my forehead, my cheeks, my lips—all while taking care not to press the wounds in my back (which reminded me, all over again, why I wanted to stay with this man forever).

"Let's not fight anymore, okay?" he whispered.

"Sounds good to me—although this making-up stuff might be worth it."

He smiled and touched my cheek. I hooked my arms around his neck and began to kiss him back, but as I closed my eyes, there it was again—

Tick, tick, tick . . . "Oh, that stupid clock!"

"What clock?" Mike glanced around the kitchen.

"In my dream, before the bomb went off, a giant clock was ticking backward. I can't stop hearing it, but it makes no sense!"

"Dreams never make sense. They're mind puzzles with scattered pieces. What else do you remember?"

"There was an Air France steward. He pointed out the clock and told me that I missed Joy's plane. So I failed to stop the bomb because I was early."

Mike made a face. "You mean late?"

"No, early."

"How can you miss a plane because you're early?"

"I told you, it makes no sense."

"Come on," he said, gently guiding me toward the kitchen door, "you need to rest—"

I dragged him back. "What else is early?"

"I don't know. It's early now." Mike pointed to the window. "Very . . ."

Outside, the world was cold and dark, a predawn January. I shivered at the black glass.

"In my dream, the airport steward looked like Eric Thorner, did I tell you that?"

Mike frowned. "That must mean something."

I thought so, too—I also thought Mike was right about dreams being mind puzzles. I stared at the black, cataloging the pieces of my dream:

A bomb going off
A backward-ticking clock
Eric Thorner saying I was early
Scolding me for missing something . . .

I broke them down even more: *Bomb. Clock. Eric. Early. Me missing something . . .*

Suddenly, I felt my jaw slackening. "Oh my God . . ."

"What is it?"

I wasn't missing it now: *"Eric Thorner was early!"*

TWELVE

∽∽∽∽∽∽∽∽∽∽∽∽∽∽∽∽

FIFTEEN minutes later, we were dressed and on the street. "Are you sure your friend is on duty?" I asked Mike, lips quivering from a full-body shiver. "It *is* the middle of a dark and frigid night."

Okay, it was closer to 4:45 AM—but it was darn cold.

My Greenwich Village neighborhood was deserted. The sky was rolling with low-hanging clouds, and the winter air was bitter with arctic blasts. Pulling me close, Quinn tried to shield me from a brand-new one. Grateful, I held on, clutching my tote bag (of culinary insurance) on one side, trying to leach a little of the man's heat on the other.

"DeFasio's in charge of the Bomb Squad," Quinn explained, long arm around me, "so I guarantee he'll be there. After the incident in front of your coffeehouse, I expect his 'Italian Squad' will be burning the midnight napalm."

I hoped Quinn was right.

For weeks, Eric Thorner had come to my coffeehouse like clockwork. Every day, he arrived at the same time, except on the day of the bombing. My barista Esther had even pointed it out. "He's early," she'd announced in surprise, but with so much chaos after the car bomb, no one (not even yours truly) had managed to count that fact as important.

Yet it was *highly* important.

"If the bomber had counted on Eric Thorner to follow his usual schedule, then the car bomb should have gone off in some *other* location," I'd explained to Quinn back in my kitchen. "Maybe there was another target—a specific building or office complex. Maybe other people should have been in that car. Wherever that vehicle *should* have been, the people there need to be warned. They need to take precautions."

Quinn had played devil's advocate, pointed out the explosives might not have been triggered by a timer. The Boston Marathon bombers had used a cell phone to detonate their pressure-cooker devices.

"How would that work?" I'd asked.

"The bomber would simply dial it up and *boom*!"

I didn't know which trigger Eric's car bomber had used and neither did Quinn. But we both knew one thing: if lives were still in danger, we had to do something.

As we hurried along Hudson, I riffled my memories for any past dealings with the "Italian Squad," as Quinn had called them. The moniker was no joke; it came right out of New York City's history, when the Mafia used sticks of dynamite to terrorize and extort immigrant merchants and residents. An Italian-American police lieutenant had formed the squad to stop these outrageous acts, which made it the city's first Bomb Squad.

Over the years, as the bombers' identities changed, so did the squad's nicknames: "Anarchist Squad," "Radical Squad." These days, members of this century-old unit were kept busy with all of the above: terrorist threats, gangland violence, and suspicious packages galore.

With their proximity to my coffeehouse, I sometimes noticed squad members stopping in. They always arrived in pairs, kept to themselves, and seldom socialized.

Unlike regular cops, who appeared constantly aware of their

surroundings, Bomb Squad detectives always seemed preoccupied—and (frankly) their military tattoos combined with the insignia on their jackets gave me the shivers. All NYPD special units had their own patches, of course, but this one was the weirdest I'd ever seen. That recollection, along with a subzero gust, set my lips quivering again.

"W-would you tell me one last thing before w-we get there?" I asked.

"If I can."

"Your friend, the head of the A-Team. What's he like?"

"Dennis the Menace?" Quinn snorted. "I wouldn't call him my friend; he's more of a colleague. I don't think DeFasio has any friends."

Great, a hardcase. "But you've worked with him?"

"Once, a few years back . . ."

As Quinn told the story, the two had first met over a car bomb case. Quinn had been running an informant undercover as part of his work investigating drug rings in the Bronx. One morning, the informant started his Caddy and the car filled with smoke; a fire erupted, and he barely escaped with his life. In the burned-out remains of his car, police found a bomb strapped to the starter.

"Lucky for Leroy, the device failed to detonate properly. But now I had a problem: someone knew my guy was a snitch and was trying to kill him . . ."

Other bombs began turning up—in a crack dealer's van, a tricked-out SUV, and a bookie's BMW. Only one of those devices detonated; it killed a freelance pimp. That death was what led to Quinn's first encounter with DeFasio.

"By then, DeFasio had examined the unexploded bombs and noticed all of them used cheap, green wires to connect the explosive material to their timers. These wires were used mostly for teaching purposes, which is why DeFasio figured them to be the work of a trade school student . . ."

The two began canvassing schools and found one that used the exact same type of cheap, green wire, even handed out spools of it to its students. Quinn cross-checked their files with arrest records and within twenty-four hours, he had a dozen leads. In another twenty-four he'd scooped up a suspect.

"DeFasio had gotten me the best clue—from the bombs themselves," Quinn explained. "The perp turned out to be a friend of some gang members who were angry about the invasion of their drug-dealing turf. When we raided the gang's den, we found dozens of devices, all of them primed. They were constructed so poorly that there was no safe way to defuse them, so DeFasio and the guys in his unit put on bombproof suits and loaded them onto a containment truck."

Quinn shook his head. "I was sweating, but DeFasio was *giddy* the whole time. I didn't understand why until he took me up to the squad's training field where we detonated the things, one after the other. He was like a kid with firecrackers, recording each explosion and chuckling with his guys over the instant replays. When the fun was over, DeFasio and his guys took me to a favorite hangout called St. Mulligan's Pub for a supper of Frito Shepherd's Pie—that was a first—and a long night of Irish Car Bombs."

"Irish Car Bombs? I hope you mean—"

"Boilermakers made from Guinness stout, Baileys Irish Cream, and Jameson whiskey." Quinn paused. "I was younger then."

You were happier then, too, I thought.

Okay, so this wasn't the time or place to discuss my observation, but I couldn't help noticing how animated Quinn had been during his story, how alive and upbeat. For a few minutes, the beleaguered Washington G-man was gone and the vital New York cop I knew and loved was back.

I vowed to point this out to Quinn—later. Right now, we were turning onto West 10th Street, a quiet, residential boulevard where the lights of the Sixth Precinct burned brightly. This Bauhaus-style brick box doubled as the headquarters for Squad 228 (the A-Team's official designation).

"A kid with firecrackers," I murmured. "Well, at least you've answered one of my questions."

"What's that?"

I gestured to one of the precinct's garage doors—the one standing next to a basement entrance labeled *Bomb Squad*. Painted against a sky blue backdrop was the unit's insignia: The central figure was a mustachioed man, dressed in black, complete with eye patch and long, dashing scarf. Between his legs was a tubular-shaped bomb, which he rode Dr. Strangelove style. Under him floated a clock face set at five minutes to midnight. The iconic Manhattan skyline (including the now-annihilated World Trade Towers) stood in the background.

To me—and probably much of the general public—the insignia's depiction of daring whimsy in the face of impending death was oddly confounding, even disturbing. In truth, it perfectly illustrated the squad's worldview.

But their strange logo was quickly forgotten. Loud voices drew our attention, and they were getting louder by the second.

THIRTEEN

∽∽∽∽∽∽∽∽∽∽∽∽∽∽∽∽∽∽∽∽∽

"COME on, Sarge, give the First Amendment some respect. People have a right to know!"

The speaker was a young news reporter, green parka too large for his small frame, press credentials swaying around his neck. He was being escorted—okay, *pushed*—through the precinct's front doors by a beefy desk sergeant who hadn't bothered with a coat.

"Sorry, pal. When Lieutenant DeFasio says you gotta go, then you're outta here!"

Despite the frigid temperatures, the sergeant waited in shirtsleeves until the young newsman disappeared down the sidewalk. When he turned, the sergeant spied Quinn.

"Mike!" he said, greeting Quinn with a smile and a handshake. "Welcome back."

"Trouble?" Quinn asked.

"Nah, just another newshound who thinks he can bypass Popeye's press conferences. So what brings you here?"

"Same thing as that reporter," Quinn replied, his breath fogging the icy air. "I want to speak with DeFasio."

The sergeant nodded, and led us through the glass doors.

The lobby smelled of cleaning fluid and air freshener. Like many older city buildings, the steam plant was running overtime. Somewhere deep inside the precinct house, an overheated radiator clanked repeatedly.

We followed the sergeant to his desk; but when he reached for the phone, Quinn stopped him. "Do me a favor, don't call us in. I'd like to surprise him."

The sergeant shrugged. "Be my guest."

A few steps away, we overheard the sergeant talking to a patrolman: "I told DeFasio the Feds would try to muscle in again, only a matter of time."

Quinn didn't appear bothered by the words, but it set me flashing on the sight of that reporter being physically thrown out.

"What if the lieutenant refuses to see anyone right now?" I asked Quinn as we moved down a cabinet-lined hallway.

Quinn waved aside my worries. "He'll see me. I'm not just a former colleague, now I'm an agent of the U.S. Justice Department. That kind of clout will get us through the door."

Maybe, I thought, clutching my tote bag tighter, *but just in case I'm glad I brought some culinary backup.*

At the end of the brightly lit corridor I spied a fire door with a not-so-friendly *Keep the Hell Out* sign taped over the official *NYPD Bomb Squad* plaque.

Quinn paused for a moment to consider the sign. Then he balled his fist and boldly pounded on the door. That persistently clanging radiator suddenly stopped (which led me to believe it hadn't been a radiator after all).

Finally, a deep voice roared, "Who the hell is beating down my door?"

"Open up, you pyromaniac," Quinn called. "It's the *Federales*!"

"I dealt with your people already. Go join your posse at One PP."

"It's Mike Quinn—and a civilian."

The lock clicked and the door opened inward. A stocky, broad-shouldered man in a form-fitting NYPD tee appeared. He ran a hand through spiky, salt-and-pepper hair. Then he folded his muscular arms and leaned against the heavy door, barring our way.

"Quinn," he said with a cautious nod. "So it is you."

Our human barricade had a generous mouth under a roman nose. He looked about forty with a rough complexion and dark, close-set eyes that went from suspicious to attentive when they met my wide-open, green ones.

"And who is *this*?" he asked with naked interest.

Quinn stepped forward. "Clare Cosi, meet Detective Lieutenant Dennis DeFasio, aka, Dennis the Menace."

"*Buona sera*, Miss Cosi," DeFasio said, gently shaking my hand. His gaze went from me to Quinn and back again. "By the possessive way the big guy is looking at you, I can tell you two are *close*. Guess this old firehouse mick is trying to improve his pedigree."

"Watch it, Firecracker. Another ethnic slur will get you a mandatory seat at a sensitivity training seminar."

"Nah. All that touchy-feely stuff is a Fed thing. But then, you'd know all about that now, wouldn't you, Mike?"

"Easy, Dennis. I'm not here for a pissing contest—"

"Then why are you here? The FBI has come and gone. They know and we know this wasn't terrorism."

"How?"

"The type of device, the lack of chatter, no claim of responsibility, and a dozen other indicators, none of which I'm at liberty to discuss. You know I pull bombs off cars and trucks dozens of times a year. They're planted by criminal rivals, disgruntled employees, angry business partners, and scheming spouses. And guess what, Mike: there's a helluva lot more of them than there are jihadists. But then, their firecrackers hardly ever go off—or make the papers. So take a hike downtown and wait for the commissioner's briefing at One Police Plaza like everybody else."

I never saw clout wither and die before. It wasn't pretty. Quinn raised his hands in surrender.

"Wait just a second, okay? I'm not here in any official capacity, *Clare* is. She's an eyewitness to yesterday's bomb blast and has information that may help."

DeFasio seemed underwhelmed. "I have a folder full of eyewitnesses. I'll be turning it over to the investigating officers first thing in the morning. Leave your name and address with the desk sergeant and—"

"And," I sharply cut in, "how many of your witnesses were speaking with the owner of the car when it blew up? I was."

"That's right," Quinn quickly added, "and Clare has pertinent information to the investigation. These statements are time sensitive, too, and may involve other victims."

DeFasio didn't budge. "Talk to the sergeant. He'll get you in touch with the investigators." He checked his watch. "In a few hours."

"Oh, come on, Lieutenant." I stepped closer. "We're here now. Aren't you curious what I have to say? What have you got to lose? Except the opportunity to sample a batch of my homemade fudge."

"Fudge?" The stonewall weakened. DeFasio's tight mouth loosened and his eyebrows lifted with interest as he watched me reach into my trusty tote. I pulled out a large plastic container and waved it under his Roman nose.

"This box is filled with freshly sliced squares of my special Baileys Irish Cream and Caramel-Nut Fudge. It's absolute heaven with a hot cup of coffee."

A groan echoed from somewhere beyond the door. Then a desperate voice cried out, "For God's sake, Dennis, let her in! The lady's got spiked fudge. *Spiked fudge!*"

DeFasio rolled his eyes—and waved us in. "Let's talk in my office."

Score!

I glanced at Quinn and he flashed me a look—half amusement, half admiration.

Fudge one, Feds none.

Honestly, I wasn't surprised. In my view, you couldn't count on people to be hungry for justice. But you could always count on them to be hungry.

FOURTEEN
~~~~~~~~~~~~~~~~~~~~~~~~~~~~~~~~~~

As soon as I stepped through the steel door, I had to make a sharp, right turn into a long hallway that led to the Bomb Squad's HQ. In that shadowy corridor I confronted my second bomb in twelve hours.

I suppose I should have expected something like this. As my grandmother used to say (in Italian, of course), "You shouldn't be surprised to find fruit at the fruit market!" Nevertheless, the sight of a missile-like explosive device dangling over my head by a few micro-thin wires was unnerving, and the shark teeth painted on the tube's pointed snout didn't help.

"Don't let Minnie scare you," DeFasio said, seeing my reaction. "Generally speaking, bombs only go off when someone wants them to."

"But that thing is hanging from the ceiling by threads. What if it dropped?"

"Even if she fell"—he loudly clapped his hands—"this old girl still wouldn't explode. A bomb is one of the most stable devices in the world, Ms. Cosi—"

DeFasio grinned impishly, his bright teeth flashing against his dusky complexion. "Until she isn't."

"Sounds like a teenage daughter."

DeFasio snorted, glanced at Quinn. "I like her."

"Yeah? Me, too."

"Come on . . ."

We followed the lieutenant to a place few civilians, or even police officers, had ever been: the Bomb Squad's inner sanctum.

The chaotic space more resembled a military arsenal than an office. Most of the desk, the shelves, the filing cabinets, and sections of the floor were cluttered with explosive devices.

Hand grenades lay scattered like overripe plums under a tree, each tagged with the country of origin. Among them were complex bombs with rainbows of colored wires attaching clocks to batteries or cell phones, missing only the explosives that would turn them into weapons of mass destruction.

Artillery rounds lined one wall, placed short to tall. Above them, jars and vials of various sizes were crammed on a shelf labeled *Molotov Cocktails.*

Lining the walls were photographs of bombs, X-ray images of lethal devices, and notices from the FBI, ATF, NSA, and Homeland Security, some of which nearly papered over official portraits of the mayor and police commissioner——the man whom the rank and file had nicknamed Popeye, primarily because he resembled the sailorman, complete with a smile that looked like a wince.

DeFasio sat Quinn and me down in dented chairs across from his gunmetal-steel desk. Then the head of the A-Team sunk into a swivel chair and faced Quinn.

"So how's the Washington gig?"

"Complicated."

DeFasio briefly held his nose. "I'll bet. Feds know how to pile it on, higher and deeper, until they stink up the room. I had my fill of G-man stuff in the army."

Quinn had told me DeFasio was an ordnance officer during the Gulf War. He'd joined the NYPD right after the military and was sent to the Hazardous Devices School in Alabama—known in the trade as "Bomb 101"—before joining the A-Team. DeFasio, like every other member of the Bomb Squad, carried a detective's shield, but they preferred to be addressed as Bomb Technician, or "Tech" rather than "Detective."

With mounting impatience (and nervous leg syndrome), I watched Quinn and DeFasio dance around the reason for our visit. Just when I was about to scream—*Lives are in danger and we're wasting time!*—we were interrupted by a third detective poking his head through the door.

"Yo, boss?"

"Something eating you, Spinelli?" DeFasio barked.

"More like something I'm *not* eating."

Younger than his commander by at least a decade, the wiry newcomer wore an identical NYPD tee but with sleeves cut away to display sinewy arms etched with military tattoos. I later discovered that Martin Spinelli was a younger version of his boss, the difference being that Spinelli got his first ordnance training in the Marine Corps, and had served in Afghanistan.

"I heard a rumor that spiked fudge was on the premises," Spinelli said.

I reached for my backpack. "If this officer could show me to the kitchen, I can brew coffee to go with the fudge."

The Bomb Squad had a kitchen, a lounge, and a barracks, too. Like firemen, at least one of the city's multi-man teams was on duty twenty-four/seven to answer emergency calls across the five boroughs—and I'd spotted the kitchen on our way in. The door was closed, but I noticed several cases of Brooklyn's Best Sweet Tea (a pricey artisan beverage) were stacked outside. It struck me as odd.

"That's an awful lot of sweet tea," I'd noted.

DeFasio frowned and his animated arms went rigid. "Techs are trying to re-create yesterday's bomb in the kitchen, so it's *off limits.*"

That explained the noises I'd heard as we passed the

door—a strange hissing rush that didn't register as any pantry sound I'd ever experienced.

"Spinelli, grab a fresh pot and bring cups for everyone."

"Roger that, boss."

Minutes later, I was arranging two dozen squares of my culinary bribe on a platter. When the coffee arrived, I poured for everyone.

Soon DeFasio and Spinelli were cooing over my happy candy. Finally, DeFasio sat back in his chair and sighed, an expression of contentment on his face.

"Good stuff, Ms. Cosi," he said before he gobbled up his fifth piece. "I'm glad you brought it."

This hardcase was getting softer. It was time for me to strike.

"I came with more than snacks," I said. "I'm here to help."

I sat across from DeFasio and for the next fifteen minutes, described in detail the moments leading up to the explosion. DeFasio, Spinelli, and Quinn listened without interruption.

"So," I concluded, "if the bomb had a timer, then it was supposed to explode someplace else. You saw the damage it did to my coffeehouse and the businesses around us. What if it was meant to explode in a crowd, or inside a building's garage? You have to discover the real target before the bomber strikes again."

Three heads nodded in agreement. DeFasio cleared his throat.

"We recovered fragments of an electric clock, so we know the bomb worked off a timer."

Question answered, I thought. *Now we need to know the real target.*

Quinn spoke up. "You'd think a software billionaire would travel with some kind of security."

DeFasio frowned. "Thorner had security."

This was news to me. "I didn't see a bodyguard with him."

"That's because his security was in the car. The individual who died in the front seat was a former New York City police officer."

Fifteen

~~~~~~~~~~~~~~~~~~~~~~~~~~~~~~~

After DeFasio dropped that info bomb, he clammed up. The more I tried to pry details out of him, the more robotic the responses became. In desperation, I tossed a grenade of my own.

"Eric Thorner already told me the victim's name was *Charley.*"

DeFasio said nothing, and the glances he exchanged with Spinelli were infuriatingly unreadable.

"Was he a detective? Was he retired? *Fired?*" Quinn asked.

"I'm not at liberty to discuss the identity of the victim until the next of kin has been officially notified," DeFasio replied, arms folded.

I was beginning to understand this man. When DeFasio lost the ethnic gestures or lapsed into bureaucrat speak, he was holding back. I pushed harder.

"So you're working furiously on this investigation, you've got guys hammering away in the kitchen re-creating the bomb. Yet you've failed to make a phone call to a wife, or visited a family missing a loved one? I find that very odd."

"Informing the next of kin is someone else's headache," DeFasio replied, robot voice in place. "Our job is to find out how the bomb was built, when it was built, why it was built—"

"And *who* built it?"

DeFasio nodded.

"Was that why you ejected the reporter from the *Daily News*? You already have a person of interest, and the journalist was getting too close for comfort."

DeFasio glanced at Quinn. But if he was looking for help, none came.

"Clare's got you," Mike said with a half-smile. "In my experience, she's better at ferreting out information than most of the people at Justice. You might as well come clean. She'll find out sooner or later."

DeFasio threw up his hands. "Okay, it's true. We have a person of interest. But we can't prove anything. It would help if we had Thorner's schedule—"

"Then you'd know where the blast was supposed to have taken place," I interrupted.

"We could also determine when and where the bomb was planted. And if it placed our suspect in the general vicinity." DeFasio shrugged. "You get it."

"Have you talked to Thorner's people?"

"Person. The investigators are at the hospital, waiting for Thorner to wake up after surgery. They tried speaking with Anton Alonzo. He's Thorner's personal and executive assistant." DeFasio rolled his eyes. "If you think I'm a blue wall of silence, you should see how *this* guy stonewalls."

"Too bad you didn't appropriate Thorner's smartphone at the hospital," Quinn said.

"Actually, we believe we have Mr. Thorner's phone. Crime scene techs scooped it off the floor of the Village Blend while we were sweeping for bomb fragments—"

"That's right!" I confirmed. "Thorner had the phone in his hand before he passed out. Then the ambulance crew arrived and he was off to the hospital."

Spinelli flicked some fudge crumbs off his shirt, and reached for another square. "You didn't notice the phone was left behind?"

"I was injured and worried about our staff and customers. Then firefighters told us to evacuate. I took my people out for drinks and left my business partner behind to deal with your forensic units."

"Why was Thorner holding the phone?" DeFasio asked.

"He had it in his hand when the glass hit him. Then he was holding it out to me, asking me to call 911."

"Wish we could access the data." Spinelli shook his head. "But that phone's locked up tighter than a virgin's legs— uh . . . sorry, Ms. Cosi. What I meant was, Thorner would have had to give you the password."

"So you've been trying to retrieve the data on that phone?" Quinn's tone made the question sound more like an accusation.

"What do you think?" DeFasio said evenly.

"You *do* have a warrant?"

"We have yet to establish ownership," DeFasio replied. "Why involve a judge at this point?"

Quinn's eyes narrowed. "You're pushing it, Dennis. You don't want to poison evidence by gathering it illegally."

Spinelli snorted. "Spoken like a Fed."

"I thought we'd gotten past that crap," Quinn replied.

"You're the one who's got to get past it." DeFasio leaned across his desk. "You used to think like a cop, Mike. Now you sound like those FBI pukes my predecessor dealt with back in '93, after the first WTC attack."

Quinn's blue eyes turned frosty. "That's a low blow, even for you."

"Yeah? I don't think so."

Now both men were on their feet. "You've got me all wrong, Dennis, and I don't appreciate—"

"Wait!" I cried.

The two men looked at me.

Fearing fists would fly, I moved between them. "Gentlemen, I don't understand your reference. Would somebody mind explaining what happened in 1993?"

Frankly, I didn't care—but if it would get these guys to "chill," as my barista Dante was fond of saying, I would listen.

"You see!" Now DeFasio was addressing his underling. "In a post–9/11 world, civilians like her have completely forgotten the World Trade Center was bombed once before!"

"And?" I prompted.

"And . . ." DeFasio threw up his hands and sat. Quinn settled down, too. Their stare-off continued, but at least both men were back in their own corners.

". . . one of this squad's technicians found the chassis of the van that carried in the explosives. The Feds told him not to touch the evidence, leave it where it was, but he was worried a cave-in might destroy it, so he violated every protocol and moved it. At the lab on 20th Street, our guys broke protocols again by dousing the chassis with acid so they could read the VIN number. When the FBI found out, all hell broke loose."

"Why did they risk breaking protocols?" I asked.

"Because it solved the case!" DeFasio replied, spearing Quinn.

"It's true," Spinelli added. "Within twenty-four hours, that VIN number led to the rental agency that owned the truck, then to the bombers themselves. Arrests were made and the perps were in custody. Doing it the Fed's way would have given the bombers time to escape and bomb again."

"That's why I'm pushing," DeFasio said. "This bomber killed one of our own. Time is critical, and I don't want the bastard who planted that bomb to get away with murder. Anyway, it's a moot point. A warrant isn't going to do us any good if we can't hack the passcode."

"Ms. Cosi . . ." Spinelli faced me. "Do you think you would recognize Thorner's phone if you saw it again?"

"I'm sure I would."

"I think we caught a little luck here," Spinelli told his boss. "Ms. Cosi could clear up the question of ownership, at least."

"We'll see . . ." DeFasio rose and stepped around his desk. "You're on the spot now, honey. Follow me."

Sixteen

~~~~~~~~~~~~~~~~~~~~~~~~~~~~~~~~~~~~~~~

"**T**hat's it!" I confirmed (with enthusiasm). "That's Eric Thorner's smartphone!"

Spinelli grinned and folded his tattoo-laced arms. "See, boss, I knew she could do it."

DeFasio still looked skeptical. "Are you sure, Ms. Cosi? Maybe we should have done a lineup."

"It's a phone, not a felon," Quinn snapped.

We were downstairs, at garage level, in the chilly heart of the Bomb Squad's workshop and storage area. Evidence cages lined one wall. A bomb disposal robot sat in the corner on rubber treads, hooked up to a battery charger.

In the center of the room, plastic bags filled with debris collected at yesterday's bomb scene were tagged and waiting to be moved to the crime lab on 20th Street. Thorner's smartphone sat, all by its lonesome, on a workbench.

"You're absolutely *certain* this belongs to Thorner?" DeFasio pressed.

"I recognize the way it's contoured to the hand. I'm far

from a smartphone expert, but I've never seen that design before."

"Neither have we," Spinelli confessed. "It's some kind of prototype. We've been trying to hack the password, but we're afraid to mess with it too much or we'll drain the battery."

"You can't recharge it?" Quinn asked, moving closer. I saw it then, that familiar look of cop interest in his eyes.

"I can't even find a way to hook it up to a power unit," Spinelli replied. "There's a slot with a weird pin configuration. I've never seen it before. That's it."

"You can't retrofit it?" Quinn suggested.

"I could try, but it's a risk. I might destroy data."

I hid my reaction to this exchange, but it did my heart good to see Mike Quinn shifting into cop mode again, warming to the details of an investigation—like the old days.

Now Spinelli was addressing me again. He lifted the black-chrome device so I could see the screen. "Do you remember seeing numbers on this display?"

I shook my head. "Too much was going on before, during, and after that car bomb went off."

"But you said Thorner held it out for you to use, right?"

"He did. He was in bad shape then. I'm sure he going into shock . . ."

I closed my eyes, tried to bring back those moments . . .

"Charley, Charley," Eric kept moaning. *"What about Charley?"*

"Stay still," I warned. *"Help is coming, but you have to keep still . . ."*

"Clare . . ."

Eric's intense, little-boy stare was back, but much different now. I could see it in his eyes: I'm scared. *I took his right hand and squeezed.*

"I'm going to get you through this. I promise. It's going to be all right . . ."

His eyes filled and he squeezed my hand back. Then his muted

*voice mumbled something. His left hand rose weakly, as if he wanted
me to take the smartphone still in his grip.*

"Nine ones squared," he said.

*That's when Tuck appeared next to me, describing the scene—
and Eric's injuries—to an emergency operator.*

"Nine ones squared," Eric repeated.

*I leaned close. "We've already called 911. Hang on now, help is
on the way."*

*"No . . ." Eric shook his head, like I'd missed something. "Nine
ones . . ." Then the smartphone tumbled from his hand . . .*

I opened my eyes. "Do you have a calculator?"

"Sure, right here," Spinelli tapped his head.

"Ninety-one times ninety-one is . . . ?"

"Eight thousand, two hundred and eighty-one," Spinelli
replied.

"Try that as the password—8281."

"Won't work," Spinelli said.

"But you didn't even try it."

"Four digits isn't long enough. The screen prompt wants
me to enter a seventeen-digit passcode."

DeFasio whistled. "Who can remember seventeen digits in
the proper sequence?"

"Maybe they're *letters*, not numbers. Like an Italian name,"
Quinn jabbed. "You could fit a lot of extra vowels and double
letters to stretch it."

DeFasio smirked. "You're a riot, mickey Mike."

"It's a seventeen-*digit* passcode," Spinelli clarified, "as in
numbers."

"Yeah, but there's a positive sign here," DeFasio pointed
out. "Our Mike is talking like a cop again. Pretty soon he
might even be thinking like a cop again, too."

"Let's start over, Ms. Cosi," Spinelli said. "Try to remember
Thorner's exact words."

"I do remember. He said *nine ones squared.*"

"Sorry, like I said, ninety-one squared doesn't work."

"Wait," I said. "What if nine ones literally means, nine ones. You know: 111, 111, 111. In that case if you squared it—"

Spinelli slapped his own forehead and shouted. "I'm an idiot!"

"This is new information?" DeFasio muttered.

"It's a kid's math riddle, boss: 111,111,111 squared equals 12 quadrillion, 345 trillion, 678 billion, 987 million, 654 thousand and 321."

Quinn snorted. "What's that mean, Carl Sagan?"

A kid's riddle, I realized. "Now I get it!"

Quinn and DeFasio stared at me. "You do?"

"Yes, the seventeen-digit code is actually easy to remember: 12345678987654321."

Spinelli grinned and nodded as he punched the numbers. "Eureka! We're in!"

Quinn turned to DeFasio, voice serious. "Dennis, you have to make that call now."

DeFasio, still looking a little stunned, nodded. "You're right, Mike. I'm on it."

As his boss dialed a nearby desk phone, Spinelli's face lit up. "Wow, this is Thorner's smartphone, all right. I'm looking at the main menu right now . . ."

DeFasio raised a hand to silence him. "Sorry to wake you, Judge Ansen, but we have a situation involving yesterday's blast on Hudson Street . . ."

While DeFasio spoke, Spinelli produced a pair of delicate reading glasses, which he perched on the edge of his Roman nose. With those wire-rim specs, and the man's brace of tattoos, Spinelli looked like a member of an Italian nonna's biker gang.

DeFasio hung up. "We've got our warrant so it's by the book now." He turned to Quinn. "Happy?"

"Yes, and you should be, too. I brought you Clare Cosi."

"I told you I liked her, didn't I?" DeFasio winked at Quinn. Then he rubbed his hands together. "Let's go fishing."

The three cops huddled around the smartphone screen. I peeked in where I could.

"There are a lot of files here, boss," Spinelli said. "What should I check first?"

"Unless you see a file titled 'People Who Want to Blow Me Up'—"

Spinelli shook his head. "Don't see one of those."

"Then go to the man's itinerary."

"Don't see one of those either—"

"Try looking for a Day-Timer, or maybe he uses an app," Quinn said.

"It's an app, and I've got it," Spinelli cried.

DeFasio raced to a nearby cabinet. "Since we can't download from this phone, I'll have to snap screen shots. We can analyze the data later."

The digital camera looked miniscule in DeFasio's beefy hands. "Start with yesterday's schedule and work backward."

While Spinelli manipulated the smartphone, his boss snapped away

"You were right, Clare. Thorner *was* early yesterday. He should have been at a server farm in Clinton, New Jersey."

Spinelli groaned. "Thorner's car crossed the state line with a bomb on board. Here comes the FBI."

"Not yet," DeFasio countered.

"What's a server farm?" I asked.

"It's a group of computers linked together to perform functions a single computer can't," Quinn replied. "Most large companies maintain a server cluster. They are very expensive to build, but vital in the computer business."

"So blowing one up would do real harm," I said.

"You bet," Quinn replied. "That kind of damage could put Thorner out of business, at least temporarily."

DeFasio continued to snap photos while Spinelli shifted screens. Quinn and I had to step back, so I couldn't see the display. It was a maddening few minutes.

Finally DeFasio spoke. "This is interesting."

"What?" Quinn and I cried in unison.

"You're familiar with a coffeehouse called Joe's?"

"I'm aware of all my competition. Joe's is a fine establishment. I highly recommend them."

"And Driftwood Coffee? How about Gotham Beanery?"

"I'm familiar with those establishments."

DeFasio raised an eyebrow. "And?"

"My nonna used to say if you can't say anything nice, don't say anything at all."

DeFasio chuckled. "I'm asking because Thorner visited all of those places on a daily basis, for many weeks."

I told them about Thorner's "Quiz Master" routine, and speculated he was pulling the same act at all of those other coffeehouses.

"The others must have failed the test, because for the last two weeks Thorner focused exclusively on your Village Blend."

"I still don't know why. He was about to tell me, but the bomb went off and the conversation pretty much ended."

"You'll have another chance to ask him," DeFasio replied. "If Thorner is that interested in your coffeehouse, he'll be back."

"The low-battery warning is blinking," Spinelli warned.

DeFasio lowered the camera "We're done shooting the itinerary. Anything else we should look at before—"

"Damn!" Spinelli cried. "There's a large file here titled 'Clare Cosi.'"

"What?! You're kidding—" I muscled my way between the men. "Open it, quick!"

"Ready?" Spinelli said, moving his thumb. "Here it comes—"

But it didn't. The smartphone screen faded to black.

"What happened?!" I cried.

"Sorry," Spinelli said. "The battery died."

"Can't you recharge it?!"

"It's a prototype," Quinn calmly reminded me. "They don't have the equipment to fit the unique pin connection."

I threw up my hands. "Then how am I supposed to find out why a billionaire has a big, fat file on me?"

"Easy," DeFasio said with a shrug. "The next time you see the guy, *ask* him."

Seventeen

∞∞∞∞∞∞∞∞∞∞∞∞∞∞∞∞∞∞∞∞∞

An hour later, Quinn and I were making our way back down Hudson Street to my wrecked coffeehouse.

We'd hung around the Bomb Squad long enough to watch DeFasio act on my information. First he notified his superiors of Thorner's itinerary and a possible new bomb target. Then he gathered a team, briefing them while they waited for the final green light to cross state lines and make the run to New Jersey.

The lieutenant refused to take me along—although he did bring the rest of my Baileys fudge. (Note to self: the next time you bribe an NYPD commander with food, plant a bug in the Tupperware.) Consequently, Quinn and I wished the squad luck, waved good-bye to their departing truck, and trudged back out into the cold, January air.

When we finally reached my duplex, the sun was beginning to rise. I thought we'd be dog tired. Instead, we were both wired. I suggested coffee and eggs. Quinn had other ideas for spending our excess adrenaline.

With a half-smile, he guided me away from the kitchen

and up the stairs, where he shed his shoulder holster, yanked his tie loose, and kicked shut the bedroom door.

Before I could get a word in, Quinn was dancing me backward. When the back of my knees hit the edge of the mattress, he began tugging off my boots, my pants, my sweater . . .

"You're *sure* you don't want coffee?" I teased.

"Don't you think I'm stimulated enough?"

"Oh, now I see. This is your way of getting me to brew decaf?"

"Bite your tongue, Cosi," he said, nuzzling my neck. "Don't ever try to serve me castrated coffee . . ."

I couldn't guess what sparked this: The excitement of the case? DeFasio's continually roving eyes? My Irish Cream fudge?

Whatever the cause, I didn't care. All that weighty darkness in Quinn was gone. No more anxious need or heaviness of heart. Just electric excitement, a thrilling buoyancy that swept me right along with it.

Soon I was the one lacking patience, and I let my fingers do the walking, unbuttoning Quinn's button-down, unbuckling his belt . . . then my mouth found his and we got busy.

Thirty minutes later, we were both (finally) as exhausted as Eric Thorner's smartphone battery. Lying on my side, still catching my breath, I touched Quinn's stubbly cheek.

His unshaven beard appeared darker than his sandy hair. That morning shadow, along with the intense look in his gaze, gave him a dangerous, almost outlaw air—an aspect of himself he let few people see.

I'd seen it plenty.

To most of the world, Quinn was a straight-laced, do-right guy, but I knew he would break rules, even skirt the law, to protect the people he cared about, me included—and I brushed his lips for that. Then I tried to thank him for his help with the Bomb Squad, but he stopped me.

"It's me who should be thanking you."

"For what?"

"It felt good to be back at the Sixth . . ." He brushed back my chestnut bangs. "I'd forgotten what being a cop felt like."

"As opposed to being a bureaucrat?"

Unlike my own post-lovemaking fuzziness, Quinn's arctic blue eyes were sharp and clear. "You were right, Cosi. Monday morning, I'm going to have a long sit-down with Sully and my squad. No more e-mails and text messages. This time I'm straightening things out face-to-face."

"What about your boss in Washington? Won't Lacey be upset?"

"I'll take the noon express back to DC. Extenuating circumstances."

"Which are?"

"You should know. You're the one who helped DeFasio figure out there might have been another target—Thorner's server farm."

"But why should that matter to your supervisor at Justice?"

"Because this car bomb incident is now crossing state lines, which means Federal officers must be a part of this case, and since I was involved in helping a witness come forward with new information—"

"I get it. I gave you a late slip for class."

Quinn smiled and pulled me across his broad chest. "Thanks, Mom."

I snuggled down and sighed. "You and I may have helped find the real target, but that's a far cry from finding the real bomber."

"No," Quinn said. "It's not."

"It's not?"

"The real target will help DeFasio and his colleagues deduce the real motive. And real motives are some of the best leads we can follow. As much as facts and evidence, a true motive can reveal a true killer."

I considered that idea along with Sergeant Franco's private words to me on Hudson the day before: ". . . *the killer . . . must have had a real hate on for his victim . . . because the device wasn't designed to blow up the car so much as roast the occupants alive . . .*"

I lifted my head. "However they catch this bomber, Mike, I hope they do it soon."

"Me too, sweetheart. Now get some rest."

I wanted to—I just didn't know if I could.

Sure, by this time my back was sore, my limbs tired, my eyelids heavy, but what would happen when I closed them?

With a deep breath, I gave it a try. No more airports, clocks, or explosions (thank goodness); the only thing my mind's eye saw was the perfect peace of blessed black.

Eighteen

~~~~~~

Monday morning came far too quickly. Before I knew it, Mike was gone and the long, cold day left me with nothing to focus on but the plight of my badly battered coffeehouse.

We still had no electricity or phone service, and I spent far too much time on my cell, trying to untie Con Edison's and Verizon's red tape. Then the insurance adjuster arrived.

I gave the man a tour of our shop's damage—interior and exterior—and strongly suggested his assessment be generous, especially for an institution as longstanding and beloved as the Village Blend.

"I'll be in touch with the owner," he said with an effortless poker face.

Meanwhile, my Tucker checked in and (hour after hour) we turned away customers, which made all of us sad.

"So how long are we going to be closed?" Tuck asked near the end of the day.

"Three weeks. And that's an optimistic estimate."

Tuck groaned. "What about the staff? How are we going to earn our living?"

"The Village Blend still has catering jobs scheduled."

"That's two days a week at most. It's not enough income."

"I know."

"Can't you afford to give us vacation pay?"

"Not for long. A week is the most the shop can afford."

Tucker shook his head. "If you put your baristas on unemployment, they'll start looking for other work at other coffeehouses—and they may never come back."

"Believe me, Tuck, I don't want to lose them."

"And what about the community groups? Our second-floor lounge is booked three nights out of seven. These groups don't have much money, and they've already spent advertising budgets to draw their crowds. Esther had a big poetry slam showdown scheduled for next weekend. What's she going to do?"

"I don't know. I'll have to think of something, I'll just have to . . ."

As winter darkness set in, I lit a fire and some candles. Tucker was gone, off to meet his boyfriend, Punch, for dinner. He felt badly about not being able to invite me, but I understood—their host was an off-off-Broadway producer eager to discuss a new project.

On my own, I took a seat at our blue-marble counter and numbly consumed a meal of sweet-and-sour Chinese takeout—which was way too heavy on the MSG. By my last bite, my head was pounding and my heart aching, but not from the MSG. I was badly missing Mike (as I usually did just after his visits), and I dreaded facing my empty duplex.

Unfortunately, there was little comfort to be found down here in the ruins.

On any other Monday, the vacant tables around me would have been filled by neighborhood regulars, students from New York University, newcomers, and tourists. My staff would be busy behind the counter; the gurgling of the espresso machine would mingle with the soft jazz from our sound system and the quiet buzz of conversation. There would be light, warmth, comfort—and caffeine—with my brick hearth adding its inviting firelight to the cozy scene.

Tonight, my only companions were a sharp chill and oppressive gloom. With slabs of wood replacing the shop's French windows, the Village Blend had all the ambiance of a cemetery vault. Even the candles I'd scattered about seemed more funereal than soothing.

And then . . . a light went on! (No thanks to the electric company.)

As I boiled water behind the coffeehouse counter, and added hand-ground beans to my small French press, I found myself studying a framed photograph I'd seen a thousand times before.

Seen, but never understood—until now.

I yanked the photo off the wall and rushed to my cell phone on the counter. The owner of the Village Blend was on speed dial, and she picked up at once.

"I need to see you! When can you come over?"

Madame Blanche Dreyfus Allegro Dubois heard the urgent excitement in my voice, and responded in kind. "Otto and his guests have just finished *il secondo* at Del Posto, my dear, but I shall skip dessert and see you *tout de suite*!"

Nineteen

~~~~~~~~~~~~~~~~~~~~~~~~~~~~~~~~~~~~

MADAME Dreyfus Allegro Dubois emerged from the yellow cab wrapped in caramel blond suede. I hurried to open the shop's front door, but she failed to move toward it. Instead, her slender form stood stiff as an ice sculpture in front of her landmark coffeehouse.

I could almost feel her heartache as she scanned the scorched bricks, burned wood, and blistered paint; then took in the rough plywood covering the shattered French windows, the broken hinges that left our hand-crafted shutters hanging askew.

A bitter gust tried (and failed) to ruffle the firm upsweep of Madame's French twist. She replied with a snap of her fur-lined collar before finally approaching me.

"I'm so sorry," I said, closing the dented door behind her.

"Don't be sorry, dear." She waved a gloved hand. "Sorrow wastes energy."

"What should I be then?"

"Be resolved. A little face-lift is all she needs. Rather like her owner." She sent me a little wink. "Now, where shall we sit . . ."

It wasn't a question. Before I could reply, my octogenarian

employer was moving with regal assurance to a table beside the hearth, where she took full advantage of the crackling fire, pulling off her blond-leather gloves and rubbing her gently wrinkled hands in front of the blaze.

I set a flickering candle on the table for added light and brought over a serving tray. Then she unbelted her long, suede coat—and I could see I'd interrupted a special evening.

Beneath her fur-lined outerwear, Madame was swathed in a suit of shimmering winter white, which dramatically complemented her silver gray hair. Draped around her neck was her *Starry Night over the Rhone* scarf. The Van Gogh's palette of sapphire, aquamarine, and purple augmented the striking hue of her blue violet eyes, but the art museum print would have been a fitting accessory for any dinner with Otto, the "younger man" in her life. (He'd been barely out of his sixties when she'd snagged his attention.)

As a gallery owner, Otto was often wining and dining clients and artists alike, and Madame's years of nurturing the latter through the most colorful decades in Greenwich Village history made her a prized dinner companion.

The only thing about Madame's appearance that seemed off to me was her jewelry—or more accurately, the lack of it.

My former mother-in-law was exceedingly proud of her jewelry collection, which spanned decades and continents, and she seldom missed a chance to show it off. Tonight, however, she wore none of her custom-made bracelets, brooches, or rings. Her only adornment was a platinum chain dangling a single teardrop pearl, its setting delicately sculpted to resemble a plumeria, the Hawaiian flower of welcome.

The necklace was a wedding gift from the late Antonio Allegro—Matt's father and the great love of Madame's life. He'd given it to his young bride during their honeymoon in the Kona District on the big island. (Matt and I had spent our honeymoon there, as well.)

I was tempted to ask about her sparse accessory display, but tabled it in favor of a cheerier subject—

"Since you skipped dessert, I'm making it up to you . . ."

"Delightful," Madame announced after a satisfying bite into my Chocolate-Dipped Crunchy Almond Biscotti. (I'd approached my biscotti-making like the gelato makers of Sicily, working on the recipe until it tasted more like a dunkable stick of chocolate-covered almonds than a cookie.)

From the coffee press, I poured her a freshly brewed cup of my new Fireside Blend. She lifted her cup to sample it, a serious expression on her face. (And I held my breath.)

"I see you're using Matt's new peaberries from that Thai hill tribe cooperative."

"Yes, along with his Guatemalan and Colombian Supremo." (I'd roasted each to bring out their respective best notes and combined them for the blend.)

"I can taste the caramel and macadamia nut . . ." she noted between appraising sips. She waited for the brew to cool a bit more. "Brown sugar . . . graham cracker, green cardamom, cinnamon . . . and chocolate. My compliments to the chef!"

For the first time since arriving, she actually smiled, and I sat back in relief. I also prayed she'd keep smiling after I made my pitch. Clearing my throat, I presented the framed photo . . .

"Madame, do you remember this?"

"Is this a memory test, dear?"

"Not exactly . . ."

I handed over the frame. The scene depicted appeared to be a Village street festival at night. The shaggy hairstyles, bell-bottom jeans, and polyester prints suggested the seventies. A guitarist played cross-legged on a blanket. Young people were gathered around him, singing and laughing.

I pointed to the edge of the photo. "Aren't those our Village Blend's French doors?"

"Indeed they are," Madame said with a wistful look, then a little smile crossed her face and she moved her hand down the photo frame in an almost tender gesture. "This is one of Nathan's—"

"Nate Sumner?" I assumed the former New York photo-journalist and activist was just one of the renowned artists, actors, and writers who'd frequented our shop. Nate was a professor at the New School now, still a regular customer. But the way she said his name . . .

"Was there something between you two back then?"

"A little something, yes, you could say that. Nathan took this during the blackout of seventy-seven."

"July nineteen seventy-seven?"

"That's right. Everything went dark around nine thirty." She pursed her lips. "Those were dark times for this city, as well, and I don't just mean the blackout."

"You're referring to the recession?"

"And the Son of Sam murders—those insane shootings had terrorized everyone that summer, six dead and seven wounded." She shook her head. "On top of that, corruption and incompetence were being exposed at all levels of our government. Too many people stopped believing in a civil society. What happened that night was the result."

"What do you mean?"

"Many of the city's neighborhoods exploded with violence. Stores were ransacked and destroyed. Buildings were set ablaze. There was so much looting and chaos that the police were helpless."

"But there's nothing like that in this photo," I noted, tapping the glass. "Tell me what went on here . . ."

"After the blackout hit, I was planning to close. It was Nate who came in with this family—a mother, father, and three adolescent children. He'd found them stumbling through the streets in abject fear. They were tourists from a small town in the Midwest who'd taken the subway to the Village so the kids could see 'where the hippies lived.' Now they were lost, stranded, and frightened, with no train, bus, or taxi to take them back to their hotel."

"So you stayed open for them?"

"Yes, and that's when Nate made me realize more people were

wandering around our neighborhood with no way to get home. Most of the businesses around our shop—the restaurants, delis, even the bars—had locked up shortly after they lost power."

Madame sighed. "Our neighborhood needed us, and I couldn't say no. Within an hour, our shop was filled to capacity. I didn't want to turn anyone away, so I came up with a solution."

"Your catering tent." I pointed. "That's it in the photo's background, right?"

"Yes, Nate and his friends erected it over the alley beside the coffeehouse. They put Chinese lanterns on poles and our regulars showed up with folding chairs and milk crates."

"Looks like you were the hub of the Village that night."

"Yes; young people spread blankets, played guitars, read poetry—but the blackout made us more than an improvised party, Clare. Those who needed serious help came to us, too: victims of crimes; people with medical conditions. Police officers began stopping by every thirty minutes to pick up new cases."

"What you did was wonderful."

"We did it together, our staff, my Nathan, and his 'hippie' friends—" She gave me a little wink. "Many of the stores that closed were looted, but not ours. Instead of shutting ourselves off in fear, becoming victims—part of the problem—we became a solution."

"A *solution*! This is exactly"—I tapped the photo—"what we should do."

"What do you mean?"

"This shop is blacked out again, but our staff and community need us to reopen. I say we do it, the very same way you did back then."

"My dear, have you been drinking something *other* than coffee? This is January, not July. It's positively freezing out there."

"I phoned Matt already. I'm borrowing one of his emergency generators from the Red Hook warehouse. We can erect our catering tent over the alley, bring out tables and chairs, warm the space with portable heaters—"

"But how will you serve the Village Blend's signature drinks?"

"Our coffee truck is garaged in Matt's warehouse for the winter, but we can take it out . . ." I was so excited I jumped up and began to pace. "We can park it at the curb and use the truck's espresso machine to bring our entire menu back to life."

I paused. "What do you think?"

"What do I think?"

Once again I held my breath, watching Madame's blue violet gaze grow wide then tearful. "I think you truly are the daughter I never had!"

Madame opened her arms, and I happily stepped into them. Then we hugged each other tight. But not for long—

BA-BOOM!

The violent noise wasn't a bomb, but it may as well have been, because we both nearly jumped out of our shoes.

What was that?!

We whipped around to face the shattered French doors, where the noise had come from. Then—

BAM!

In the flickering firelight, we watched one of the long plywood planks covering the broken glass violently shudder then fall away. With a hollow *BONK,* it fell to the coffeehouse floor.

The black rectangle that appeared looked like a postal slot to the abyss.

Madame and I stared at it in dead silence. We sensed movement beyond the darkness. Suddenly the bright beam of a flashlight appeared and slowly began moving around the shop.

"It's a looter," Madame whispered.

I froze for a moment, but Madame was already moving toward the counter.

"Call the police, dear," she calmly advised. "I'll get the baseball bat."

Twenty

∽∽∽∽∽∽∽∽∽∽∽∽∽∽∽∽∽∽∽∽

DESPITE Madame's instructions, I didn't phone the police.

Yes, the minor vandalism scared us, but what if this "looter" was simply a curious Village Blend customer? Before I put some poor patron in handcuffs, I had to be sure there was truly a threat.

"Who are you?" I called. "Who's there?!"

The flashlight beam stopped moving for a second. Then it zigzagged wildly around the wood-plank floor until it found my feet, then my torso, and finally—*my eyes*!

Blinded, I raised my hand. "This shop is occupied!"

"I can see that . . ." The voice sounded male, not young, maybe middle-aged? And somewhat hoarse.

"So what do you want?" I demanded.

Dead silence and then—

"Were you there?"

"I'm right here! Don't tell me you can't see me. Your flashlight is burning my retinas!"

"Were you *there* when the *bomb* went off?" The man sounded irritated, as if I should have understood him the first time.

By now, Madame was by my side, bat on her shoulder like Mickey Mantle. "Say the word and I'll take a swing," she whispered.

"Not yet," I whispered back.

"Did you *see* it?!" the man pressed, his voice quiet but emotional. "The bomb?"

"Yes, I saw the bomb go off. Why do you want to know?"

"Then you saw her?"

Her? I took a step closer and saw dark eyes, dark hair, and a red knit cap. "Who?"

"Don't play games with me!" The man's sudden roar rattled me—and Madame.

"I'll have you know we've called the police!" she cried. (Okay, we hadn't, but *he* didn't know that.)

The flashlight beam vanished. I ran to the open slot in the boarded-up French door, saw the back of a man, and heard his heavy footsteps moving away, down the sidewalk.

As the man passed under a working streetlight, I took a quick mental snapshot. He wore construction-like, tan work boots, dark blue denims, and a light gray parka. The parka was bulky so it was hard to tell what his build was like. His height appeared several inches less than Mike Quinn but taller than most New York men (about my ex-husband's height of six feet). His hair was probably short because the bright red knit cap covered it completely. There was something written on the cap in white lettering—*ARE* was all I could make out.

"Give me that bat!" I grabbed the weapon and took off.

"Where are you going?!" Madame demanded.

"After him! That man was no looter . . ."

I sprinted to the front door, but it began opening before I got there. *Holy cow! How had he doubled back so fast?!* Planting my feet, I lifted the bat high and cursed my decision to delay the police. Madame was like a mother to me, and I'd do anything to protect her.

As the door swung toward me, I cocked the bat back, ready to swing it forward when—

"A little early for spring training, isn't it?" (The voice was male, but it wasn't the stranger's.) Standing on our doorstep in black jeans and a battered leather bomber was Matteo Allegro, my ex-husband.

"Get out of my way!" Off and running again, I lunged for the sidewalk as Madame called—

"Stop her, son!"

Unfortunately, this was one time Matt listened to his mother.

Twenty-one

~~~~~~

"**For** heaven's sake, Matt, let me go!"

"Forget it."

"That man is getting away!"

I tried to break away, but Matt's grip on my waistband rivaled the one on his bank account.

"You don't even know why you're stopping me!" I cried, squirming. "Be reasonable!"

"Be reasonable?!" He tightened his hold. "You're running out into a freezing-cold January night, swinging a baseball bat after some 'man'—and I'm the one who needs to be reasonable?"

With a grunt, I finally twisted with enough force to dislodge his hand. *Freedom!* Unfortunately, Matt's other hand had already snaked around my torso. Before I could get away, his muscular arm jerked me back against his hard chest. I wasn't going anywhere.

"Listen to me," I snapped, "I'm not going to assault him or even try to stop him. I only want to talk to him!"

"Him who?" Out of patience, Matt addressed his mother. "Will you translate *crazy*, please?"

"Some awful looter tried to break in . . ." she explained. "I told Clare to call the police, but she wanted to speak with the man for some reason."

"Not for *some* reason! For a *very specific* reason. The guy was emotional—and his questions were bizarre. I think he may have been the bomber!"

Matt let out a groan. Then he wrapped his other arm around me, lifted me off my feet, and swung me back into the shop. When he finally released me, there was nowhere to go. He shut the door firmly, leaned against it, and crossed his arms.

I threw up my hands. "You're being ridiculous, autocratic, tyrannical—"

"I'm fine with that—as long as the mother of my daughter is safe."

"You're not my husband anymore."

"No, but I'm your business partner, and your friend. And it's *your turn* to act reasonable. That man, whoever he was, is long gone by now."

"I should at least tell the NYPD Bomb Squad." I pulled out my cell phone.

Matt grabbed it. "Tell them what? That some poor slob got tipsy, got curious, and when you caught him in the act, decided to pull your chain?"

"Arsonists are famous for watching their fires. Criminals often return to the scene of the crime. Even if he's not the bomber, I think he may know something, and—"

"And it's not your job to solve this crime. It's the NYPD's job, and the police don't need your help."

I should have bit my tongue. Instead, I blurted the truth. "They already did!"

"What?" Matt frowned as he studied my face. "Oh no. I know that look!" He turned to his mother. "What are you two up to?"

"I'm not entirely sure." Madame arched a curious eyebrow at me. "What are we up to, my dear?"

"Over the weekend, Mike Quinn introduced me to the

head of the squad, that's all. I had some pertinent information, which he was happy to get. He told me to contact him with any leads. This might be one—"

"Well, it's not," Matt cut in.

"You don't know that."

"Come on, Clare, think it through. By now, the police certainly have some person of interest under surveillance. If it's this looter guy of yours, there's probably a tail on him already. Tell me you can live with that."

I folded my arms.

Matt sighed. "Please."

"Okay . . ." I took a calming breath. "Like you said, he's gone by now . . ." *But he'll probably be back,* I silently added, *and that's when I'll talk to him.*

KNOCK, KNOCK, KNOCK!

This time it was Matt who jumped. Bracing himself for a fight, he pulled open the door. Otto's driver tipped his cap—

"Good evening, sir, I'm here to pick up Madame Dubois."

"I'll be right there!" she called. "Otto's hosting nightcaps at his gallery," she explained as she gathered her things. "It's an intimate gathering of international buyers. I'd invite you both, but . . . I believe you two have things to *discuss.*"

On the word *discuss,* she sent Matt a meaningful look. Then she pecked his cheek, waved at me, and headed out the door.

Twenty-two

∽∾∽∾∽∾∽∾∽∾∽∾∽∾∽∾∽∾∽∾∽∾

"So?" I asked, holding out my hand.

"So?" Matt echoed, slapping my mobile phone back into it.

"What exactly are we supposed to 'discuss'?"

"Got anything to eat?" Matt said, ignoring my question.

"I have some extra Chinese takeout," I said and offered to reheat it.

"You didn't cook something special for the flatfoot?"

"*Mike* ate every bite—but I did bake up a storm for his kids and his squad meeting. Your mother ate the last of the biscotti."

"Damn."

"But I still have a few Chocolate-Bottom Banana Bars upstairs."

"Lovin' from the oven . . ." He clapped his hands together and rubbed. "Now you're talking!"

Matt always did look forward to my home cooking. His new wife, Bree—disdainer-in-chief of *Trend* magazine—was many things, but a baker of banana bars wasn't one of them.

"Sit tight," I said.

Unfortunately, he didn't.

After climbing the stairs to my duplex apartment and venturing into the kitchen, I heard Matt's familiar footsteps. Turning, I found my ex-husband leaning against the doorjamb, hands in the pockets of his tight black jeans.

"What are you doing up here?"

He shrugged, a bad-boy look on his black-bearded face.

"*Matt?*"

"It's warmer up here."

"No, it's not. Go back down to the shop."

"Why?"

"Because you don't *live* up here. Not anymore."

Matt's slow-spreading smile was beyond smug.

"What's so funny?"

"The reason you don't want me up here," he said. "It's obvious: you don't trust yourself around me."

"Oh, please!"

He crossed his arms. "Prove it."

"You're a child sometimes, you know that?" I expelled a frustrated breath. "Fine! Sit down, then."

"Not here. We'll be more comfortable in the parlor. I'll start a fire for you there . . ." He caught my eye as he peeled off his jacket. "Unless you'd like one in the bedroom."

"Don't get cute or I'll put you on the sidewalk—by way of a third-floor window."

"Just checking."

Ten minutes later, I was sitting by a roaring blaze again, this time on the rosewood-framed sofa in the duplex's well-appointed salon.

Matt's mother had decorated the place herself, collecting and placing gorgeous pieces over many decades. The main room—with its carved rosewood and silk sofa and chairs, jewel-toned Persian prayer rug, cream-marble fireplace, and French doors opening to a narrow, wrought-iron balcony of flower boxes—felt more like something you'd find in a Paris arrondissement than a New York walk-up.

As a girl who grew up in a Pennsylvania factory town, I continued to feel grateful and blessed for the privilege of sitting here amidst this Old World elegance, sipping my hot, fresh cup of Fireside Blend. Matt, who had grown up in a sophisticated world of beauty and culture only to become an extreme sports nut and cocaine addict, was acting as he usually did in his mother's apartment—aloof to civilization.

Barely chewing, he stuffed three of my Chocolate-Bottom Banana Bars into his mouth inside of two minutes.

"Didn't you have dinner?"

"Many hours ago," he garbled mid-chew and brushed crumbs from a black, cashmere V-neck just tight enough to show off his sculpted pecs. "Bree and I went to her favorite sushi bar before she hopped a flight to LA. But, I'm sorry to say . . . no matter what Bree treats me to, it seems I'm never completely satisfied . . ."

He threw me a suggestive smile. I rolled my eyes.

Matt and Bree had an open marriage, and when the cat was away, Matt loved to play. But there was no playing around here, which I'd made clear enough *multiple* times.

"Enjoy the baked goods," I told him, "because they are the *only* goodies you'll get from me tonight."

Unfortunately, the thickest muscle in Matt's body was in his head. All he did was smile wider.

"Okay, talk already," I demanded. "What did your mother want you to discuss with me?"

"The artwork." The swipe of a napkin wiped his smile, too, and his mood shifted. "I know it's not a happy conversation, Clare, but you have to make the decision."

"What decision? I don't know what you're talking about."

"What do you mean, 'you don't know'—" He stopped abruptly, studied my perplexed face, and cursed (in several languages). "She didn't tell you!"

"Tell me what?!"

"I can't believe she dumped this on me," he muttered.

"Matt, explain!"

He closed his eyes and took a breath. "The insurance adjuster called Mother this afternoon. The news wasn't good, Clare . . ."

"How bad is it?"

"Bad . . ."

He went over the numbers with me, and my heart sank.

"Our insurance company contacted Thorner's insurers. They're hiding behind their legal skirts. They refuse to pay a cent until the legal issues surrounding the case are resolved."

"You mean the bomber needs to be caught?"

"And convicted. Then they can go after the guilty party in civil court to claim damages."

"But even if they arrested someone tonight, the trial wouldn't come up for at least a year!"

"I know. Our insurance company is prepared to cut us a check and wait for Thorner's insurers to reimburse them, but it's nowhere near what we need . . ."

Because our coffeehouse was located in the Village historic district, exterior restoration would have to comply with strict codes. We'd need to hire construction companies with specific expertise, which meant repairs wouldn't be cheap. The estimate was astronomical.

"Mother refuses to mortgage the place or sell any of the furniture, but she is going to have a fire sale with her jewelry collection—"

"So that's why she only wore one piece tonight?"

Matt nodded. "The rest is being appraised. In a few days, she'll select which pieces to sell—"

"That's going to break her heart!"

"And she wants you to number the pieces of artwork from the coffeehouse and the duplex. Give her a list of items you're willing to part with, in descending order. Otto will appraise them and you can make the final decision."

"Decision on what?" I gawked in horror as it hit me. "On which ones to *sell*?"

"Or auction, yes. We'll only sell off what we have to until we reach the amount we need."

"But, Matt—it's a hundred years of Village Blend history!"

"I know."

"I can't believe this is happening to us . . ."

"Believe it."

I couldn't sit still any longer. On my feet, I began to pace. "Your mother should be the one to choose which pieces."

"She wants you to do it, Clare."

"But she's the one who has the most personal attachment to it all! Oh, Matt, imagine her memories!"

"That's why she wants you to do it. It's too painful for her, and Mother said . . ." His voice trailed off.

"What?" I whispered.

Matt's expression looked sadder than I'd seen it in a long time. "Mother said you'll be the one living with the remaining artwork for the next thirty years, not her—and that's why the choice should be yours."

His voice was even, but his eyes were damp. The words made me think of losing her, too, which made my own eyes well.

"Aren't you going to help me choose?" I asked, my voice barely there.

"Clare . . . I'm no art expert. I spent most of my adult years traveling the globe. You're the one who went to art school. You and my mother—that love was something you two shared from the beginning." The firelight flickered, casting shadows of regret across Matt's olive complexion. "It was always your thing, not mine . . ."

He rose. "So you'll let me know? Give me the list sometime tomorrow, then?"

I moved to the door with him, swiped the moisture off my cheeks. His strong arms reached for me; I stepped back.

"Sorry," he said, slipping into his bomber. "Old habits die hard . . ."

The words made something inside me lurch. More than anything, I wanted to fling my arms around the father of my daughter and cry my eyes out, but I held myself in shaky check.

Matt would be happy to give me comfort with his hard body, and I would gladly take it—possibly too far.

I'd never admit it, but he was right. Alone and hurting, seeing that tenderness in his liquid-brown gaze, feeling that desire to console me in his soft touch, I didn't trust myself.

"Good night, Matt," I said stiffly. "I'll see you tomorrow."

"Chin up, okay?" He cleared his throat. "I'll bring that generator from the warehouse, like you asked. We'll set up the catering tent and you can start serving our customers again. That's something to look forward to, isn't it?"

"Sure."

I closed the door, bolted it, and faced the apartment—four walls and two floors that contained a bounty of treasures from more than a century of Greenwich Village history.

There were pen-and-inks, portraits, cityscapes, prints, sketches, poems, manifestos, even doodles on napkins from legends of the New York art world—and each and every piece carried a memory of a wonderful tale Madame told me (once, twice, a dozen times) about how she and the Village Blend were connected to it.

Every piece in this building was an irreplaceable gem. Like a curator, I proudly cycled them in and out of the main shop downstairs and its second-floor lounge to delight (and educate) young and old about this neighborhood's indelible place in art history.

Selling off these pieces would be like parting with tangible parts of my dear friend and mentor, my daughter's beloved grandmother, a woman who'd been like a mother to me for the past twenty years.

How can I choose? How?

"I can't . . ." I whispered. "Not tonight."

I doused the fire and blew out the candles.

The night felt black and cold as death as I trudged up to bed. Numb as a zombie, I changed into my nightshirt and slipped under the pile of covers. Only when my face kissed the pillow did I let the tears flow.

Twenty-three

~~~~~~

My heart nearly stopped the next morning when I heard it again.

BA-BOOM!

I was shivering in the shower, reliving pioneer days with a rustic sponge bath when the downstairs tremors began. In my haste to get to my cell phone, I knocked over my pail of stovetop-heated water. I didn't care. If that heavyset "looter" in the light gray parka and red knit cap was back, I needed to find out fast.

Without a stitch of cloth covering my curves, I raced across the freezing parquet floor of my bedroom and speed-dialed my ex-husband. *Voice mail—*

"Matt, get over here! It's an emergency!"

BA-BOOM! BA-BOOM!

The pounding was getting stronger, rattling the glass panes in my window frames—in broad daylight.

That's it, I'm calling 911.

The dispatcher would need a description of the man

assaulting our shop. With the sun up, I could probably get a decent look at him from up here.

Throwing on my short, terry robe, I raced to the window. Using two hands, I ripped open the long drapes—and came face-to-face with a telephone lineman.

What the . . . ?

The big, burly guy with a battered Verizon hard hat stood staring at me from a cherry picker bucket on a crane that had him nearly bumping up against my fourth-floor window.

Dumbfounded, I stumbled backward, and my loosely tied robe fell open. For a mortifying second, I just stood there, generous curves naked as a newborn to the man's widening eyes.

Flashed before breakfast, the big Verizon guy nearly fell out of his bucket.

I screamed and shut the drapes.

Blushing and cursing in tandem, I yanked a shapeless wool sweater over my head, tugged jeans over my hips, and dived into a pair of power flats. I'd just grabbed the shop keys when my cell went off.

"Matt?!"

"No, boss, it's your favorite barista—and I am in the weeds here! Help!"

"Esther? Where are you?"

"Downstairs!" Clearly in a state, she was shouting into the phone over sounds of pounding and whirring. "Can you hear me? We're suddenly surrounded! All Tucker and I did was unlock the dang shop and the cast of *This Old House* descended like locusts!"

"Hang on! I'm coming!"

I rushed into my shop to a blast of cold air from the wide-open door and an army of workers in bulky jackets.

"There she is." Esther and Tucker pointed. "That's her!"

"Miss Ko-see?" A workman in a hard hat approached, clipboard in hand. "You the shop manager?"

The man was speaking loudly, trying to be heard over a jackhammer in the street. Behind him, men were cutting a hole in Hudson, surrounded by a half-dozen trucks and a forest of emergency orange cones.

Con Ed, Verizon, the Department of Environmental Protection (aka the water company) were all represented. A glazier's truck pulled up with taped-up windowpanes strapped to its flanks.

"Yes, I'm Ms. Cosi!" I yelled back.

"I'm Stan, your project manager. I have all the permits ready to go. The electricians have already started working. The job's urgent, we understand, and we're on it . . ."

Is this Matt's doing? I wondered in astonishment. *How can it be? We haven't even raised the funds for this yet!*

I noticed a yellow cab dodge several construction vehicles as it pulled up to the curb. A well-built, black-bearded guy in jeans and a leather bomber emerged from the backseat.

Speak of the devil . . .

Matt threw bills at the driver, dodged a gauntlet of construction workers, and raced to my side. "Are you okay? What's the emergency? And what the hell is all this?!"

"You didn't arrange this? Did your mother?"

"No!"

"Then who?" I waved over Stan, the project manager. "Sir, can you tell us please—who's footing the bill for this work?"

As my question hung in the air, Matt, Tucker, Esther, and I drew closer, waiting for his answer.

"You don't know?" Stan asked in surprise.

"No!" sang our curious chorus.

"THORN, Inc., arranged the construction. The certified check came through Sunday morning, signed by Eric Thorner, the CEO himself. We received your building owner's approval to do the work about an hour ago—a Mrs. Dubois. She signed the papers."

Tucker, Esther, and I gaped in happy awe.

But for some reason, Matt was grimacing.

He confronted Stan: "Are you telling me that in some mystical fashion, you and Mr. Thorner acquired all the necessary construction approvals and licenses from the appropriate city agencies in record time?"

Stan smirked. "I think the magic word you're lookin' for is *money*."

"How long are these repairs going to take?" Matt fired back.

"We guaranteed Mr. Thorner the work would be completed in three days."

"Three *days*!" I nearly fainted.

"Oh my goodness!" Tucker cried. "I thought it would take three to four *weeks*!"

"And that's not even the best part . . ." It finally sunk in that I no longer had to choose artwork to sell. All the artifacts of precious Village Blend history could stay with us now. "Isn't Eric Thorner a wonderful man?!"

Esther whooped and we all hugged—all except Matt.

"Don't be such Pollyannas," he snapped. "The jerk was probably scared."

"Of what?" I asked.

"Of us taking him to court, suing him for damages."

Okay, that annoyed me. "Why would a man like that be afraid of a lawsuit? He has a team of lawyers on retainer, and you said his insurance company was handling it."

"I did, but . . ." Matt looked away.

I shook my head, tears of happiness blurring my vision. "I was about to put the staff on unemployment and sell off precious pieces of our Village Blend history. Now we'll be open for business in just a few days! I'm sorry, but this is astonishingly decent of Thorner, and you should be grateful, too."

"Why? Thorner's the one who caused all this damage."

"No," I said. "Thorner was a *crime victim*, just like us . . ."

After a few more minutes of verbal Ping-Pong, Stan interrupted us with a tap on my shoulder.

"Good news, Ms. Cosi. You now have hot water and electricity."

"It's Christmas!" I cried.

"No, Clare, it's January."

"And you're still in Grinch mode. Why?"

"Because you're acting like this is some kind of generous gift, and it's not. You should be angry at Thorner, Clare. He brought that bomb here. Fixing our shop is something he *owes* us!"

"Ms. Cosi, excuse me," Stan interrupted, "but we also have a special delivery for you. They're rolling it in now . . ."

Twenty-Four

⟨∾∾∾∾∾∾∾∾∾∾∾∾∾∾∾∾∾∾∾⟩

"It" turned out to be a wooden crate the size of a small refrigerator laid on its side. Strapped to a wheeled cart, the box was pushed by a smiling man in a ski parka.

"It's bigger than a bread box," Esther declared. "But what is it?"

John F. Kennedy Airport air cargo tags were stamped on the box, one marked *SEATTLE to NYC: SAME DAY AIR.* Then I read the sender's name and address.

"My God," I sputtered. "Is this . . . ? Could this be . . . ?"

The deliveryman extended his hand. "Ms. Cosi? My name is Terrence. I'm here to install your brand new Slayer."

Esther's scream of unbridled joy halted construction for a moment. Tucker staggered backward, clutching his heart in a mock swoon. When Esther stopped jumping up and down, she grabbed Tucker and they did a barista tribal dance around the wooden box.

"Slayer! Slayer! We've got a Slayer!"

My eyes were too blurry with tears to join them so I

pumped the deliveryman's hand. I had to ask, though I already knew the answer.

"This espresso machine was ordered for us by . . . ?"

"THORN, Inc. Mr. Thorner insisted on immediate delivery."

I turned to Matt. "He didn't owe us *this*."

Matt glowered. "Slayers are handmade to order. How could Thorner possibly buy one so fast? Isn't there a waiting list?"

"You're right, sir, there is," Terrence replied. "This Slayer was scheduled for a coffeehouse in Cambridge. Apparently Mr. Thorner bought out their contract."

"Apparently, huh?" Matt speared me. "I wonder what else he's *apparently* planning to buy around here."

I reached up and shook my ex by his hard shoulders. "For goodness' sake, man, don't be so cynical! It's Christmas in January, and Eric Thorner is our Santa Claus! So, ho-ho-ho!"

"Sorry, but I think the guy wants to turn us into his 'ho.'"

"Enough. I'm going upstairs to take a hot shower—"

"Before you go, Ms. Cosi," Stan interrupted again, "there's a Bubba from Verizon who has a question for you."

Bubba? Uh-oh. "He wouldn't be that big, burly guy who was up on that cherry picker crane, would he?"

"That's the fellow. He, uh . . ." Stan's expression turned sheepish. "Well, he wants to know if you'd like to go out with him on a bowling date Friday."

I groaned.

Matt frowned at me in befuddlement. "You know the guy?"

"Let's just say he's *seen* me around—" (*A little too much of me.*)

I turned to Stan. "Please tell Bubba that I have a boyfriend, but I wouldn't mind a break on my next Verizon bill. He'll know why."

"I have a package for Clare Cosi!"

More?! The announcement came from a man in a private

courier uniform. He handed me a large, long box. I broke the tape seal and opened it, to stare at white paper.

"Flowers?" Esther guessed. "Who's your secret admirer?"

Matt chuffed.

"Let's find out." I ripped the paper away. Esther and I both gasped.

Tucker came over to investigate and nearly swooned, for *real* this time! "Are those *blue* roses? Actual, real-life blue roses?"

Apparently they were, though the word *blue* was too prosaic to describe the brilliant beauty of these blossoms. The only hybrid "blue" roses I'd ever seen were in a flower show, and they had been more lilac in color.

These were a striking cobalt, a vibrant hue that, until now, I'd thought impossible to produce in a flower—unless you were Claude Monet with a brush in your hand.

"I found instructions." Esther untied a string which released a small plastic card. "How to Care for Blue Velvet Roses," she read.

"They're so lovely," Tucker said with a sigh. "He must have sent you three dozen. And the name is so romantic—*Blue Velvet*."

Esther rolled her eyes. "Don't gush, Broadway Boy, they're Franken-flowers—"

"What?"

"It says on the card that these roses are genetically engineered and not yet available commercially."

"Prototype flowers?" Tuck cried. "They must be priceless!"

"What makes you so sure? Are you a horticulturalist in your spare time?"

"No, Snark Queen, a *dramatist*, and when I played Laura's gentleman caller in the off-Broadway revival of *The Glass Menagerie*, the director wanted every audience member to leave with a blue rose. He insisted that nothing else would do. The set designer priced those Suntory True Blue Roses from Japan, and informed the producer that if they used them, one-fourth of the daily box office take would go to the florist."

While Tuck shared his backstage anecdote, I discovered a gold-embossed envelope secreted among the blossoms. The missive was hand-addressed to me in an elegant script.

"Open it! Open it!" Esther chanted.

Matt loomed over me, but not to admire the flowers. "What's in the envelope?"

"I can't believe this. It's an invitation—Eric Thorner wants me to have dinner with him at the Source Club on Thursday night."

"The Source Club," Tuck said in awe. "Whoa . . ."

Mouth gaping, Esther was speechless (a rare occurrence).

Matt didn't share my baristas' shock or enthusiasm. Instead, with a glower, he announced, "There is *no way* you are going to dinner with that tech brat!"

His voice was so loud that the men installing our new windows stopped to stare. *Oh, for heaven's sake . . .*

I grabbed the box of roses with one hand, hooked Matt's arm with the other. "Come help me put these in vases," I said, and dragged my ex into the back pantry.

"Stop making a scene," I hissed.

"Better than watching you make a fool of yourself."

I nearly hurled the flowers at him. "You want to see a fool? Look in the mirror!"

"You're too naïve to know what Thorner is really after."

"Don't make me slap your face."

"Slap away; it wouldn't be the first time. I just don't want you involved with this guy—"

"Listen to me. There's a very good reason I'm going to dinner with Eric Thorner. When I was with the Bomb Squad, they accessed his private smartphone files—and he had a file on me."

"You?!" Matt's eyes bugged.

"Before that bomb went off, Thorner said he wanted to make me an offer—"

"Offer? As in proposition? It really is *ho-ho* time!"

"Will you please get your mind out of the gutter? A billionaire wants to do *business* with us."

"With you, you mean."

"Me *is* us—I mean this coffeehouse, the Village Blend. And you know we could really use that kind of business."

"Says who? We were getting along fine before the Quiz Master showed up—"

"You have a short memory, Matt. Before any of this happened, we were having major money problems. That's why I'm going to dinner with Thorner—"

"Not while this guy has a big, fat target painted on his back. We don't even know who wanted to blow him up or why!"

I began to separate the roses. "Okay, then why don't you let me find out?"

"Don't get cute."

"I'm not kidding. Going into business with this man could resolve all of our financial woes. The only problem is—"

"Somebody is trying to bump him off!"

"Yes, that's right—and I can be of assistance."

"Assistance? We're not talking about mopping up spilled coffee here. We're talking about a killer who used a firebomb!"

"You know I'm good at asking questions, finding answers, uncovering—Ouch!"

I shook my finger as bright red droplets appeared. "You'd think the science that created these blue roses could have eliminated the thorns."

"Oh, no . . ." Matt blanched.

"It's not that bad," I said, washing the wound. "Anyway, the guy's company is called THORN, Inc., so I guess I should have known, right?"

Matt didn't reply. He was mumbling in Spanish while clutching the talisman hanging around his neck.

"What are you doing?"

"Warding off the bad luck."

"What?"

"You pricked your finger on the man's flowers. That's an omen, Clare."

"Of what?"

"In Ethiopia they'd inform you of an Arabic legend about a man who stole a prince's bride by pricking her with a thorn from a *zizouf*—"

"Ziz-who?"

"A magical lotus. And then there are the Yanomami, who'd warn you about their tribal beliefs through the story of a woman held in thrall to a lustful man after being pricked by a thorn from a Brazilian spider flower—"

"I think you've been in the bush too long. Don't turn native on me."

"Sorry, but I don't want you anywhere near the man who gave you those."

"It's not your decision. The billionaire is sending his limo for me at eight o'clock Thursday night, and I'm going to be in it."

"A limo?!" Matt's face turned so red I thought he was going to pop an artery. "And I'm the one with a short memory? It was his limo that exploded in front of our coffeehouse, remember?"

"Yes, so what are the chances it could happen again? Astronomical, probably."

"No! The mother of my daughter is not getting into Eric Thorner's limousine. Not Thursday night, and not any night! Do you hear me? I absolutely forbid it!"

Twenty-five

~~~~~~~~~~~~~~~~~~~~~~~~~~~~~~~~~~~~~~

"**And** that pretty much brings you up to speed, Mike . . ."

I switched the cell phone to my other hand and gazed at the city lights rolling by the limo's window. It was Thursday evening, and I was Cinderella, on my way to the most exclusive club on the Eastern Seaboard—and in vintage style. Even jaded New Yorkers were gawking at the antique Rolls that Eric sent for me.

"Don't you think this invitation is a little rushed?" Quinn's deep voice rumbled in my ear. "Thorner was injured in the bombing. What's the damn hurry? There's got to be an ulterior motive—"

"For all I know, a nurse is going to wheel Thorner to the table and right back into an ambulance after dessert. If he's willing to take such pains to be gracious, then how could I refuse?"

"Your powers of deduction are failing you, sweetheart. Or maybe the air in that limo is a little thin—"

"Don't patronize me. I have Matt Allegro for that. He actually forbid me to go to this dinner. Can you believe that?

I reminded him we were living in the twenty-first century, not the sixteenth."

"Sounds like the guy was worried. I know how he feels."

"There's a security escort in a black SUV, right behind this limo as I speak. And Eric's driver assured me both vehicles were checked for bombs, by a member of the NYPD Bomb Squad, before they picked me up. And speaking of bombs, do the police have a person of interest yet?"

"I know they haven't arrested anyone," Quinn replied.

"Well, I plan to ask Thorner about it." *Along with a whole lot of other things . . .*

A traffic light switched to green as the limo approached the intersection, and the mute driver turned onto Water Street.

"The Source Club is just up ahead. I have to say good-bye."

"Well, order something expensive, thank him, and part company. I'll give you a call at eleven or so—just to make sure you're home safe and sound."

I knew that tone. "You're not fooling me with that 'safe and sound' stuff. Like I said, this is a business dinner." I lowered my voice. "Really, Mike, if I were going to step out on you, would I call you to tell you about it? If you think so, then *your* powers of deduction are slipping."

I knew I'd said the wrong thing the moment I said it. Only now, I couldn't set things right. The limo had stopped at the curb, and an usher in a tux opened the door for me.

"Good evening, Ms. Cosi," he said, extending a gloved hand. "May I escort you to Mr. Thorner's table?"

"We'll talk at eleven. I love you," I whispered into the cell. But Quinn had already hung up.

Twenty-six

I was a good thing Eric Thorner stood as I was shown to his table or I might not have recognized him.

I was no expert on the Tribe of Tech, but one thing I did know about the young lords of the digital domain was that they had an aversion to formalwear. Business attire was anathema, jackets seldom worn, and neckties were as welcome as a silver cross on a Victorian vampire.

This club, however, had a dress code for dinner service and Thorner had mothballed the denims, flannel shirt, and Yankees cap in favor of a gray, London-tailored wool suit and a buttoned-up shirt so white it seemed luminous in contrast to the ebony-silk tie knotted tightly around his neck.

"Mr. Thorner, I can't believe how fabulous you look—"

"Wow, Ms. Cosi! You look amazing—"

We halted our overlapping compliments and laughed.

"I guess it's a good thing we both clean up so nicely," I said and meant it because I still couldn't believe I was here.

Last year, the *New York Times* magazine had done a splashy spread on the Source Club, highlighting its art, architecture, spa, cigar room, and world-class wine bar. The membership roster was a who's who of Wall Street's most successful investment bankers; the digital world's newly minted tech founders; and the actual world's wealthiest aristocrats (the ones who maintained a pied-à-terre with a 212 area code, anyway).

Tucker had drooled all over the *Times* spread, bringing it in for me and the rest of my baristas to shake our heads over. (The palatial enclave carried annual membership dues north of $50,000—and that didn't include the costs of drinking, dining, squash court time, personal trainers, plastic surgery, overnight accommodations, intimate concerts with rock legends, lectures by Nobel laureates, or anything else the club offered.)

As for the architecture, the street entrance through which I'd been escorted was sufficiently grand (no surprise, since the century-old building was once a bank). Its vaulted, stone archway and busy Beaux Arts base felt like a nod to the more traditional private clubs of New York like the Harmonie, Metropolitan, Knickerbocker, and the oldest of them all, the Union Club, with a "past members" list that included John Jacob Astor, Cornelius Vanderbilt, William Randolph Hearst, and Ulysses S. Grant.

While those old-guard clubs were primarily located in Midtown, downtown was the new place to be, and the barely ten-year-old Source Club was considered the hippest haven in New York.

The dramatic River Room, in which I now sat, was an architectural marvel. An ode to modern minimalism (and maybe Frank Lloyd Wright's Fallingwater), the three-story-high structure of one-way glass had been built to extend off what was once an old pier along the Manhattan side of the East River.

Beneath our feet, the river ran. Beyond the glass, boats floated by and fast-moving ferries crossed to Brooklyn's shore where lights twinkled from the high-rises of hipster Williamsburg and the tech town that ate DUMBO (no, not the adorable little Disney elephant but the shorthand way New Yorkers referred to the area "Down Under the Manhattan Bridge Overpass").

I couldn't help feeling nervous when I walked into this glittering dining room of crystal and orchids, but Thorner's earnest greeting put me at ease.

"Thank you for coming, Ms. Cosi."

"Please, call me Clare."

"I'll grant that wish, as long as you call me Eric."

"Of course . . ."

The last time I saw Eric, he had had a jagged eight-inch thorn of glass pricking his neck. Mere days later, there was no outward sign of injury—no bandages, slings, and no stiffness. His movements appeared fluid as he elbowed the maître d' aside to pull out my chair himself.

As he smiled down at me, Thorner's expression was all warmth and camaraderie (no smirking this time). His golden, surfer hair had been trimmed, making him appear older— until those killer dimples flashed, revealing the boy inside the man.

He returned to his own seat and for a long, uncomfortable moment he studied me without speaking. Embarrassed, I glanced away, only to be reminded that pretty much everyone else in this dining room was staring at me, too.

Stranger still, some of those gawking were public figures themselves—a network news anchor; an award-winning actress; the scion of an Italian fashion house.

Why in the world are they curious about me? Do I look freakish? Out of place?

On my way to the dining room, the usher had led me across a transparent sky bridge, and I caught my reflection in the tinted glass: the beaded Chanel dress looked stunning. Madame had selected it for me from her own vintage closet. Her seamstress friend had speedily custom tailored the garment, letting it out here and there (and there!) to accommodate my curves.

Maybe it's simply the dress they're staring at . . .

"Does everyone merit this sort of attention?" I whispered to Eric.

"You're a beautiful woman, Clare, inside and out, and you should be admired. But . . . I think they're staring because tonight you're a mystery woman—to them, at least—and you happen to be my date."

That's when I understood.

Thorner was of no particular significance in this company, just another billionaire member of the club. But a week ago, the bomb in his limo made him worldwide news, and this was his first appearance in public since the explosion.

"Honestly, I'm not convinced you really are Eric Thorner. You might be a corporate double, or a clone. Or was it the clone that was taken away from my coffeehouse in an ambulance?"

Eric laughed, loud enough to turn heads. "I assure you it was me, and I can prove it." He lowered his voice. "Later, I'll show you my scars."

The waiter delivered the menu, but I hardly glanced at it. "Are you as uncomfortable as I am with all this . . . attention?"

"Ridiculous, isn't it?" Eric's gaze remained on the menu card. "Is there anyone *not* staring at us? I can't look. You'll have to tell me."

I raised my menu in front of my face and peeked over it.

Though scrutiny seemed intense, I discovered that not everyone was paying attention. There was a young prince from the House of Saud who didn't seem interested in anything more than the model-perfect trio of women who were his dinner guests. Another table had a pair of Hong Kong businessmen who hadn't stopped talking (in Cantonese) since I arrived, leaving their ignored wives to sip their drinks with bored expressions.

Then my eyes were drawn to a raised table in the corner, where a broad-shouldered man in an exquisite, black, pin-striped suit was holding court with a pair of tieless younger men in sport jackets.

In his mid- to late fifties, the big man was bald and blustery, a larger-than-life rooster type. It was the deliberate manner in which he ignored us that made me curious. It felt like a ruse—as I watched his table, I noticed his companions stealing glimpses in our direction, and then the rooster himself snuck an intense peek.

"There's a Mr. Clean in Caraceni across the way—" I subtly tilted my head. "He's dining with a young pair of techie types. They seem to be trying very hard *not* to stare at us."

Eric masked his smile with his menu. "I'm impressed with your powers of observation. That's Grayson Braddock, and the guys with him are his nephews. More than anyone else in this room, those Aussies would kill to know what I'm up to."

"I'm sorry, did you just use the word *kill*? Given what happened last week, you don't actually think . . . ?"

"I do, Clare." He met my eyes. "And I've told the authorities as much."

I blinked a moment, unable to believe what Eric had so easily admitted—and as coolly as if he'd just conveyed the weather.

I glanced around, wondering where the undercover detectives were. If Braddock was a person of interest, he had to be under surveillance by the NYPD. Not quite sure how to act, I followed Eric's lead, tried to remain calm, and cleared my throat.

"Can you tell me why Braddock is so angry with you?"

"He and I are competing head to head on a time-sensitive project. So I'm sure the man would poison us both with Mulga snake venom if he thought he could get away with it." Suddenly Eric grinned. "By the way, enjoy the food. It's a very special night. Grayson Braddock is hosting this dinner service. His favorite celebrity chef is cooking."

I nearly dropped my menu.

"I'm joking, Clare. Chef Harvey wouldn't dare poison us. Not here. For one thing, it would ruin the sales of his new cookbook—Braddock's publishing company released it just last week. All bets are off when it comes to his boss though."

"If Braddock blew up your server farm, he would have the advantage in this race of yours, wouldn't he?"

Eyes on the menu, Eric nodded. "He would. Braddock is a legacy mogul, a gatekeeper of the old order. His latest social networking venture failed miserably—remember the jokes? *The InZone is out.* And, of course, *Who's in the InZone? Nobody!*"

I had no idea what Eric was talking about, but when he laughed I smiled and nodded appropriately. "I guess that failure embarrassed him?"

"Big time. His systems thinking is outdated, and his empire is crumbling. It matters not that he's launched Interweb equivalents for his magazines and newspapers because he can't monetize sufficiently to plug the leaking revenue—and he detests the very idea of me. In his *Forbes* magazine profile last month, Braddock had the nerve to call me a 'baby billionaire in a carnival business.'"

I wanted to know more—about exactly what they were trying to get to the market and who exactly might have planted that bomb (certainly Braddock wouldn't have done the dirty work himself)—when I saw movement from Braddock's direction.

"Heads-up," I warned. "Your favorite legacy mogul is approaching this table right now."

Twenty-seven

~~~~~~

GRAYSON Braddock loomed large as he approached our table. Standing well over six feet, the Australian-born magnate had draped himself in hand-sewn Italian silk.

If Mike Quinn were here, he would have mumbled something about an easy target. That would have been true on the firing range; in this dining room, I wasn't so sure. Men like Braddock didn't get where they were without learning how to dodge a few bullets.

"Good to see you, Thorner." Braddock's tone was formal, but he didn't offer his hand.

Eric didn't bother to rise. "Good to be here, Braddock."

While the two exchanged vague pleasantries, I studied the man. The cut of his dark jacket accented his broad shoulders and thick-muscled arms, and Braddock's beefy hands, though manicured, would have done a professional boxer proud. (Actually, if it wasn't for his expensive clothes and the civilized surroundings, I could easily mistake the billionaire for one of the bodybuilding stars of *Live Studio Wrestling,* a show my cigar-chomping pop watched every Saturday when I was growing up in western Pennsylvania. I could almost imagine Braddock, with some name like the Aussie Annihilator, going toe-to-toe with Bruno Sammartino at the old Civic Arena.)

"Rough business the other day," Braddock was now saying, "but I see you've recovered nicely."

"Yes," Eric returned, "I *couldn't wait* to get back to work on a *certain project*."

"Well, you're not working *now*, are you?" Braddock rested his hand on the back of my chair. "Good to see you finding new . . . *diversions*."

The tone of Braddock's voice pricked me into risking a glance up. I found his gaze fixed on my cleavage.

From this angle, only I could see his little invasion. He didn't appear bothered that I'd caught him in the act. Instead he slowly moved his attention from my breasts to my eyes, finishing his bit of fun with a leer.

The message was clear—*a man like me does what he wants and feels no shame about it.*

Another woman might have blushed or looked away in embarrassment. But I'd taught my daughter (just as Madame had taught me) never to allow any man to make you feel uncomfortable for simply looking like a woman.

Natural interest and admiration was one thing, lack of respect another, and I returned the man's open leer with a disdainful smirk worthy of any self-satisfied tech brat.

Grayson Braddock arched an eyebrow when our gazes locked. My reaction had surprised him, and he faltered for the slightest second.

"Anyway . . ." He glanced back across the table. "I find it's always better to move on and forget the things you *can't control*—ah, I see my guest has arrived. You know Donny Chu, don't you, Thorner?"

Eric's eyes widened at the approach of a stocky, young Asian man with a buzz cut and an open-collared shirt under a navy blue blazer.

Braddock gripped the newcomer's hand, then hooked a

possessive arm over Donny Chu's shoulders and led him back
to the raised table. Braddock's corporate cronies greeted the
Asian man like he was a long-lost relative—hugs, pats on
the back, laughing grins.

Eric gritted his teeth and quietly cursed.

"What's wrong?"

"Donny Chu was my special projects director until I fired
him about a year ago. We were working out of Los Angeles
then—"

"Why did you fire Chu?"

"We clashed over . . ." He waved his hand. "It was personal stuff. Anyway, last I heard, he'd gone back to Silicon
Valley to launch his own start-up, but I always knew Donny
didn't have what it took to go it alone."

A burst of laughter erupted from Braddock's table. "Looks
like Mr. Chu found a new employer."

Eric nodded. "His nephews must have brought him in,
probably met him at Stanford. It seems they've joined forces
to combat me, but I'm not going to let that happen. Maybe
you could help me with that?"

I raised my palms. "I shouldn't be involved in a corporate
throwdown."

"You're involved already, Clare. Braddock just saw you
with me."

"But he doesn't know who I am."

"Believe me, by the end of the evening he will."

"What does that mean?" I glanced around. "Does this restaurant have some kind of face recognition system I should
know about?"

"No . . ." Eric flashed me a cryptic smile. "Let's just say . . .
you're bound to make *an impression*."

I was dying to know what prompted that remark, but Eric
quickly changed the subject. "See anything you like on the
menu? Chef Harvey's featuring *Poulet de Bresse*—the real thing,
too, not Blue Foot chickens from Canada. They're flown in special from France."

I groaned (couldn't help it).

"What's the matter? You don't like chicken?"

"No, it's my daughter."

"Your daughter doesn't like chicken?"

"Bresse chickens are the reason my daughter is too busy to do more than text me a string of trite abbreviations."

I briefly told Eric about Joy, her apprenticeship in Paris, and the Bresse chicken incident, which resulted in her promotion to saucier. The story made him laugh till he cried (I guess flying chickens and irate French chefs can do that).

Wine appeared and soon we were both laughing. Eric was so easy to talk to that I ended up telling him all about Joy's relationship with Sergeant Emmanuel Franco—a good man and a good cop—and my wish to sprout wings and fly to Paris to talk some sense into her before she lost him.

And the wine *kept* flowing . . .

Looking back on it now, I'm firmly convinced the Source Club waitstaff mastered some sort of service kung fu mind trick where they refill your wineglass without your ever noticing. Whatever the case, their superb service made drinking effortless, and before I knew it, nature called.

TWENTY-EIGHT

~~~~~~

IF I had known the challenges that would come with one trip to the powder room, I (frankly) would have held it.

The first challenge was finding the room itself.

A waiter discreetly pointed toward one end of this giant, glass cage, but I was lost until another waiter explained that the twenty-foot waterfall in the corner was a hologram, complete with falling-water sound. As I approached, I could see it was a canard—a mere display of dimensional lighting, and I walked right through (staying dry as a bone, thank goodness).

On the other side, I found an empty corridor, eerily backlit by that holographic spigot. One end of the corridor appeared to house the men's facilities with faux-stone columns guarding the darkly lit lounge of leather sofas and heavy oak paneling.

In the other direction, I saw a flowery bower of an archway. Inside was a lounge of sumptuous sofas and antique, gilt-edged mirrors where twin girls gently strummed identical harps, their sweet strains mingling with the sounds of that holographic waterfall.

Okay, now I really had to go!

Moving faster, I found the stalls.

Everything was gilded in here—the sink, the mirror, the TP dispenser, even the . . . well, *everything*. Frank Lloyd Wright might have been the inspiration for that dining room, but someone had gone all Donald Trump on the ladies' lounge—1990s-Atlantic-City-casino Trump, to be exact, which brought to mind one of Madame's many axioms:

"Wealth is not a singular idea, dear, and money does not equal taste."

True, taste was never a given where money was concerned, but wealth could certainly buy you *space*. These bathroom stalls were bigger than some Manhattan apartments, with amenities catering to a girl's every personal need.

On the way out, I paused at one of the antique mirrors to check how the seams in this vintage dress were holding out against my formidable curves. Gazing at my reflection, I noticed a blond Amazon enter the ladies' lounge and storm right up to me.

Draped in a jewel-trimmed gown of aquamarine with a daring slit up one leg, and a décolletage nearly to her navel, she seemed wobbly as she walked, but I couldn't tell the cause—the six-inch fetish heels on her pedicured feet? Or the oversized martini in her manicured hand?

Her loose, flyaway locks formed a blunt-cut Jazz Age halo of yellow fire around her scowling face. Looming over me, she tossed her sun-kissed crown and addressed my reflection in the mirror.

"Who the hell are you?"

"Excuse me?" I turned to face her.

"Eric's last fling is hardly out of the morgue, and he's already sniffing up a new cougar?!"

The strident pitch of her voice might have embarrassed me, but this wasn't the kind of restroom with an echo. The pink-fabric wallpaper (thick as soundproofing), effectively absorbed the ear-splitting decibels, and I noticed those twin harpists began to strum louder. (Now I knew why they were here—to drown out the catfights.)

I also solved another mystery: the blonde's wobbling wasn't caused by her Everest heels. She fairly reeked of overpriced gin.

"How do you know Eric?" Her eyes, the same aqua shade as her gown, had narrowed into pissed-off slits. "Are you his maid? The cook? Or just another hired babysitter like that sniveling rat Anton?"

"I don't know who you are, but stop it," I replied, voice level but firm. "You're causing a scene."

With a crooked smirk, she placed an index finger on her chin and looked me over like I was a horse at auction. Her appraisal was so obvious I half expected her to check my teeth.

"I'll admit you have more class than his last piece of trash. But hopping from a B-list actress to a divorcée—well, it's no wonder someone tried to blow him to kingdom come."

How does she know I'm a divorcée? I thought, and then I realized, *She doesn't.*

The "B-list actress" was clearly Eric's late girlfriend, Bianca Hyde. But who was this other woman, this divorcée?

"Back up," I said. "Exactly what divorcée are you talking about? And who are *you*?"

"Age before beauty—I asked *you* first."

"Look, whatever you think is happening, it's not. Eric and I are having a business dinner—"

"*Monkey* business, you mean!" Aqua eyes flashed, and her scowl morphed into a smug grin. "I'll bet Eric's already sent you those damn blue roses, hasn't he?"

My silence was all the reply she needed. The martini glass slipped from her fingers and shattered on the pink-marble floor. I leaped back to dodge flying glass as an attendant rushed over to make the mess vanish.

The blonde was already gone, heading for a vacant stall.

"Bad things seem to happen to the women around Eric," she called over her shoulder. "Keep your distance, honey, or something bad might happen to you."

As soon as she closed the carved (and, yes, gilded) stall door, I bolted for the dimly lit corridor. But I was so busy watching my back, I accidentally smacked into a solid wall of Outback muscle.

" 'Ere, hold up there, sheila," a voice both masculine and familiar commanded. "What's the rush? You and I have some things to discuss."

Twenty-nine

෴෴෴෴෴෴෴෴෴෴෴෴෴

I was astonished at how much larger Grayson Braddock appeared with my nose buried in his chest. I took a quick step back—away from the aroma of expensive cigars and even more expensive cologne (a little too much of it).

"Been meaning to ask since I saw you with junior. Didn't I see you skiing in Telluride over the holidays? Or maybe it was that New Year's bash at Lighthouse Bay in Barbuda? You look mighty familiar."

"I work for a living, Mr. Braddock, and I spent the holidays here in New York. Now, if you'll excuse me—"

"If you spent December in this dismal town, you must have been working, and it must have been profitable." He folded his arms, tapped his cheek. "Finance? Hedge funds? No, I would have heard of someone like you."

"I really have to get back to Eric's table."

Braddock sidestepped, using his larger body and outspread arms to block my run to the end zone. He must have seen my reaction because he threw up his enormous hands.

"Easy now, sheila. Just want to talk, that's all."

"My name is Clare, not Sheila."

"Aw, don't take offense. That's just my Down Under show-ing. Beautiful name you have, Clare. Please call me Gray. All the ladies call me Gray . . ."

I didn't feel threatened—*yet*—but I checked my surround-ings. Though the restaurant was populated, this area behind the faux waterfall was out of sight and nobody was in this dimly lit passage at the moment. (Where was a sloshed, angry blonde when you needed her?)

"We must have met before, Clare. Give me a hint."

"You're fishing, Mr. Braddock."

"Fishing, eh? Okay then, tell me: What will it take to reel you in?"

"Better manners."

He chuckled, a deep rumble. "In my experience, that's *not* what women want, but . . ." He stepped closer. "As heuristics go, trial-and-error should find me the right bait."

Maybe I should bait him.

"Have the police paid you a visit yet . . . Gray?"

He stopped laughing. "Is that what *he* told the police? I'm not surprised; I make a mighty convenient scapegoat."

"You're also an unconvincing victim."

"Don't believe everything that baby genius says. Have you ever heard the real story about how that first little mobile phone game of his became a hit? Little Donny Chu gave me the scoop. Quite a tale . . ."

"You're talking about the game that launched his busi-ness? *Pigeon Droppings*?"

"That's the one." He laughed again. "Bet the story of how he got those birds off the ground was never a subject of your pillow talk."

"Don't make assumptions, Mr. Braddock."

"What? You're not Junior's girlfriend?"

"No."

He rubbed his prodigious chin. "You don't strike me as a

techie, and you're not a member of this club . . ." He thought a moment and smirked. "Oh, now I get it."

"What?"

"That boy . . ." He shook his head, tossing the infuriating insult before swaggering away: "He just can't keep his hands off the help, can he?"

THIRTY

~~~~~~~~~~~~~~~~~~~~~~~~~~~~~~~~~~

I returned to the table with a strained smile, attempting to shake off the slimy encounter with Braddock by way of a vow to nail the SOB for planting that car bomb.

As soon as I sat down, the main course arrived. Eric dug in, and so did I . . .

"So tell me, Eric, how is the investigation going?"

The straightforward inquiry changed his mood. He shifted on his chair. "Let's enjoy our dinner, Clare, and skip the dark talk."

"Let's not."

Eric blinked, surprised at my bluntness.

"I'm sorry," I said, "but I have some stake in the situation. My coffeehouse was wrecked, my life disrupted, I was injured, and my baristas nearly forced into unemployment."

"You were injured?" He looked stricken. "Nobody told me."

"Just some shrapnel in my back, it's practically healed now." I lowered my voice. "That's why I couldn't go strapless."

"I'm so sorry . . ." Eric set his glass aside. "And you're right.

You deserve an explanation, though a little bird told me you've already been briefed."

"That bird wouldn't have a military crew cut, would it?"

"You know DeFasio?" Eric shook his head and chuckled. "Now I understand."

"What's so funny?"

"The lieutenant had his dog sniff up my limo *twice* when I told him who my dinner companion was going to be."

"I noticed you have extra security watching your car, as well."

Eric shrugged. "That's the way I'm going to have to live from now on. One driver with bodyguard training isn't enough." His expression went from serious to glum, and I suspected he was thinking about the death of Charley, that former NYPD officer.

"If you're sure Braddock was the one who had the bomb planted, he had to have hired someone, right? You fired Donny and he's now obviously working for Braddock. Could anyone else in your business have a bone to pick with you?"

Eric snorted. "I'm on top of a thirty-billion-dollar-a-year industry, Clare. I didn't get here without stepping on a few toes. And I'm not alone. The digital domain is like the Wild West. There aren't any rules, only winners and losers. The winners are sitting all around us. And because we're the winners, we've made enemies. Sometimes we *are* enemies."

"Well, someone got access to your limo—and your schedule. Could someone in your company be working with Braddock, behind your back?"

"No way."

"How can you be so sure?"

"I staked my family fortune to start this corporation, and the people with me now were with me in the beginning. We all worked together and we all got rich together. My company is like a family . . . hell, some of us *are* family."

"What about old girlfriends?"

Eric looked stricken. He stopped eating and put down his fork. "What do you mean by that, Clare?"

"One of your ex-lovers confronted me in the restroom."

"Who?"

"That one there," I said, pointing to the sloshed blonde with the daring gown who'd just emerged from behind the holo-fall.

"Eden?" Eric laughed. "That's *my sister*, Clare! Eden Thorner-Gundersen—she used to manage my late father's business, but she works for me now. She's my New York office manager."

Eric glanced at the shaky woman, and then met my gaze. "You'll have to forgive Eden for any misunderstandings. She's protective of me; and she's really only unreasonable when she drinks. You'll meet her again soon—under better circumstances. I think you'll find her quite likeable."

Hard to imagine, I thought.

Eric noticed my expression. "I mean it. Eden is a very interesting person. One of her passions is protecting wildlife. She just came back from tagging wolves in Wyoming."

That did sound interesting, but it failed to win me over.

With a wary gaze, I tracked the woman's less-than-steady course to a table across the room. She sat down with a single dinner companion, a lean, middle-aged man with a salt-and-pepper ponytail. He wore the required jacket for the club's River Room, but the embroidered blue green Nehru didn't look anything like the business attire around him.

"I'm glad she's having dinner with Garth," Eric said, tilting his head toward their table. "A talk with the Metis Man will straighten her out."

I blinked. "Did you just say *Medicine Man?*"

"No, but you're not far from the truth. Garth Hendricks is a very important person in my organization. Sometimes I think of him as the Energizer because he inspires me and my staff. Sometimes we joke that he's the Ventilator—because he allows my people to vent. He's like a father confessor and court jester rolled into one. But his official title at THORN, Inc., is Metis Man."

"Metis . . . that's from Greek mythology, isn't it? Metis was a goddess?"

"Goddess of wisdom, spouse of Zeus . . ." He smiled and nodded. "I'm totally impressed that you know that, but somehow I'm not surprised."

Of course you're not surprised, I thought. *You probably have my whole life outlined in that secret file of yours.*

"So Garth doesn't mind being named after a goddess?"

"He chose the name! And he's always been big on gender equality. Garth was a mentor of mine before I ever met him."

"How could that be?"

"I read his books—more like devoured them. *New Management for a New Century, Make It Don't Break It, Puncturing the Donut—*"

"Did you just say *Donut* as in coffee and—?"

"It's part of a bigger philosophy. In that sense, Garth is like a medicine man. He runs our youth outreach and talent scout programs, *App This!,* and the local chapter of the Junior Rocketeers, and he's the unofficial company psychologist. I'll introduce you."

"I'd like that."

And for a very good reason . . .

If I was going to learn this company's secrets, including who might be working with Grayson Braddock to undermine Eric, then this ponytailed father confessor was clearly the "Metis" man to ask.

Thirty-one

∾∿∾∿∾∿∾∿∾∿∾∿∾∿∾∿∾∿∾∿∾∿∾

By the time the dessert menu arrived, I was starting to feel fatigued (the night had thrown me more to deal with than I'd bargained for), but Chef Harvey's whimsical selections managed to perk me up, including something called the Billionaire Twinkie.

"Now, that I've got to try."

"Oh, yes, me too—"

Unfortunately, we never got the chance. Before we could order, a waiter arrived with a silver tray.

"Excuse me, Mr. Thorner, I have a special dessert tray prepared just for you and your lovely guest by Chef Harvey himself."

"A surprise?" Eric said, slightly wary. "What's on it?"

"Chef Harvey has titled his offering Baby Carnival Treats, and it comes with the compliments of Mr. Grayson Braddock."

Eric's eyes narrowed with anger, but he quickly masked it behind a stiff grin. The waiter set the tray in front of us along with a special mini dessert card, which described the beautifully presented entrees.

"We have two candied apples, glacéed with Calvados and raw honey, and garnished with shredded Tanzanian coconut and crushed macadamias. These sweet, tiny apples are a Fuji and crabapple hybrid grown in Chile. Beside them are mini–cotton candy clouds in flavors of pink champagne, candied Meyer lemon, and sweet jasmine tea . . ."

While the waiter spoke, I glanced in the direction of Braddock's table. The bald billionaire lifted his wineglass. The predatory grin rattled me enough to miss the skinny on the gourmet popcorn balls, the Sno-Cones laced with flavored vodkas, and the cute, little funnel cakes drizzled with roasted white chocolate.

"Shall I carry a message to Mr. Braddock, sir?" the waiter asked.

"In a bit," Eric replied through gritted teeth. "For now, could you please bring us a coffee service? The chef's special selection, please."

"Right away."

As the waiter departed, Eric faced Braddock and lifted his own wineglass, returning the shark's grin with a bitter smile of his own.

"What's this about?" I whispered. "Should I expect the candy apples to be injected with Mulga venom?"

"Braddock doesn't need to poison us," Eric whispered back. "His insult was enough; the news is already traveling."

Eric was right. The little "special dessert" menu cards were being distributed to every table and people in the know were taking out their smartphones. The gesture reminded me of the *Forbes* magazine profile he'd mentioned earlier—the one where Braddock had called Eric a "baby billionaire in a carnival business."

Eric gestured toward the goodies. "He just doubled down on the insult with this tray of 'Baby Carnival Treats.'"

Before I could reply, the coffee service arrived. The waiter French-pressed, poured two cups, and waited for us to taste. Eric hadn't touched the dessert tray, now he ignored the coffee.

"Tell me what you think, Clare."

With Eric waiting and the waiter hovering, I quickly sampled the brew. I found the coffee smooth and generally flavorful, but unbalanced and one-dimensional.

"It's fine."

Eric narrowed his eyes. "What's the problem?"

"I'm your guest, Eric, and my nonna always told me, if you can't say anything nice . . ." I shrugged. "Sorry."

"Don't be sorry for having an opinion, Clare, especially about something on which you are an expert." Eric tasted his own cup and frowned at the waiter. "This is not what I ordered. I asked for the chef's selection coffee."

"Yes, sir," the waiter replied. "This *is* our guest chef's coffee selection for the evening—Ambrosia."

"What?!" I couldn't believe it. "You can't be serious!"

"Perhaps madam does not understand," the waiter replied with a sniff. "The cup of coffee you have been served was prepared via the French press method from a single-origin bean harvested from a plantation in Brazil. The Ambrosia was sourced and roasted by the Village Blend, a landmark coffeehouse here in New York."

With a condescending smile, the waiter departed.

I racked my memory, but could not recall ever selling the Source Club or Chef Harvey a consignment of the now-unavailable bean. *Could Matt have done it without telling me?*

Gripping my cup with shaky hands, I drank again. Rolling the warm liquid around in my mouth, I searched in vain for the perfectly balanced brightness, the notes of berry, of shortbread, of cherry lambic—notes that sadly, never came.

I swallowed, shuddering. I was horrified, mortified, and temporarily speechless as I set my cup aside.

How can it be? This club of the rich and powerful has been completely duped. Someone's passed off this dud of a bean as the Village Blend's signature Ambrosia, which it decidedly is not! Not even close!

"Clare?" Eric said, obviously sensing my distress.

Scene or not, I could not let this situation stand. "Please call the waiter back."

"Another question, madam?"

"No. Just a simple statement. I'll say it loud and clear so you understand . . ." I placed my hands flat on the table and locked eyes with the haughty man. "This is *not* Ambrosia."

The waiter paled.

Eric's reaction was instant outrage (almost too instant). "Not Ambrosia?" he cried. "Are you sure, Clare?"

"This is not Ambrosia," I repeated, but a moment later, I was sorry I had.

Eric rose to his feet, threw down his napkin, and spoke loudly enough to be heard in every corner of the glittering dining room.

"This coffee is a fraud!"

Oh, my God, what is he doing?

"Management had better explain this *insulting deception* to everyone dining here tonight!" He eyed the waiter. "Get *Grayson Braddock's guest chef* out here—*at once!*"

ᒿHIRᒿY-ᒿWO

ⵙⵙⵙⵙⵙⵙⵙⵙⵙⵙⵙⵙⵙⵙⵙⵙⵙⵙ

ᙓRIC'S public act of outrage ended with a gaggle of waiters stampeding our table, followed by the flame-haired fire-cracker known to America's food TV aficionados as Chef Clarke Harvey.

A Down Under version of a certain world-renowned British chef (minus the profanity), Chef Harvey speared us with steely gray eyes. Jaw outthrust, the chef placed his hands on his hips and frowned down at us.

"'Ere now, mate, what seems to be the problem?"

"The problem is the coffee," Eric replied. "My guest tells me that what you are serving is definitely *not* Ambrosia."

Chef Harvey faced me. "You're familiar with Ambrosia?"

"Intimately," I replied. "You see, I—"

"This is Clare Cosi," Eric interrupted, "manager and master roaster at the Village Blend."

In a world where chefs were suing importers for passing off inferior oils as extra virgin and billionaires were hiring private eyes to nail vintners for selling them fake vintages, my charge was serious business, and Harvey knew it.

Without hesitation, the chef turned to the nearest waiter and snapped his fingers. "Take this coffee away and bring out a fresh service for three. You make damn sure it's Ambrosia. I'll press it myself."

The old coffee and cups were whisked away, and a pair of waiters set up a portable tray beside our table. The new coffee service appeared after a few uncomfortable minutes.

We were an open show now. Everyone in the dining room was craning his or her neck to view the Source Club Coffee Showdown. Some of the people in the back were on their feet and moving closer for a better look.

Grayson Braddock and his cronies, including Donny Chu, had fluttered over from their perch. Braddock glared at me until I felt goose bumps appear on my arms.

Meanwhile Chef Harvey poured three cups and, without asking, pulled up a chair and sat between Eric and me.

"Shall we try again?" he challenged.

Again, Eric ignored his cup, his expression strained.

I placed the cup to my nose and sniffed, swirled it a little, then sipped. I let the coffee wash over my tongue, breathing with an open mouth to aerate.

Chef Harvey didn't bother to test the aroma; he just gulped and swished the hot liquid around in his mouth, cheeks bulging.

I finally swallowed and set my cup down. Chef Harvey spit his coffee back into the cup and frowned.

"Ms. Cosi is right," the chef declared. "This is not the coffee I sampled when I made the purchase. The vendor pulled a switcheroo before delivery. I humbly apologize to Mr. Braddock, and to everyone who's dined here tonight. I shall amend the menu accordingly!"

Chef Harvey rose and shook my hand. "I *have* sampled Ambrosia, though apparently that's not what I bought for the club. In any case, I congratulate you on an amazing cup. I hope we meet again, Ms. Cosi, under cheerier circumstances."

The chef hurried back to his kitchen. Eric rose and faced a stunned Grayson Braddock.

"Sorry about the *carnival* atmosphere, Braddock." Thorner's tech brat smirk was back. "This must be quite embarrassing for you, given that tonight's menu was your *baby*."

Braddock's reaction to his chef's confession, Eric's taunt, and the curious gaze of nearly every diner in the room was to spin 180 degrees in his wingtipped Guccis and stride away so fast that he left his associates to play catch-up.

Eric held himself erect until the group was out of sight and the diners' attention was back on their whimsical desserts; then he slumped back into his chair.

"That felt *so* good," he said with a relieved sigh.

I frowned at the sudden pallor in his complexion—the change was alarmingly dramatic. "For someone who 'feels good,' Eric, you look terrible."

Dark circles had appeared under his eyes, but this was more than fatigue. His expression had gone rigid, as if he were in great pain. Now he leaned forward for a sip of water and winced. When he sat back again, he actually gasped and cursed.

"What's wrong?" I whispered.

"It must be close to midnight. Anton warned me not to play Cinderella tonight."

I glanced at the vintage Cartier watch Madame had lent me. "It's eleven forty-five."

"Damn. The painkiller wore off fifteen minutes ago—"

"Why didn't you say something?"

"I'm saying it now. We'd better go, Clare, before I turn into a passed-out pumpkin."

"I'll call the waiter to help you—"

"No," Eric said sharply and winced again. "I'm going to have to tough this out, I can't show weakness."

"But you can hardly stand."

"Oh, I can stand . . ." He smiled weakly. "It's the walking I'm not so sure about . . ."

"Please, lean on me then." I rose. "Put your arms around my waist. I'll put my arm around you, too, and we'll fool everyone."

Eric pressed against me, but managed to make the gesture look lusty, not wobbly. "Hey, I like this," he whispered.

But someone else didn't. From her corner table, Eden Thorner-Gundersen glared glass splinters at me. This "business dinner" appeared to be ending as anything but. *Great, now she'll assume I was lying to her in the ladies' lounge. Oh, well . . .*

"Should I call your car?" I asked Eric.

"I've got it . . ." He brought his wrist to his lips and spoke into what looked like a large watch. "Bring the car, Anton."

"*Rrrri*ght away, Mr. Thorner," a tiny voice replied with an impressive Castilian *R* roll.

"I can't believe you just did that," I couldn't help murmuring.

"What?"

"Are you old enough to get a Dick Tracy joke?"

"Dick who?"

"Oh, never mind."

"Mr. Thorner . . ." another voice beckoned from the watch, this one with military crispness.

"Yes, Walsh?"

"We have a situation, sir."

"What?"

"I'll apprise you in the lobby, sir."

"Very good," Thorner replied tightly, but I got the distinct impression it was anything but.

Thirty-three

≈≈≈≈≈≈≈≈≈≈≈≈≈≈≈≈≈≈≈≈

With Eric clutching me, we crossed the dining room, sky bridge, and finally entered the grand lobby area. As we paused by the cloak room to wait for our wraps, an unsmiling, tall, lean African-American man in a dark suit greeted us.

"Good evening, Mr. Thorner, madam . . ."

"What's the issue, Walsh?"

"Paparazzi, sir, and Solar Flare."

Eric frowned. "You'll get us through?"

"Of course."

As Walsh turned to lead us to the grand oak doors, I felt myself tensing.

"It's midnight," I whispered to Eric. "How could the paparazzi possibly know you were here?"

"Remember all those smartphones in the River Room? Either someone there informed the press or Braddock tipped off his own reporters."

"And what exactly is Solar Flare?"

"You're about to find out."

* * *

WHEN I'd first arrived this evening, the Source Club's vaulted stone archway was lit so expertly it glowed golden, but I didn't get a second chance to admire the architecture. The moment we stepped outside, I was blinded by the sudden glare of dozens of photo flashes exploding at once.

With quiet authority, Eric's bodyguard led us into what (at first) seemed to be a civil crowd. Like a linebacker, he used his shoulders to push a path through the bodies.

I could see Eric's antique Bentley on the street. But it seemed so far away, and impossible to reach with the human tide in front of it.

Meanwhile, Walsh was doing a good job clearing a space on the sidewalk; we stayed behind him and kept moving forward. More cameras flashed, and I had to blink blue spots out of my eyes as we continued walking.

Keeping my head low to avoid the glare of camera flashes, I heard a few angry voices begin to shout. More voices joined in until it became a chant—

"Turn off. Tune out. Unplug!"

We were maybe six feet from the limo, the chauffeur waiting with the door open, when I heard grunts and caught movement to our right. Like a human bulldozer, three burly men with arms interlinked surged forward. I thought for a second that Eric and I were going to be crushed, but they weren't aiming at us. Their target was Walsh.

With a collective roar, the trio slammed into the security man, and all four tumbled to the sidewalk in a tangled, chaotic bundle of flailing arms and legs.

The security wall broken, the mob surged forward. Signs and placards came out, and I felt rough hands on me, heard Eric moan as we were jostled. Flashes exploded, turning night into day. Blindly I lashed out, pushing the flat of my hand into a hairy, bearded face. More people crowded us, but I continued to push the man back.

Finally my eyes cleared and I discovered I had my hand in the elderly face of Village Blend regular and Madame's old flame, Professor Nate Sumner from the New School! (Not that he noticed.)

"Nate!" I cried. "What are you doing?!"

With a quick brush of his arm, Nate knocked my hand aside and lunged at Eric, shouting, "Unplug!" and "Get real!" as loud and passionately as the rest of the pack.

In the end, the biggest shock wasn't the presence of Madame's ex-boyfriend, or the naked aggressiveness of this political demonstration. What really rattled me were the identical wool caps Nate and the rest of the demonstrators wore.

Each and every placard-waving member of this group had a red cap with white lettering that spelled *Solar Flare*.

My mind flashed on the "looter" who'd come to the Village Blend the other night. The man had worn a red wool cap just like these. I'd even caught three letters on his cap: *ARE* . . . as in *Flare*!

That's when I absolutely knew. That looter was no looter. He'd been a member of this organization—one whose enraged members had swarmed us!

Then all of a sudden, the crowd began to scatter. A wild man was now flailing among them. In the next moment, I realized the wild man was the same formerly quiet chauffeur who'd brought me here. Transformed into raw energy unleashed, he rushed the protestors.

"Back off, all of *jou*!" the Spaniard shouted.

Ducking, diving, kicking, and swinging his fists, the chauffeur effectively cleared the area around us without actually striking anyone.

Some of the snapping paparazzi regrouped, but Eric's manic chauffeur would have none of it.

"No pictures! Stay away from my man, you stinking *rrrr*ats!"

As the driver continued to threaten the mob with karate

chops (and Castilian *R* rolls), Walsh regained his footing and was joined by a second security man. As the two formed a barrier around us, the chauffeur helped Eric into the rear seat. I jumped in beside him, the door closed, and the driver gunned the engine.

Protestors shouted, running after our limo, and a new chant began: "Analog, analog, analog!"

Analog? What the—

"Who are those people?" I cried as we sped away. "They made no sense! And they're all wearing red wool caps!"

"Red wool caps?" Eric blinked. "Did you get cracked in the head, Clare?"

"I'm fine. But listen. This is important. Those nutjob protestors were wearing the same cap as a man who came to my coffeehouse the other night. He tried to break in, scanned the place with a flashlight, and scared the life out of me. From the way he acted, and the questions he asked, I got the feeling he was connected to the bombing. Maybe he *was* the bomber!"

I took a breath. "Now people wearing the same caps attack you? It can't be coincidence."

"Forget about Solar Flare," Eric said as he sank into the soft leather. "Let the police handle it. I, for one, don't want to think about those Luddites tonight."

Maybe Eric was willing to forget, but I wasn't. First thing tomorrow, I would speak with Professor Nate Sumner. And after I got some answers, I was going to the police.

"How is he?" the chauffeur asked, eyes on the road.

Eric gave me a feeble thumbs-up, but I didn't buy it.

"He's in pain," I told the driver. "His eyes are dull, and he's too weak to sit up. He should see a doctor."

Police cars roared past us, going in the opposite direction.

"They're heading for the Source Club, I think . . ."

Sirens drowned out the rest of the chauffeur's words.

In the light from the passing police cars, I could see that Eric was sweating, so much that he didn't protest as I loosened his coat and tie. That's when I saw the bandages he'd kept hidden under his stiff collar, and that they were bright with fresh blood.

"Anton, I want you to take Clare home," Eric called.

"For heaven's sake, forget about me. You're bleeding. You need medical attention. Let's get you to a hospital."

"No hospital. I mean it."

"Then at least let me help you."

Eric sank deeper into his seat. "Okay, but no hospital. Take us home, Anton."

A moment later, I was wincing at the look of Eric's bloody bandage when I caught him smiling up at me.

"Looks like I'll be keeping that promise," he said.

"What promise?"

"I told you I'd show you my scars."

THIRTY-FOUR

〰〰〰〰〰〰〰〰〰〰〰〰〰〰〰〰〰〰

THE Bentley rolled into an underground garage beneath a spanking-new luxury apartment tower overlooking Central Park. Anton drove the limo through a second set of automatic security doors, into a paneled car park that contained several other luxury vehicles and a dark SUV with tinted windows.

Thorner's security detail pulled in with us and parked beside the second SUV, but neither bodyguard emerged from the vehicle.

Thorner lifted his watch to his lips. "Walsh?"

"Yes, sir."

"We're good."

"Ring if you need us, sir. We'll be here, on call."

"See you in the morning."

Anton pulled up beside a private elevator. Then he and I helped Eric out of the backseat. With Eric's arms draped over our shoulders, we paused long enough for Anton to press his thumb against a glass sensor.

"Anton Alonzo cleared for entry," a robotic female voice declared.

The doors opened, and we entered the compartment. The myriad reflections inside the mirror-lined elevator (coupled with more wine that I was used to) made my head spin.

As we rapidly ascended to the thirty-fifth-floor penthouse, Eric wasn't looking so good, either.

"Almost there, boss," Anton whispered reassuringly.

When the doors opened, lights sprang to life in a thick-piled entryway. The same robotic voice greeted us.

"Welcome home, Eric, Anton, and . . . guest."

"House, activate the master bedroom, please," Anton replied. "Lights low, blinds drawn. Adjust the temperature to a constant 78 degrees Fahrenheit—"

"House, turn on the fireplace, too," Eric added, voice weak.

"Affirmative," the fembot replied.

"And House, please double-filter and boil two quarts of water," Anton added.

"Immediately, sirs."

Eric was steadier now, but he gripped my hand as we moved through the expansive penthouse.

The entranceway opened into a glass and chrome wet bar stocked with bottles of premium wine, liquors, and soft drinks. The ultramodern steel and glass motif continued in the spacious living room, where a freestanding staircase ascended to a second-floor gallery.

Lights snapped on as we moved through each chamber, muted and recessed in the living room so as not to interfere with the view of Central Park. The vista was spectacular, of course, but I didn't get more than a glimpse of shadowy parkland ringed by the city's twinkling lights, before we entered another dark hallway.

Everything was so futuristic, so *Streamline Moderne* . . .

"You wouldn't have a neighbor named George Jetson, would you?"

"Who?"

"Never mind . . ." (*Just another antiquated reference.*)

The invisible fembot spoke up again. "Master bedroom is ready for occupation . . ."

"That's it!" (*I couldn't help it.*) "If a robot teddy bear appears in a Napoleonic outfit, I'm looking for an origami unicorn."

"*Blade Runner!*" Despite his pain, Eric snorted. "That one I got."

"Not to worry, Ms. Cosi," Anton quipped. "Our house may be smart, but I am no replicant."

Like the rest of this apartment, the bedroom's décor was minimalist chic, with high ceilings, windows for walls, and sheer shimmering-pearl curtains that only partially veiled the panoramic view. Cozy flames flickered in a hooded fireplace in the center of the room, and concealed lights illuminated the room with a warm glow.

I helped Eric stretch out on the largest bed I'd ever seen. As I took off my coat, Anton used scissors to ruthlessly cut away the tailored jacket and starched shirt. Finished with that, the jack-of-all-trades chauffeur examined the wound and hurried off "to fetch the medical kit."

Eric reached for my hand again and tugged me close. I sat on the edge of the bed.

"How are you feeling?"

Eric's smile was tortured. "I don't know what's worse, the painkillers wearing off or the crash after the amphetamine rush."

"You're kidding. You took amphetamines?"

"I checked myself out of the hospital against the doctors' advice, so I needed a little something to get through dinner without collapsing."

"That's crazy. Why did you risk going out in public if you were in such bad shape?"

"To prove to the world that I'm *not* in bad shape and, in fact, I'm perfectly fine." Eric chuckled—then gritted his teeth. "I would have stayed fine, too, if I didn't get jostled by those extortionists from Solar Flare."

"How exactly are they extortionists?"

"It's a strategy employed by many activist groups. They say they have a mission, but what they're really angling for are dollar donations, or a paid 'advisory position' on some board of the very companies they claim to despise, including mine."

Anton arrived pushing a metal cart with medical tools and supplies spread across a virgin white cloth. Without a word, he thrust a hypodermic needle into the muscle around Eric's torn stitches. Then he donned a pair of rubber gloves.

"You'll be floating in a minute, boss, and I'll stitch you up again."

"But don't you need a doctor?"

"Anton is a doctor—well, sort of," Eric replied. "He was in Timmy's Uncle's Opera Cone Special."

"I'm sorry—is that some kind of drag show?"

Eric smacked his lips. "Sowwy . . . the shot made my mouf numb. Tell her, Anton."

The wiry man was threading a needle, but paused to look at me through darkly flared eyebrows. "I was a medic in the *Unidad de Operaciones Especiales*, the Spanish special forces."

"See," Eric said, flying now, his pronunciation improved. "Anton can do everything!"

The shot appeared to lower Eric's inhibitions, not unlike truth serum—and I decided it was an opportunity I couldn't pass up.

"You were telling me about Solar Flare?" I prompted.

"Publicity hogs and camera hos," Eric said with a dismissive wave. "They showed up tonight because they knew the press was sniffing around, and the press is only interested in me because of that car bomb."

The stress lines on Eric's face faded as the painkiller worked through him.

Meanwhile, Anton cleaned the wound with hot water, applied an antiseptic, and started sewing. Eric was so numb he hardly flinched.

"The night was worth it," he said dreamily. "It felt great to get one up on Braddock for a change."

"Glad I could help, even though you did trick me into it."

Eric frowned. "Tricked?"

"Don't play me, Thorner. You knew about the fake Ambrosia ahead of time. You were waiting for my reaction, hoping I'd cause a scene."

Eric tilted his head. "Actually, sweet Clare, I was counting on it . . ."

Anton cut the thread, added more antiseptic, and finally applied a fresh bandage. "Fit as a fiddle, boss. I'll be outside."

Anton took the medical cart with him. When the door closed, I faced Eric.

"On the day we met, you said you wanted to make me an offer. That Ambrosia stunt was my final job interview, wasn't it? A last test from the Quiz Master?"

Eric had not released my hand since he hit the mattress. Now he squeezed my fingers, gazed up at me with little boy eyes, and smiled.

"Congratulations, Clare, you're hired."

"What is it you want me to do, exactly?"

"Two jobs," he said, flashing fingers on his other hand. "First I want you and your staff to cater the launch party for THORN, Inc.'s Appland."

"Appland?"

"Our Chelsea office. We open in a few weeks, and my people will finally be moving out of that crappy cinderblock bunker at the server farm. I want a real celebration."

"It would be my pleasure—"

"Don't thank me yet. Half of my staff won't touch wheat gluten or dairy. The other half lives on junk food. Good luck pleasing everyone."

"No sweat. Pleasing everyone is practically the definition of a good barista."

"Anton will supply you with a list of my gang's likes and dislikes. You can start there." He noticed my frown. "You look worried. Is the job too intimidating?"

"It's not the catering. Look, Eric, I want to be straight with you. My partner in the coffee business actually forbade me to have anything to do with you, or your organization."

Eric frowned. "Is it because of the bomb?"

"Partly . . ."

"Partly, huh?" Eric sighed. "I get it. It's the testosterone thing, which is a shame, because Matteo Allegro is a very talented coffee hunter, one of the best in the business. I could use his expertise, and yours, for a very special project—that would be the *second* job."

"I'd like to help, but you don't know my ex-husband—"

"Actually, Clare, I think I do. And I believe I have an offer even Mr. Allegro won't refuse."

I listened intently as Eric explained why he really wanted to hire us.

I couldn't believe it, but Eric was right. No matter how threatened Matt's ego was by this incredibly successful baby billionaire, there was no way any self-respecting coffee hunter would refuse this challenge.

Thirty-Five

〜〜〜〜〜〜〜〜〜〜〜〜〜〜〜〜〜〜〜

Holding my hand the entire time, Eric finished outlining his proposal for me and Matt before falling into a deep sleep. I gently detached myself, left his bedside, and quietly retrieved my things.

As I opened the door, the bedroom lights automatically dimmed until the flickering fireplace and glow of the city were the only illumination. The view was stunning, and I couldn't help lingering another few minutes to imagine what it would be like waking up to this vista each and every morning.

A little voice answered (but it wasn't robotic).

Like much in life that becomes commonplace, dear, this, too, would be taken for granted.

"Yes, it would, Madame . . ." I whispered in reply, and with a little smile, I turned away.

I'd barely crept into the darkened hallway before stumbling into Anton Alonzo. "Goodness, you startled me."

He looked at me strangely. "But I informed you that I would be waiting outside, did I not?"

"Indeed, you did."

Anton smiled, his white teeth luminous in the low light. "It appears everything went according to Mr. Thorner's plan, so I suspect you never received your after-dinner coffee service?"

"Actually I was served two, but neither was worth drinking."

"I could prepare some for you now, if you wish?"

This compact, intense man, who I thought a mere chauffeur at the start of the evening, was obviously much more. The Spaniard seemed to know Eric and his business better than anyone I'd encountered.

And who knows? I thought. *He might even dish over a cup of Joe.*

"Thank you, Anton, I would love some coffee."

Anton lifted his chin and spoke to the invisible fembot. "House, heat thirty-two ounces of filtered water to a constant of 196 degrees Fahrenheit. Grind seventy-seven grams of beans from coffee basket three, medium fine."

"Yes, Anton."

The lightest whirr of a burr grinder sounded from another part of the penthouse.

"Please excuse me a moment, Ms. Cosi, I must freshen up after my medical duties."

"I should visit the powder room, too."

"The door to your right," Anton said. "When you are finished, simply ask Miss House to lead you to the kitchen. She will point the way." Anton bowed. "I will expect to see you in ten minutes, Ms. Cosi."

He began pushing the medical cart through a nearby door.

I slipped in and out of the lavish, marble- and copper-fixtured bathroom in record time. Back in the hall, I saw Anton had left the medical cart lodged in the door, wedging it open. I called Anton's name, but there was no reply. I called his name again, this time pushing the cart through the doorway and all the way into the room.

Lights turned on and my jaw dropped at what I saw.

The walls in this side room were lined with row after row of dolls—Ken dolls, to be exact—placed side by side on backlighted glass shelves. Each little plastic Ken sported a different outfit, and some even had accessories. A quick survey revealed a heavy emphasis on casual wear.

One Ken had been placed on a center podium, and I realized this doll was clad in a miniature version of Eric's formalwear for the evening, down to the ebony silk tie.

Okay, that's creepy.

Though they all wore the same painted smile, I couldn't help but think that these were a lonely bunch of Kens, for there was nary a Barbie in sight.

A peek through an inner doorway revealed that this space was part of an immense closet, which explained the lack of furniture. On the wall, I noticed some pictures.

One framed photo showed Anton Alonzo armed to the teeth in camouflaged combat fatigues, surrounded by other soldiers. A second showed his small frame in combat, lifting a man twice his size in a fireman's carry. A third featured him in dress uniform, Spain's flag draped off a flagpole behind him. A final picture also featured Anton. Snapped on the nude beach at Fire Island, he romped with a different set of manly companions. Their snug swimsuits (or lack thereof) revealed that these tanned, muscular men were certainly *special*, but they weren't Special Ops.

Interesting . . .

I glanced at Madame's jeweled watch. *I'm supposed to rendezvous with Anton in three, so I'd better hustle.*

Back in the hall, I turned my eyes skyward. "Oh, Miss House? Hello there?"

"Yes . . ." Miss House paused then added (to my shock), "Clare."

Okay, yes, that was creepy, too.

I cleared my throat, feeling silly, but—"Would you show me the way to the kitchen, please?"

"Certainly, Clare. Follow Mr. Arrow, please."

"Mr. Arrow . . . ?"

A holographic blue arrow appeared in the air three feet from my nose. About the size of a bread knife, it pointed to the end of the hall, where another transparent, floating arrow directed me to turn left. Following several more of the ghostly beacons, I descended a chrome and glass staircase so delicately constructed it seemed almost ephemeral.

The kitchen, as expected, was immense, and filled with a wonderland of gadgets, from a soda machine to a pair of deep fryers, to gas pizza ovens, and a grill and smoker combination.

I didn't require any more holographic arrows to find Anton. I simply followed my nose and the aroma of freshly brewed coffee.

Anton waited at a small breakfast nook by the window. He directed me to a chair.

"It smells delicious."

"Thank you, Ms. Cosi. But my compliments go to the roaster."

About then I recognized the aroma of my Wake Up the Night roast, and acknowledged the compliment.

Anton sat across from me. The formerly intense ball of energy seemed more relaxed now that he'd replaced the starched chauffeur suit with loose, black chinos and a soft, cocoa brown cashmere sweater.

"To your health," he said, lifting his cup.

"Perfect." I sighed after a satisfying sip.

"This is Eric's favorite roast. He thinks it's amazing."

"You're pretty amazing yourself, Anton. You make superb coffee, you're a chauffeur, a bodyguard, a butler, and a para-medic, too."

"I have an exceptional patient," Anton replied. "Eric is no stranger to pain."

"Oh? How so?"

"He was born with a spinal deformation that worsened

with age. It took a dozen operations over many years to correct. He suffered acutely through childhood and adolescence."

I could hear the empathy in Anton's voice as he related Eric's ordeal, and I had to ask, "You and Eric seem awfully . . . tight. Just how close are you two?"

"I would never let anything happen to my man."

"No, I mean are you really, *really* close? You know, are you . . ."

"Are we lovers?" Anton finished for me.

I nodded.

"No, Ms. Cosi. Eric is as straight as Mr. Arrow." He gave a wave of his hand. "His tastes are really quite prosaic."

"I'd hardly call Bianca Hyde ordinary."

Anton frowned. "Eric had his reasons for allowing Ms. Hyde to insinuate herself into our lives. The end was messy, but it ended."

"Yes, it did . . . which makes me wonder."

"What?"

"I met Eric's sister tonight. She warned me that bad things happen to the women around Eric. She said 'women.' Plural. She also mentioned something about a divorcée. Do you know what she meant?"

Anton appeared stricken for a moment, but quickly recovered.

"Eden was probably drunk. She's very protective of her younger brother, and not very discreet when she imbibes."

"But what she said sounded so . . . ominous. Was it a threat?"

"Pay no attention," Anton insisted. "Bianca's death was one thing, Charley's quite another—"

"Charley?" I put down my coffee cup. "Are you saying that Charley, the ex-cop who died in the explosion—Eric's dead driver—was a *woman*?"

Thirty-Six

≈≈≈≈≈≈≈≈≈≈≈≈≈≈≈≈≈≈≈≈

"You didn't know this?"

"No, I didn't."

"Charley was indeed a woman," Anton confirmed. "An attractive one who intrigued Eric from the start. But Charley was not what she appeared to be . . ."

"Eric was intrigued? Then Charley and Eric really were . . ."

Anton nodded.

Well, I thought, *at least now I understand Braddock's comment about Thorner sleeping with "the help"—not to mention Eric's desperate behavior after the first explosion.*

In the moment it took for me to process the fact that Charley was a woman, I almost missed the second half of Anton's statement—almost.

"Not what she appeared?" I said after a pause. "You mean because she was an ex-cop?"

"No; Eric knew her credentials. That's why he hired her, both to drive him and provide protection. But Charley had her own agenda, and she wanted the job for her own reasons."

"And those reasons were . . . ?"

"Not for me to say." Anton shrugged. "In any case, you have nothing to fear."

"Excuse me?"

"You have no rivals for Eric's affection, Clare. He has thought of nothing but you since he awoke from his operation."

"But you misunderstand. I'm not interested in Eric. Not *that* way."

Anton rolled his eyes. "Then why quiz me about his prior affairs?"

"After everything that's happened tonight, I'm curious, that's all. And I already *have* a boyfriend."

Anton tapped the Omega chronometer on his own wrist. "Are you referring to the man who was supposed to call you at eleven?"

I slapped my forehead. *Not only had I forgotten Quinn's call, I'd turned off my phone at the Source Club.*

"I can't believe I forgot. What's Mike going to think?"

Anton mirrored his boss's smirk. "He will suspect the worst, of course. Perhaps you should have told him you loved him before he hung up."

I frowned. "Eavesdropping is bad form."

"My dear lady, ears come with the job."

"Apparently so do Ken dolls."

"Snooping is bad form, too."

"I'm sorry, but the door was open—and I thought you were inside."

"Did you?"

"Okay, I was snooping. So what's with the Ken dolls?"

He shrugged. "Understated luxury."

"Excuse me?"

"It is my job to help Eric straddle two very different worlds. In this city run by money, the financial class dresses for success. The more tailored and elegant their attire, the more respect they garner."

"That's true."

Anton paused to finish his own cup. "The situation is very different in his world of digital commerce and computer technology, where a fashion heuristic states that only two types of men wear suits and ties: funeral directors and assholes."

I bit my cheek. "Who told you that one? Let me guess . . . Eric."

Anton leaned across the table. "This is Eric's world, not mine. I was born to an esteemed and aristocratic Spanish family. I attended military school and became an officer, like my father and grandfather before me. I grew to be a man around elegant things, and I understand the world of wealth and power in ways Eric cannot."

He sat back. "So you see my dilemma. Two worlds, two cultures. But Eric must function in both of them, so I dress my man in clothes that are distinctive, casual, yet classic— and expensive enough to impress bankers and financiers, and their women."

"Unless they *are* women."

"Touché."

"Those hand-sewn denims and the Florentine leather bomber jacket Eric wore when I first met him—your idea?"

"They're all my ideas, Ms. Cosi. I order the outfits tailored in miniature, from the materials that will be used to make the finished product. I show the dolls to Eric, and he makes his selections."

Anton owned his pride, and why not? He got to dress his own living, breathing, billionaire Ken doll.

"It's a more efficient system than trial-and-error, Ms. Cosi, even if it's not perfect."

"What heuristic is perfect? A heuristic is basically just a rule of thumb, isn't it? Helpful, maybe, but a rule of thumb is just an easy shortcut, like stereotyping. It doesn't work all the time, does it?"

Anton smiled and nodded appreciatively. I glanced at my watch. It was after one in the morning. I thought about turning on my phone, but I knew Anton would eavesdrop on any call, and I didn't want to deal with a concerned or angry Quinn until I had privacy.

"It's very late, Anton. I'd better head home before the seams on this vintage dress give way."

Anton rose. "I'll drive you."

"No, don't leave Eric alone. I insist. Call me a cab and I'll be fine."

Thirty-Seven

~~~~~~~~~~~~~~~~~~~~~~~~~~~~

Was *that a whimper?*

As my taxi pulled away, I was buffeted by an arctic blast. My coat, more stylish than functional, leaked like a New Orleans levee, and the beads on my vintage Chanel dress felt more like ice chips.

The coffeehouse was closed, the shop dark, the newly installed French doors shuttered. I was fumbling for my key when I heard the sound, like a whimper of pain or despair. *A lost pet?*

I moved to the dim alley beside the shop and tried to peer into the darkness. Then I heard it again. A sob, and definitely human . . .

It could be a homeless person or even a drunk, in which case I'd call the authorities for a non-emergency to help the person find shelter on this frigid night. But if this were a crime victim or someone who'd been seriously injured, he'd need help right away.

"Hello?" I called.

A large figure burst out of the shadows—so fast I had no

chance to run. Heavy shoes scuffled on the cold concrete and thick arms wrapped around me in a crushing bear hug. I struggled and felt the delicate dress tear under my coat, but I couldn't break free.

When I tried to scream, a gloved hand covered my mouth and nose. I could barely breathe, and within seconds I was seeing stars.

I looked down, hoping to spot a foot to stomp on or leg to kick.

What I saw were tan construction boots and dirty denim cuffs. Then something else tumbled into view—a red wool *Solar Flare* cap had fallen from my attacker's head.

That's when I knew the man holding me was the looter from the other night. And here I was, helpless as a bundled baby to do anything about it!

I groaned in frustration. He must have thought I was suffocating, because the glove came off my face.

"Stop struggling," he hissed.

For the second time that evening, a noxious alcohol cloud wafted over me. This time it was cheap malt, not premium juniper berries.

"Okay," I said, willing myself calm. "Do you want money? Jewelry?"

I couldn't see his face, but he gripped me so tightly I felt his head shake.

"This is where it happened. This is where they killed her. You were there, right? You saw it?"

When I didn't reply, he squeezed until my ribs bruised.

"Right, right!" I yelped.

"Now she's dead and they're looking for me." His grip relaxed a little. I might have been able to escape him, but suddenly I didn't want to.

"We can talk about it. Let's go inside, have coffee—"

"No!" His cry was anguished. "It's a trap. There's someone inside already. It could be the police. They're looking for me. They think I did it."

"There's no one inside. The coffeehouse is empty."

"You're lying!" He shook his head. "You saw how they killed her, right?"

"Charley?"

"Yes, Charley. Charlene Kramer Polaski; my ex-wife. She was too close to the truth so they murdered her."

"What truth?"

"The truth of who *really* killed that young actress Bianca Hyde."

"Are you telling me that Charley was the target of the bomb, and not Eric?"

"Yes. They didn't know about me. They couldn't. She was sending notes for safekeeping, deleting them from her phone before midnight."

Midnight? Why? Was Charley a PI Cinderella?

I cleared my throat. "So who is *they?*"

Before he could answer, the sound of keys rattling in the Blend's front door interrupted us. The man released me so fast that I nearly stumbled to the pavement. Snatching up his red cap, he took off, legs pumping, heavy construction boots smacking the pavement.

I lunged for the door just as Matteo Allegro yanked it open.

"Clare?!"

"Matt! I was nearly assaulted!"

"I knew it!" He took one look at my gaping coat and torn dress and (despite his sub-Saharan tan) turned redder than a chili pepper. "I don't care if Thorner is a billionaire! I'm going to kill the little son of a—"

Thirty-Eight

～～～～～～～～～～～～～～～～～～

Of course, I straightened Matt out and he calmed down—then he calmed *me* down. After plopping me on a stool at our espresso bar, he rummaged around for my container of home-made Kahlúa, and grabbed ice from the freezer and a bottle of vodka.

"What are you making?"

"Espressotinis."

I rubbed my arm, sore from the manhandling. "Make mine—"

"A double. I plan to . . ."

As he mixed our drinks, I told him everything, starting with the Source Club dinner, the coffee showdown with Grayson Braddock, and the fact that Eric Thorner had endured excruciating pain—just so he wouldn't miss the chance to embarrass a business rival who'd insulted him.

"Sounds like you had dinner in a shark tank."

"More of a shark aquarium, complete with its own holo-fall."

"Hollow-what?"

"It doesn't matter. Let's just say there were plenty of predators swimming in money, and Thorner must have been planning his 'got-ya' moment for some time."

"The kid's obviously very smart," Matt conceded, straining my espresso martini into a glass crusted with cocoa and sugar. "Maybe too smart for his own good . . ."

I took a long sweet hit of refreshingly cool burn and kept talking, explaining how a group called Solar Flare had gathered to protest Eric (for *what* exactly, I still didn't know), then I'd come back here, and—

"It was one of their members who grabbed me. The man outside claimed Charley—*Charlene*—was his ex-wife, and he was trying to tell me what he knew about the car bombing outside our coffeehouse, until *you* scared him off—"

"You think I'm sorry?" Matt snapped. "The guy was obviously unbalanced."

"He was upset. And some of what he said didn't make much sense. He's mourning his ex-wife's death, after all, and he thinks the police suspect him of being the bomber, but I don't think he's crazy."

"He told you the police think he's the bomber? Maybe he is, Clare, and the last thing you should have proposed was a one-on-one sit-down with him in this coffeehouse."

"But I believe him. He said his wife was murdered because she was close to discovering the truth behind the death of Bianca Hyde. He also used the pronoun *they*, which implies a conspiracy, so I'm going to speak with Nate Sumner first thing tomorrow—"

"Mother's old hippie friend? That geezer who teaches at the New School?"

"Yes."

"Why? What does Sumner know about reality after all those psychedelic acid trips?"

"Nate is a member of Solar Flare; he was at the demonstration tonight; and the man who grabbed me was wearing one of their red caps, so Nate might know him—"

"I don't like this."

"Look, all I need to do is locate that man and get his statement to Quinn or Lieutenant DeFasio at the Bomb Squad. DeFasio owes me, and I know he'll listen."

"Well, don't get your hopes up. Not after Nate saw you on a date with Thorner. You're sleeping with the enemy."

"I am *not* sleeping with—"

"In Nate's eyes, you're in bed with Eric—metaphorically, anyway, and before this is all over, who knows?"

"Stop it."

"No. That Thorner kid got you into his bedroom tonight, didn't he?"

"Well, truthfully, he did but—"

"I knew it!"

"It was only to help his butler administer medical aid!"

Matt smirked. "Face it, Clare, the rich are used to getting what they want, and from where I stand, that rich kid wants you in his bed."

"I really don't need your insulting negativity right now. What are you doing here, anyway? Don't you have a wife . . . I mean *life?*"

"I'm here because *your boyfriend* asked me to check up on you. The flatfoot called me around midnight and said you *never answered your cell*. So he—"

"Assumed the worst?"

"He called me because he was worried about your safety. Are you going to call Quinn or what?"

"When I go upstairs and have some *privacy*. But since you're here, we need to talk."

"We are talking."

"About something else—"

"You know, it's odd how you claim that creep tore your dress under the coat. Are you sure you're not making up a story to protect the boy billionaire?"

"Eric was a perfect gentleman, which is more than I can say for the guy who grabbed me. Or Grayson Braddock."

Matt scratched his black beard. "Braddock's a playboy, that's true. Bree and I went to one of his parties at last year's South Beach Wine and Food Festival. The guy lives large. A mansion playground in Coral Gables. Women. Fast cars. Kinky parties. A yacht called *Made in the Shade*—"

"Your eyes are glazing, Matt. Who are you jealous of, Braddock or Thorner?"

"Both, frankly, and I'm wary of both. Those men are players—in business and monkey business, too—and they play to win, so I wouldn't believe what either of them tells you. Thorner probably steered the police toward Braddock just to foul him up."

"Don't compare Eric to Braddock. I like Eric. He struck me as an earnest, trustworthy young—"

"Don't waste your time selling me on the kid. Sell your flatfoot boyfriend."

"Actually, Matt . . ." I took a long hit off my nightcap. "I do have to sell you."

"Why?"

"Because tonight Eric offered us an incredible, once-in-a-lifetime opportunity—"

"The answer is *no!*"

"Hear me out." I gestured to the bar stool beside me. "Why don't you sit? When you hear this, I think you'll need to."

Matt didn't budge. Standing even taller, he folded his arms. "There's no offer Thorner could possibly make that I would accept. Ever."

I took another vodka-laced sip of courage and launched into my pitch (the one I'd rehearsed in my head on the cab ride home).

"Eric wants us to create the ultimate coffee. A world-class cup of excellence called Billionaire Blend. He wants us to use the rarest, best, and most exclusive coffee beans in the world. I do the roasting, after *you* source the beans."

Matt snorted. "I'm supposed to go broke scouring the world at the behest of the boy billionaire?"

"Eric wants to pay for everything—up front. Money is no object. You can fly anywhere and pay any price; all you have to do is buy the best with Eric's money, and I'll do the rest right here in our basement."

Matt went silent for a very long moment.

"So, what do you think?"

"I think I have to sit down."

Yes! "Does that mean you're in?"

Matt raised a hand. "Not so fast. What about this 'they' the man who grabbed you mentioned?"

"What about it?"

"What if whoever 'they' are killed Charley to cover up Eric's murder of Bianca Hyde?"

"You're just saying that because you're jealous of a handsome, young man who has it all, and earned it all, by himself."

"And you're just saying that because you *want* Eric to be innocent. Money changes everything, doesn't it, Clare?"

"If that were true, I would have stayed to watch the sunrise in his Central Park bedroom."

"You don't think there's even a *chance* Eric is guilty? Not even a little bit?"

"No. And try this on for size: you're being incredibly selfish."

"Me? Selfish?!"

"Think about all the good you could do with Eric's money."

"What?"

"Remember that tribe in Uganda you told me about—the one without a washing station? How about those struggling farmers in Haiti? And what about Costa Gravas? They finally dumped their dictator, but that's just a start. Their new democracy needs to rebuild its coffee industry from the ground up."

"That's true . . ." Matt frowned and took his own long drink as he thought about that. "Costa Gravas is so close to Jamaica, they have the same microclimate. In a few years, they could be producing beans with a rep that rivals Blue Mountain. But the farms have no infrastructure support, their situation is even worse than Haiti's, they've got sink-holes for roads, antiquated methods—"

"Things you could help change by directing Eric's money to the right places, to worthy people. A ten-thousand-dollar grant to every farm or cooperative you single out could help change lives."

"As if Thorner would care."

"I think he would, if you educated him. Offer to take him with you on your sourcing trips. Teach him how the farmers who grow coffee live, what they struggle against every day. Convince Eric that he can create real change in the real world simply by helping them."

"Fine!" Matt threw up his hands. "You win, okay? I'm on board with the rich kid's scheme—as long as the twerp doesn't turn out to be a mad bomber."

"He's not."

"Or a lady killer—literally."

"He's not that, either."

"I know you, Clare. Your lips may say *he's not*, but those worried green eyes say you're not entirely sure."

"What you see in my eyes is exhaustion. Let's call it a night, okay?"

I closed and locked the door behind my ex, then headed upstairs.

Dreamland was calling, but the night wasn't over yet. There was one more man I had to calm down, and (heaven, help me) ask for a favor.

Thirty-nine

~~~~~~

"Clare?"

"I hope you're looking at your caller ID."

"I am."

"Then you know I'm home safe—and I'm so very sorry, Mike. Things got crazy, and I lost track of time—"

"I was worried. I called your ex-husband—"

"I know."

"And DeFasio—"

"DeFasio? At the Bomb Squad? Why?"

"I told you, I was worried. I asked if there were any bomb scares in Lower Manhattan. He answered—and I quote—'No, Mike. I swept Eric Thorner's limo for devices myself before he picked up your lovely lady.'"

Oh, geez. "So how angry are you?"

"What I am is a little embarrassed, but I'll live."

"You didn't have to call him."

"*You* could have called me."

"Let's not argue . . ."

I heard the hard exhale on the other end of the line.

"I love you, Mike, you know?"

"I know. And you know the feeling is mutual—otherwise, I would have waited for the morning news to see if you survived the night."

"You won't be angry all weekend, will you?"

"Does that mean you're coming to Washington?"

"Yes, of course. It's my turn to travel, isn't it? I'll be on the afternoon Acela—you can pick me up at Union Station. I'll even bake you that Triple-Chocolate Cheesecake I've been promising, if . . ."

"There's an *if*? After what you put me through, I don't get the cheesecake free and clear?"

"I need a favor."

"You're pushing it, sweetheart."

"True. But it's for a good cause . . ."

I explained what I needed. By the end, I was so exhausted (from the day and the vodka), I nearly drifted off.

"No promises," Mike said at last. "But I'll see what I can do. Now, get some rest and do *me* a favor . . ."

"Anything."

He lowered his voice. "Dream about me."

"I plan to . . ." I said, then hung up and (on a stifled yawn) placed one last call.

"Clare?"

"I'm so sorry to disturb you at this crazy hour, but I need a very important favor . . ."

Madame listened to my request. *Yes*, she agreed. First thing in the morning, she'd call her old flame and invite him for coffee.

"Thank you," I said.

Then I bid her sweet dreams and promptly passed out.

FORTY

"**B**ootsie Girl!"

Nathan Sumner's cry interrupted the chatter of our late-morning rush. From behind our counter, I watched as the old professor, eyes only for Madame, strolled across our restored plank floor.

"Bootsie Girl?" Esther and Tucker said in unison before I shushed them.

Madame rose to greet the plus-sized man. He opened his arms wide, and they shared a lingering hug and affectionate pecks.

In his youth, Nate had been a passionate young man with a baby face, golden ponytail, and idealistic fire in his hard, brown gaze. The ponytail was still there, though shorter now, and as silver as Madame's pageboy. He wore rimless glasses over those brown eyes, and his baby face now sported a close-trimmed white beard and more than a few creases. As for the rest of him . . .

"By God, Bootsie Girl, you never lost your figure, unlike

we less fortunate ones." Nate patted the wool vest jacketing his own impressive middle.

"You've gained more than a few pounds," Madame conceded, still holding his hand. "You've also doubled up on the charismatic charm that bruised the hearts of so many young coeds."

The tweedy professor was pushing seventy, but when he gazed at Madame, his dark eyes danced like a man in his lusty prime.

"Passing fancies," Nate said with a wave of his wrinkled hand. "My heart was forever stomped by you, Bootsie Girl."

My former mother-in-law struck a coquettish pose and lifted her maxi-length lamb's wool skirt just enough to display what I'd foolishly thought was a rare fashion faux pas—white, knee-length leather go-go boots with pointed toes and stacked heels.

From Nate's excited reaction, however, I realized Madame was merely dressing to rekindle some provocative memories. (I also guessed it was Madame's *boots* that had done some walking all over Nate Sumner's heart.)

The pair returned to Madame's quiet corner table arm in arm. I'd set a vase with a few blue roses on the table, and Nate eyed them suspiciously before slipping off his leather shoulder pack. As he pulled off his coat, he yanked a tall, brown paper bag out of one deep pocket and set it on the table.

"What's this?" Madame pointed to the paper bag with disapproval. "Brought your own drink?"

"Oh, that's just my favorite iced tea. I talk so much, I guzzle a dozen cans a day. Anyway, this one's empty, and you know I'd never refuse a Village Blend espresso."

That was my cue to enter the scene, bearing a tray with a *doppio* each for Madame and Nate—and a third for me.

"So, Blanche, what's up?" Nate asked while I served. "We haven't sat for coffee since we pressured the City Council to expand landmark zoning rules to the entire Village."

"What a day," Madame said. "The mayor was frothing at the mouth."

"Flipping the bird to power is a blast, Bootsie. You should do it more often," Nate said with a self-satisfied chuckle.

"Is that what you were doing in front of the Source Club last night?" I interjected. "Flipping the bird to power?"

"Oh, Nate," Madame cooed. "Perhaps you know Clare Cosi, my manager?"

"Yes, I saw her just last night, though this is our first *formal* introduction . . ." Nate didn't look happy to see me. I didn't care—

"May I join you," I said, sitting before Nate could object.

Nate sampled his espresso, drained the demitasse, and set it aside. "So, Ms. Cosi, you must have had an interesting dinner last night."

"It's what happened *after* dinner that concerns me."

"Ah," Nate said with a stubbornly proud smile. "My little protest."

"Your mini riot, you mean."

"Some of my followers are . . . enthusiastic. Things may have gotten out of hand."

"Saul Alinsky tactics?" Madame asked, referring to the political anarchist's notorious guidebook, *Rules for Radicals* (a sort of *Robert's Rules* of disorder).

Nate laughed. "They were General Patton's tactics, Bootsie. We outflanked the enemy."

"What were you protesting, exactly?" I asked.

The good humor drained from Nate's bearded face. "The digital age, Ms. Cosi. The insidious use of computers to control populations. The cancer of social media in all of its forms."

"Goodness!" Madame blinked. "And I thought you were an advocacy group for solar *power*."

Nate patted Madame's hand. "I chose the name *Solar Flare* because of my original concern. Our rush to computerize our infrastructure, to digitize our libraries, records, and financial transactions, ignores a hidden danger—"

"A solar flare?" I assumed.

"Precisely, Ms. Cosi. A solar eruption could potentially

destroy all computers and the data they contain, obliterating two thousand years of human endeavor in an instant, should we abandon our history of traditional print and paper. Why, a solar hiccup could disrupt power grids for months, even years."

"A terrifying possibility," I acknowledged. "But like an asteroid striking the earth, what are the chances of it actually happening?"

"A valid point, which is why, in order to become more relevant, our group's emphasis has shifted to the immediate and insidious threat of cyberization."

"Cyber-*what*?"

"I coined the term to illustrate our increasing dependence on high-tech gadgets. We are becoming cyborgs, fusions of man and machine." Nate pulled a small, thin hardcover from his shoulder bag and handed it to me. "I outline it all in my book—and I'd like you to give it to Eric Thorner."

"Cyberization and Control: The Totalitarianism of New Technology," I read.

The dust jacket art depicted a photo of a young man draped in technology. Devices covered his eyes, nose, mouth, even his arms. Wires rose from each machine, leading to crosshatched puppet master's sticks floating under the title.

"At present, the man/machine commingling is only psychological. Separate any one of the customers around us from their smartphones and you'll see what I mean. Within a few hours, they exhibit many of the same withdrawal symptoms as an addict deprived of heroin."

"Heroin?" I echoed, slipping the book into my apron pocket. The statement seemed ludicrously extreme to me— although a few months ago, Matt *did* climb the walls after he'd smashed his own smartphone in a tantrum and had to live without it for all of a half day.

"The results of studies are disturbing," Nate continued. "The Internet is turning into the new opiate of the people— especially young people. Privacy is violated, civil rights trampled upon. If we're not careful, the digital domain is going to control our bank accounts, our thoughts, every waking moment of our lives—"

"You don't think you're overstating it?"

"What the future holds is terrifying. The cyber-world gives people the illusion of anonymity and power, but neither of those things is true. It takes away our power. It sells out our privacy. And as these clever devices insinuate themselves, tempting us with easy lives and glib replies, I believe we'll become like machines ourselves. Soulless and sociopathic, if not out-and-out automatons."

I saw the somber change in the old man's demeanor and took a shot in the dark. "It sounds like you're speaking from personal experience."

"Yes, I confess: it *is* personal, Ms. Cosi. Eric Thorner, the man you dined with last night, is responsible for the death of my niece."

Forty-one

~~~~~~~~~~~~~~~~~~~~~~~~~~~~~~~~

The statement shocked me. I assumed Nate was talking about Eric's old girlfriend, the young actress Bianca Hyde. Before I could ask, however, Madame set me straight.

"You're speaking about Eva, your brother's child? I remember when she was born, but that must have been—"

"Eva would have been seventeen last month. She died almost two years ago."

"I'm so sorry, Nate," Madame said. "I didn't know."

"You didn't know because my brother's company transferred him. He placed Eva in an exclusive private school. Eva was the new girl, and the students there were cruelly cliquish. By the end of her first semester the cyber-bullying began."

Nate told us how one of Eva's female tormentors secretly took a candid photo of Eva half dressed in the locker room after gym class.

"The bully used Eric's popular *Pigeon Droppings* app to place Eva in the game without her consent, and then spent an entire weekend circulating screen grabs among her friends. By Monday, one of the little sadists posted printouts all over the school. When Eva saw the pictures of her half-naked body covered in cyber-crap, she ran home and locked herself in the bathroom."

Nate paused. When he spoke again his voice was shaking. "By the time the school alerted my brother, it was too late. Vince found his daughter hanging dead in the shower."

Oh my God . . .

I heard the air leave Madame's lungs in a rush, and her violet eyes welled. I felt tears welling, too, but I had to point out the obvious.

"I'm so sorry, Nate . . . what happened was awful, *criminal*, but the bullying was the issue. Eric Thorner only created the game, not the abuse."

"The game became a tool for abuse, Ms. Cosi. As a society, we regulate tobacco companies, gun manufacturers, and distillers of alcohol because we know their products have the potential to do harm or be abused."

"I see your logic, but how do you propose apps be regulated? The online shops that carry them do so already, don't they?"

"Yes, but more must be done. Solar Flare has been effective in the past. We were instrumental in the banning of those vile *Pigeon Droppings* T-shirts. We made sure Thorner took a financial hit for those!"

"I'm sorry to tell you that Eric doesn't see what you're trying to accomplish. He believes you simply want his business to pay for your advocacy."

"What's wrong with that?" Nate replied. "Tobacco companies fund lung cancer research. Gun manufacturers are the leading promoters of firearms education, and alcohol manufacturers support substance abuse programs. Why shouldn't tech companies like Eric's fund Solar Flare, so we can effect much-needed change from within? We're committed to our public protests against him until he pays up."

I nodded like a good student—even though it seemed to me that Nate Sumner was treading a fine line between activism and extortion. But now was not the time for debate. Now was the time for me to find out what Nate knew about Charley's husband.

With care, I shifted topics and told Nate about my encounters with the man in the red Solar Flare cap.

"I need to know. Is he a member of your group?"

"Yes, Joseph Polaski is a member of Solar Flare," Nate said, "but I don't know where you can find him, and I wouldn't tell you if I did. I will also add that Joe is another victim of the digital domain."

Nate then told me all about Joe and his ex-wife, Charlene Polaski. The two were once cops; they'd met on the job. He was the veteran, she the rookie. Things were fine between them until Joe's retirement. He started drinking, and they began to drift apart. The marriage ended when Joe discovered Charley was seeing a lover she'd met on a website that facilitated extramarital affairs.

"Joe reacted badly. He slapped Charley, and she got a restraining order against him. Joe joined Solar Flare shortly after."

"Is he a volunteer, or is he paid?"

"Solar Flare has no paid staff, Ms. Cosi. I run the organization with a few dedicated interns and many volunteers. Joe is a responsible member of the community. He prepares food at a Bowery homeless shelter, collects clothing for the local Salvation Army, and performs maintenance work for the Friends of the High Line Committee."

"Does he build firebombs in his spare time, too?"

"Joe had nothing whatsoever to do with the murder of his ex-wife. He still loved Charley, and they'd recently reconciled—well, after a fashion. When Charley became a licensed private investigator, she asked Joe to help with her first major undercover investigation."

Now I understood. Eric's butler, Anton, said that Charley was *not what she seemed*, and that she had *personal reasons* for taking a job at THORN, Inc. After what Nate just revealed, I easily guessed the rest.

"Charley was investigating Bianca Hyde's death, wasn't she?"

"She was." Nate nodded. "From what Joe told me, the girl's family hired her. They blamed Eric Thorner for what happened to their daughter, and wanted Charley to find proof that Thorner was responsible for her death. Charley knew Joe was a member of Solar Flare so she asked him to feed her information about Thorner's company. But from what Joe told me the last time we spoke, it was Charley who was feeding him information toward the end—and lots of it."

I leaned forward. "What kind of information?"

"You'll have to ask Joe."

"But you don't know where he is?"

Nate shrugged. "Sorry."

I was about to suggest refills when I spied a trio of men in dark suits approaching our table. Alarmed, I slid my chair back and bumped into another man hovering behind me. More suits flowed out of the crowd, to surround our table. NYPD officers in uniform and several detectives followed. To my horror, one of them was Lieutenant Dennis DeFasio of the Bomb Squad.

The original trio displayed their FBI credentials.

"Nathan Sumner," the one in the middle said. "You are under arrest for detonating an explosive device for terrorist purposes, and for the murder of Charlene Polaski."

"No!" Madame cried, leaping to her feet to block the agents. "You're making a terrible mistake. This man is innocent!"

One agent deftly pulled Madame aside while the other two cuffed Nate. The old professor seemed as stunned as the rest of us. He didn't resist in the least, which made the regiment of FBI agents and NYPD officers there to arrest him look like ridiculous overkill.

One agent lifted Nate out of his chair; a second grabbed his shoulder bag.

On his feet, Nate quickly recovered some of his old spirit.

"Pass my book to your friend, Ms. Cosi," the old professor told me quickly. "It has *good information*."

The authorities who filled my coffeehouse pulled back,

taking their prisoner with them. Moving toward the door, Nate cried out one last chant—

"Roses white and red are best!"

His words barely registered as my focus fixed on Lieutenant DeFasio, bringing up the rear. I rushed forward, grabbing his arm before he got out the door.

"What are you doing, Lieutenant?"

"The FBI has made an arrest," DeFasio replied, tone stiffer than his military crew cut. Then he grabbed my arm and pulled me into a corner.

"Nate is no killer," I hissed. "He's an opinionated old man, that's all—"

"An old man with a past that fits the crime."

"What past?"

"We also have physical evidence."

"What evidence?"

"I can't tell you, not officially . . ." He lowered his voice and held my eyes. "I can only discuss the case with *Federal agents*."

Quinn, I thought. *DeFasio is telling me to talk to Mike.*

The lieutenant hurried out to join the others—and I joined my own stunned customers, staring like zombies at the departing police vehicles. I noticed Tuck at the espresso bar, comforting a distraught Madame, and I wanted to do the same. For the moment, however, I couldn't move that far. I simply sank back down at the table where they'd arrested Nate. In the process, I bumped his paper bag. It tumbled to the floor and an empty can rolled out—

Brooklyn's Best Iced Tea.

I stared at the can.

Where have I seen that before?

At the Bomb Squad headquarters, I realized. Cases of the very same iced tea were stacked outside the kitchen where DeFasio claimed his people were *re-creating the bomb*!

Not just a bomb. A firebomb, using liquid accelerants, according to Sergeant Emmanuel Franco.

Oh my God. Whoever built that bomb used a can just like this one—Nate's favorite brand. I just knew it wasn't a coincidence.

Madame approached me, grasped my arms. "We have to help Nathan," she said, drying her eyes. "He's a good man and a gentle one. He abhors violence. You know he's innocent, don't you?"

"I do, Madame."

"Then you'll help him? You'll find a way to clear him of these terrible false charges?"

"Yes, I promise—because I know exactly how he was framed."

Forty-two

❧❧❧❧❧❧❧❧❧❧❧❧❧❧❧❧❧❧

"**They** have Nate's fingerprints," Mike confirmed when I saw him that weekend. "They pulled the prints off recovered bomb fragments and singled him out as the person of interest very quickly."

It had been less than a week since we'd last seen each other, but after Nate's arrest, it felt more like a month, so I didn't object when Mike asked if we could go straight back to his DC apartment.

Alone at last, Mike wanted to make love, but I was anxious to hear what he knew. "Talk," I demanded, and he did. Unfortunately, I didn't much like what he had to say . . .

"Enlighten me please, Mike. If the NYPD and FBI had Nate's fingerprints so quickly, then why did they wait a week to arrest him?"

"Their theory is that Nate had an accomplice so they put surveillance on him. But after last night's protest at the Source Club, they decided to take him into custody, try to break him in an interview."

"This is so wrong! Nate didn't set a car bomb to kill Eric Thorner or anyone else!"

"Getting emotional won't help your friend."

"I know. It's just so frustrating."

"Then what's *your* theory, Detective?"

"Someone framed Nate—obviously."

"How?"

"The killer must have watched Nate finish a can of Brooklyn's Best Iced Tea and discard it, then recovered the can from the garbage pail. The killer then built the bomb using that can, knowing it would be linked back to Nate, who appeared to have strong motives to want to hurt Eric Thorner."

Mike nodded. "I agree—and between you and me—DeFasio does, too."

"What did he tell you?"

"They went back six months but found no records of the professor purchasing accelerants. They found nothing on his computer or cell phone that indicated he'd been planning a car bombing. They found no traces of bomb-building material where he lives or works or in the Solar Flare offices."

"So why arrest him?"

"Because the agents and detectives running the investigation have enough of a case to pacify the politicians, public, and press who put the pressure on for an arrest."

"So they're betting on Nate confessing and naming an accomplice who built the bomb?"

"Yes."

"He won't, you know, because he's innocent."

"I'm with you, Clare, I am. But who framed him? And why?"

"That's where your favor comes in. Did you do it for me?"

"I did. I spoke with a friend in the LAPD."

"So you got the information?"

"It's locked in my briefcase, but only one thing will persuade me to give up the combination."

"Let me guess: my Triple-Chocolate Italian Cheesecake?"

"Okay, two things. Come here . . ."

THE next morning, I woke to the heavenly smell of buttermilk pancakes on the griddle. In a nice switch, Mike made breakfast for me. As I stuffed myself with comfort-food carbs, he retrieved his handwritten cop notes. Then I made a big pot of coffee and he sat down to give me the skinny on Bianca Hyde's death and the police investigation that followed— straight out of the Los Angeles Police Department files.

"Okay," he began, "Bianca Hyde died at the Beverly Palms Hotel via blunt force trauma. Officially, it was determined that Ms. Hyde was intoxicated, stumbled, or passed out; struck her head against a heavy glass table, and bled to death."

"That much I knew from Tucker's tabloid account."

"Patience, Cosi . . . The investigating officer was convinced her death was foul play, and from the files he seemed eager to pin the crime on Eric Thorner."

"His evidence?"

"They were recently estranged. He'd had enough of her drinking and insisted she check into rehab. She refused and checked into the hotel. The Beverly Palms had been sued the previous year and forced to provide camera footage for a divorce trial, so they removed most of their interior security cameras, promising discretion to future guests."

"What about the elevators?"

"There were cameras in the elevators and in the underground parking garage. The police viewed the footage closely, but there was no visual evidence that Eric Thorner, Anton Alonzo, or any of Bianca's other former boyfriends, who sometimes had jealousy issues, appeared on camera."

"That's it?"

"The police brought Thorner in for questioning. He claimed to be at his Silicon Valley residence that day, all day. It turns out that Mr. Thorner owns considerably more security cams than the Beverly Palms, and the LAPD quickly found time-stamped video images showing Thorner and his butler, Anton, at the residence in the hours leading up to Bianca's death and many hours after."

Mike set his notes aside to pour another cup of coffee. "That's about as solid an alibi as you can ask for, so the LAPD had no choice but to back off."

"Then Eric is innocent."

"Maybe," Mike said.

"Maybe's pretty vague. What's *your* theory, Detective?"

"I'll put it to you this way: What sounds more believable to you? A chubby, out-of-shape old man like Nate Sumner constructs a bomb and finds some way to plant it in a car that's always either in a secure garage or driven by a former NYPD cop? Or . . . a tech genius like Eric Thorner and a former member of Special Ops like his butler, Anton Alonzo, find a way to trick their own security cameras and falsify an alibi?"

I blinked. "You think Nate was framed by Eric and his butler?"

"I do."

"You're crazy."

"And you're willfully blind. Brush those dollar signs away from your eyes, Cosi, and maybe you'll be able to see the truth."

"Don't be insulting. For your theory to work, that means Eric would have planned to kill Charley and almost kill himself."

"Every insurance adjuster knows that the easiest way to appear innocent of starting a fire is to make sure you get burned in it."

"I can't listen to this!"

"DeFasio did."

"You think Eric Thorner murdered Bianca Hyde and then—"

"Yes."

"No, I can't believe it."

Mike exhaled. "More like you don't want to believe it. Like that daughter of yours who broke up with Franco because of his salary."

I held my head. "Don't make things worse."

"Sweetheart, listen to me. I know Nate Sumner got a raw deal, but it's his problem now—and his attorney's problem. I want you to stay away from Thorner."

I swallowed hard. "I promised Madame I'd help. But even if I went back on that promise, I can't live with the situation the way it is. I'm going into business with Eric, and I want to know the truth about him. I really don't think he framed Nate."

"Then who did?"

"I don't know. We don't have enough facts yet to conclude anything."

"And how are you going to get your facts?"

"I'll continue to work with Eric and keep my eyes open."

"But I don't want you *anywhere near* Thorner or his people. I'm worried about you."

"Look, someone around Eric has to be guilty—someone close enough to know his schedule and get to his car without suspicion. I don't know if the motive was personal or monetary, but I'm going to find the truth."

"The truth? Okay, Clare, you think about this truth on your train ride home: the last person to investigate the truth around Eric Thorner was an ex-cop named Charley. And if you're not careful, you're going to end up where she did—on a cold, steel slab at the city morgue."

Forty-three

~~~~~~

For the next few nights, I tossed and turned. Matt was off on his hunt for the best coffee beans in the world. Madame was inconsolable with worry. And me? I was feeling powerless and without a clue (literally).

To make matters worse, Eric himself remained out of touch. He'd left the city upon Nate's arrest and had yet to return. His behavior was beginning to feel suspicious, and I couldn't help wondering whether Mike was right.

On Wednesday night, I tried to call Quinn. His voice mail declared that he was on an unexpected special assignment and temporarily unreachable. I lay awake, hoping he'd get back to me, my mind playing our last conversation over and over again . . .

"You're willfully blind. Brush those dollar signs away from your eyes, Cosi, and maybe you'll be able to see the truth . . ."

On Thursday morning, Tucker took one look at my eyes and gave me a brotherly hug. He didn't see dollar signs, he saw dark circles.

"Listen, CC, there are two remedies for insomnia: physical exhaustion or better *ZZZ*s through chemistry."

I gave the former a try by taking a long afternoon swim at the 14th Street Y. By my tenth lap, I could swear I heard someone gurgling my name under the chlorinated water.

"Ms. Cosi!"

I popped up to find Anton Alonzo at the edge of the pool, wearing full chauffeur livery, standing stiff as a towel rack—complete with a fluffy, white one on his arm.

I climbed out of the water, and he wrapped the soft material around me.

"What are you doing here?" I asked (uncomfortably aware that a dozen of my fellow swimmers were wondering the same thing).

"I have something for you from Mr. Thorner." He pulled a small, gold gift bag from his pocket and opened it. "Please . . ."

"But I'm soaking wet."

"No matter."

I dipped my hand into the bag and brought out a mobile phone, but not just any mobile phone. This was a prototype THORN, Inc., smartphone. The sleek, black design was beautiful, gently caressing my wet hand.

"This phone is shockproof, fireproof, and waterproof to a depth of one kilometer," Anton briskly informed me. "All new data is backed up daily at midnight."

"How do you turn it on?"

"Phone on!" he commanded.

"Good afternoon, Ms. Cosi . . ." I shivered at the familiar fembot voice, the one from Eric's cyber-wired luxury apartment.

"It's Miss House," I whispered to Anton. "Now what?"

"Wait for it," he whispered back.

The fembot spoke again: "I have an incoming call from Mr. Eric Thorner. Will you take the call?"

"Yes," I said.

Eric's visage instantly filled the little screen. "How's my favorite coffee lady?"

"Dripping wet and dog tired."

"Good," he said with a feline grin. "You'll get some good sleep tonight, and when you wake up, we'll have a late breakfast meeting."

"At the Village Blend?" I assumed.

"Anton will give you directions. Trust me, Clare, and I'll see you tomorrow."

"Wait! I have some important questions for you—"

"If you do as Anton says, you can ask me anything."

Then the screen wiped his image, and I shivered in my swimsuit, certain the billionaire's Cheshire Cat grin was the last thing to disappear.

A few hours later, I was shivering again, this time from the winter weather. As snow lightly fell, Anton pointed to a rabbit hole in the form of a Gulfstream jet, sitting on the tarmac at Teterboro Airport.

"I should have taken the sleeping pill," I muttered.

This was Eric's private plane, I was told, which I would have guessed anyway from the THORN, Inc., logo of barbed-wire thorns stenciled around the G5's blue and white tailfin.

"Where am I going?!" I called over nearby roaring engines.

"The pilot will answer your questions, Ms. Cosi! Please board now!"

The pilot answered none of my questions because he was busy flying the plane. The copilot, who acted as steward, wouldn't tell me, either.

"It's a surprise, Ms. Cosi," he said. "My apologies, but I'm under strict orders from Mr. Thorner to keep it that way."

The jet was set up like the cabin of a small yacht—all polished, blond wood and cream-colored cushions. Its small help-yourself galley was stocked for a baby billionaire: champagne, chocolate, caviar, Coca-Cola, Doritos, and Reese's Peanut Butter Cups . . .

At the very back was a private bathroom, complete with a

shower, and a bedroom with a large mattress and a flat-screen TV set up with high-speed Internet and a head-spinning selection from Thorner's personal movie library.

I'd been told to pack light—a change of clothes, underthings, and a nightgown. I changed into sweatpants and an oversized T-shirt, collapsed onto the cloud-soft bed, and slept like a dead person.

Maybe it was the purring sound of those jet engines, maybe it was the relief that I would finally get a chance to question Eric about Professor Nate Sumner's arrest, but my insomnia was officially over and my last thoughts before drifting off: a Ping-Pong match between "How cool is this?" and "What kind of *Interweb* did I get myself into?!"

FORTY-FOUR

~~~~~~~~~~~~~~~~~~~~~~~~~~~~~~~~~~~~~~~

"**Bonjour**, madam . . ."

The sounds of our jet landing had woken me, but the airport didn't look familiar. I washed up, changed into clean slacks and a sweater, and disembarked. As I knotted my topcoat on the chilly tarmac, a bulky man approached.

"Please to follow me," he said, his breath steaming as he took my Pullman. He had a barrel chest and wore a microphone bud in his ear. From the cut of his jacket, I assumed he was carrying a shoulder-holstered gun—and I didn't know whether to feel safe or threatened.

"Excuse me?" I asked him. "Are we in France?"

"*Oui*, madam."

"Where?"

His reply was to pull open the back door of a black SUV. "Please to go inside."

"Won't you tell me where I'm going?"

The big guy didn't answer. He just slid behind the wheel and took off, but when I saw the sign for the A1, I knew: we were driving into Paris.

* * *

As we rolled through the early traffic of tiny cars and giant trucks, all I could think of was Joy. Whatever Eric wanted me to do here, I would absolutely insist on the chance to see my daughter before we left.

As billionaires go, Eric would likely be staying in the center of the city at an ostentatious hotel, something near the majestic Palais-Royal or Champs-Élysées, maybe the Hotel Le Meurice along the Tuileries Gardens.

Frankly, all I cared about on this bright, winter morning was how far we would be from Joy's restaurant.

Could she get a few hours off for a visit? Would Eric let me make the time . . . ?

I prayed it would all work out.

Nose pressed to the car window, I watched the egg-like domes of the Sacré-Coeur basilica draw closer—and closer! With growing excitement, I realized we were heading into Montmartre, where Joy lived and worked.

Tears filled my eyes as we moved through the narrow, cobblestone streets. Then my heart was in my mouth. The SUV pulled up right in front of Les Deux Perroquets!

I burst out of the car before it fully stopped. The restaurant wasn't yet open, but I saw her immediately, sitting in her chef's whites at a table near the window. My daughter rose, opened the front door, and then her arms—

"Mama!"

"Joy!"

Together at last, we held on tight.

FORTY-FIVE

~~~~~~

"MOM, I can't believe you're here!"

I couldn't, either, and it was hard to find my voice.

As we headed into the restaurant, arm in arm, I tried to sense how she was doing. Her chestnut hair appeared shorter than the last time I'd seen her (nearly four months ago), and was presently scraped back into a kitchen-ready ponytail. Her curvy figure was hidden by the blocky chef's jacket, but it was her face that worried me. It looked thin and pale. Shadows under her eyes and a tightness around her mouth made her look older than her years.

In my view, there were two likely causes for this: anxiety about her work or love life (or both).

I was about to launch into a battery of Mother Hen questions when a gentleman roughly the height of the Eiffel Tower rose from a table to greet me.

"Good morning, Ms. Cosi. How was your flight?"

The last time I'd seen this man, he'd been having dinner with Eric Thorner's half-crocked sister in the Source Club's River Room.

Eric had described Garth Hendricks as his medicine man—after a fashion. He'd replaced *medicine* with the Greek term for wisdom, but "Metis Man" was a title I'd never heard before. And I still didn't understand his function at THORN, Inc.

"Sometimes I think of him as the Energizer," Eric had attempted to explain, *"because he inspires me and my staff. Sometimes we joke that he's the Ventilator—because he allows my people to vent. He's like a father confessor and court jester rolled into one . . ."*

Given Garth's penchant for brightly colored clothing, the court jester part was easy to believe. I recalled the jacket he'd worn in the Source Club's formal dining room—shiny, turquoise silk with a Nehru collar.

On this morning, he stood before us in billowing, black slacks and a shocking red Indian kurta with gold embroidery around the dipping neckline. His long, salt-and-pepper pony-tail was held in place by a beaded leather tie that caught an eagle feather in its webbing.

Despite his odd attire (for a Caucasian man in a Montmartre eatery, anyway), Eric's consigliere radiated confident authority.

"Where's Eric?" I asked, glancing across the leather ban-quettes and brass rails of the empty dining room.

"Busy in meetings," Garth replied, "but he has a View-Mail message for you."

"View-Mail?"

"Check your THORN phone, Ms. Cosi."

I pulled the sleek, black smartphone from my bag.

"Phone on!" I said (a little too loudly).

"Mom," Joy whispered, "are you crazy—oh, wow . . . cool phone!"

Miss Phone lit up and with my command to play new mes-sages, the device displayed Eric's image in a prerecorded visual communiqué.

"Bonjour, Clare!" he began (that cryptic grin back on his face). "Did you get what you wished for?"

A chill went through me. On the night of our dinner, I had indeed wished for this chance—an opportunity to speak with my daughter face-to-face about her life and the direction it was taking.

Eric's View-Mail continued: "I can't imagine either of you would be able to concentrate on the little assignment I have for you both—"

Assignment? I thought. *For us both?*

"—So please, take the morning to catch up and enjoy each other's company. Joy is off today; I've arranged it with her employer—"

"Oh, my goodness, thank you!" Joy told the recording.

"I'll see you both tonight for dinner. My treat," Eric cooed. "Until then, *au revoir!*"

During the playback, I noticed Garth seemed distracted, glancing several times at his very own THORN, Inc., "Dick Tracy" phone watch on his skinny wrist. When my own phone's screen went black, I turned to him.

"Mr. Hendricks, will I get a chance to question Eric?"

"Question him?" Garth's skyscraper body stiffened. "About what, if I may ask?"

About his feelings on Nate Sumner being arrested, I thought, but said: "About . . . what we're doing here. About this secret 'assignment' for me and Joy?"

"Ah, I see . . ." His posture appeared to relax. "Patience, Ms. Cosi. Enjoy this bit of time with your daughter, stretch your legs after that long flight, and walk these beautiful, old streets, and I'll catch up with you both this afternoon."

"Where?" I asked. "What time?"

"When the time comes, I'll find you."

Then Garth Hendricks left the restaurant, folded himself into the SUV that had brought me, and spoke intensely into his wrist phone while the armed chauffeur drove him away.

"MOM, who was that odd man?"

"His name is Garth—"

"I know his name, he introduced himself, but what is

going on? He showed up an hour ago, spoke to my boss, and the next thing I know I'm having coffee with him and answering questions about living and working here. Then he tells me, 'Your mother is going to pay you a visit this morning.'"

"What else did he tell you?"

"That his boss is a client of yours. Who's his boss?"

"His name is Eric Thorner. He's a very successful young businessman who hired your father to source the most expensive coffee blend on the planet . . ." (I conveniently left out the stickier aspects of the story, including Quinn's theory that Eric killed his actress-model girlfriend then doubled down by blowing up the ex-cop who'd been hired by the girl's family to investigate.)

"Wow, that's so exciting, Mom, tell me more!"

"Later. Right now all I want to hear about is you . . ."

FORTY-SIX

〜〜〜〜〜〜〜〜〜〜〜〜〜〜〜〜〜〜〜〜〜〜

Joy and I did exactly as Garth suggested. We walked and walked and talked—and talked . . .

The crisp winter air felt refreshing in our lungs and on our cheeks as we traversed Montmartre's hilltop maze of quiet cobblestone streets. Every so often, Joy would sing *"Bonjour"* to a neighborhood acquaintance while we strolled past town houses rich with the patina of age and galleries tucked into tiny storefronts.

The legendary painters who once lived in this arrondisse-ment had different names than those of my storied New York neighborhood—Monet, Picasso, van Gogh, Dalí—but the sensibilities were the same, and (like my own Village, an ocean away) Montmartre remained a magnet for the young, the artsy, and the offbeat, be they iconoclasts or romantics.

I wasn't surprised my daughter was having the time of her life here. Joy was a true Allegro. Though she had my green eyes, chestnut hair, and heart-shaped face, her height and gift for languages, not to mention her audaciousness, ambition, sense of adventure, and headstrong stubborn streak were totally Matt—and his intrepid, French-born mother.

But the need to climb mountains wasn't always a blessing, and I wasn't surprised to hear that Joy's daily life was far from perfect.

"We're grossly overworked," she confessed.

"In Montmartre? In *winter*?"

"The news is getting out. We received a Michelin Rising Star award . . ."

This was a rare honor for this district of the city, which was known for cheap eats, not fine dining. I was so proud when my daughter told me she'd made contributions to the new menu. Clearly, she'd played an important part in the brigade that was getting this coveted recognition.

But even that shining news had a dark side . . .

The Rising Star honor was really a public challenge. The Michelin guides gave such restaurants a two-year window of evaluations to bring their menu and service up to star level.

Joy's executive chef was determined to earn that star—but the pressure was driving everyone to drink.

"And that's really what led to his second-in-command losing it," she told me. "The perfectionist pressure!"

Apparently all of the Paris food world had heard of the Bresse chicken-throwing incident, thanks to a television news report—and that crazy story brought even more customers to Les Deux Perroquets.

"We're killing ourselves every night in that kitchen. Our hours are longer, we're open seven days instead of six, but the owner refuses to bring in more help for the brigade . . ."

An hour later, Joy thanked me for listening to her vent—in English and French. (Like her father, she sometimes switched out of her native tongue without even noticing.)

Finally, she suggested we warm up at a café.

With my fingers, toes, and cheeks thoroughly chilled, I quickly agreed.

* * *

Joy chose a little café on the Place du Tertre, an open square of cobblestones where artists (good and not so good) set up chairs and easels all year long. In the rainy spring, they placed large umbrellas over their little spaces. In the dead of winter, they bundled up and drank steaming cups of coffee.

At a café table near the window, Joy ordered us our own coffees and a plate of her favorite French pastries: *canelés*, small cakes made with rich egg batter and laced with the fragrance of vanilla and rum.

Like French madeleines, our *petit canelés* were baked in special molds. A mixture of beeswax and butter painted on the molds was the secret to the cakes caramelizing in the oven. The result was a Proustian-like treat that would forever remind me of this sweet morning with my daughter—crisp as winter on the outside with a texture that made getting to the inside even more warm and tender.

Cozy in our battered, cane-backed chairs, I finally turned our conversation to a more tender topic (or at least a more delicate one): Joy's love life.

"So, what's going on with Franco?" the Mother Hen in me prodded.

Joy's mood shifted with the subject. The buoyant color that had reappeared in her cheeks began to fade, her shoulders slumped. "I don't know what to do, Mom. I think he must hate me."

"Hate you? Joy, Emmanuel Franco is devoted to you."

"Oh, come on . . . how would you even know that?"

"Because two weeks ago, on Hudson Street, I watched two gorgeous, young women throw themselves at him. He couldn't get rid of them fast enough. He wants you, Joy; he loves you."

Joy turned down her emerald gaze, as if searching for her lost steam in the coffee cup. At last, she confessed what I already knew—

"Manny and I had a terrible fight when he was here over the holidays . . ."

I poked her for details, and finally it all poured out. Her best friend, Yvette, had been pressuring Joy to date a well-heeled cousin of her wealthy fiancé . . .

"We went out a few times—but as a *group*. The last time, Yvette and her fiancé found a reason to leave us alone, forcing me into a date with his rich cousin. He was a total jerk, Mom, so arrogant, completely in love with himself, but Yvette wouldn't let it go. She kept saying I wasn't giving him a fair chance because of my long-distance relationship with Manny. Then when Manny came to see me over the holidays, she showed him a cell-phone photo of me and this Frenchman. She said I was 'going out with him,' which made it sound like I was dating him, which I wasn't! She told Manny that if he broke things off with me, it would 'free me' to hook up with this wealthy Frenchman who 'has the means to make life much easier for me.'"

"What did you say to that?"

"I didn't even know the conversation happened until after Manny left! I could have murdered Yvette when I found out! While he was here, he started acting tense, prodding me with questions. What did I want out of our relationship? Was I ever coming back to New York . . ."

"What did you say?"

"I said I couldn't give him a timetable! Not yet! Our Rising Star designation threw everything out of whack. We were getting flooded with new customers, and my boss revoked half my holiday vacation. It was a major mess—and from the semi-hostile way Manny was acting, I thought he wanted out. I told him he could break it off if he felt this long-distance thing was too hard. Then we parted bad . . . and I decided that maybe it was for the best. Maybe he changed his mind about me."

"Well, he hasn't. Look . . . I know the kind of guy Manny Franco is. He's sown his wild oats, and now he's fed up with cotton candy. He wants something lasting and sustaining, and if you truly reject him now, he'll move on, find a life with someone else. The question is—are you all right with letting him go? You've sown your own wild oats, as I recall, and had a lot of bad boyfriends."

"Manny is the best. I know that, Mom. He's patient and loving and so brave. He makes me laugh and our physical chemistry is . . ." The color came back to her cheeks. "Well, it's amazing. Anyway . . . I never met anyone like Manny Franco, and I just love being with him—and I do love him. But that's not the issue."

"That's the only issue."

"Look, he's there, and I'm here—and I *need* to be here at least another year. We have a chance to earn that star designation, and if we do—oh, Mom, I could write my own ticket back in New York, and I've worked so hard for this!"

"Then give Franco a chance to wait for you. I think he's willing. He just has to know you are."

"I am."

"Joy, you know that old saying 'All that glitters isn't gold'?"

"Mom, I don't need—"

"Just listen. Real gold doesn't start its journey in a display window at Tiffany. It's dug out of the dirty earth. Sometimes true gold doesn't glitter. It may need a little polishing, but don't let that bit of needed patience or effort trick you into discarding what could be the greatest treasure of your life."

Joy said nothing to my little lecture. She simply sipped her coffee, nibbled her *canelé*, and gazed into the square, as if thinking things over.

I gazed out, too, watching artists' pencils sketch lines— some with subjects, some without. Only time would tell what the finished drawings would be . . .

"Would you like to light candles at the Sacred Heart?" Joy finally asked.

"Very much," I said. Then we finished our cakes, drained our cups, and stretched our legs one last time.

* * *

We rode an electric tram they called a funicular up the steep hill to the basilica. This was the "mount" in Montmartre, which made the Sacré-Coeur the highest point in Île-de-France, and one of the prettiest views in all of Paris.

"I'd like to see you walking down an aisle like this one day," I whispered to my daughter inside the quiet, century-old church. We'd lit candles and said prayers together. Now we were walking out.

"I want that, too, Mom," Joy said. "For you."

"For me?"

"How are you and Mike doing? I noticed you haven't mentioned him."

"We're . . . working things out."

"Long-distance relationships aren't easy, are they?"

"No. I guess that's clear enough with what you and Franco are going through. But then, you know what my nonna used to say?"

"Absence makes the heart grow fonder?"

"It does for me. I miss Mike every night. But that's not exactly how the Italian proverb goes. For two lovers, it's more of a warning."

"What does it say?"

"Absence is the enemy of love."

Forty-seven

∽◌∽◌∽◌∽◌∽◌∽◌∽◌∽◌∽◌∽◌∽◌∽◌∽◌∽

As we moved outside the church into a cloud of chattering tourists, a strikingly tall figure approached us wearing an Eskimo parka and a placid smile.

"Mr. Hendricks!" Joy sounded amazed. "How did you find us?"

Garth Hendricks's little smile grew wider. "Oh, I had a feeling you'd come up here . . ."

And I had a feeling my THORN phone was broadcasting a GPS tracking signal. Uneasy with the continued weirdness of all things Thorn, I opened my mouth to ask for some answers when Joy beat me to the first question.

"So what is this secret 'assignment' for me and my mom? The one your boss mentioned. I'm dying of curiosity here."

Garth looked to me. "Check your phone's messages, Ms. Cosi."

"View-Mail?" I assumed.

After a swift greeting, Eric Thorner's prerecorded image began to tell us a story: "Every year, on the first of May, a group of very wealthy and very influential people in the world of food and drink get together for a . . . well a sort of potluck dinner—"

"Ohmigawd, Mom!" Joy cried, tugging my coat sleeve. "He's talking about the Billionaire Potluck!"

"You've heard of it?"

"It's legend in the foodie world! I didn't know it was *real*!"

"The dinner is one of the most prestigious and exclusive meals on the planet," prerecorded Eric continued. "No amount of personal wealth can buy you a ticket, yet I would *very much* like a ticket to this dinner. Garth will tell you the rest. I'll see you tonight, ladies. *Au revoir!*"

"Why does Eric want in to this Billionaire Potluck?" I asked Garth. "For culinary kicks?"

Metis Man stepped closer. "Eric has a business proposition he is pursuing that involves many of the regular attendees of the Billionaire Potluck. He would like to propose this business in a casual way at this exclusive dinner. It will give him a much better chance of achieving his goal than approaching each particular attendee alone—in less cordial circumstances."

"So how does Eric get into this dinner?" I asked.

"The same way everyone gets in. He must be invited."

"And how do you get invited?" Joy pressed.

"It involves some tasteful politicking," Garth admitted. "But one requirement for the invitation is unavoidable: the attendee must offer to bring an item to the potluck that these gentlemen and ladies would like to eat or drink."

"That's a tall order for people who continually eat and drink the world," I said.

"It is," Garth agreed. "It's a matter of exotic ingredients used in an intriguing way. And we're more than halfway there. The Billionaire Blend is a coffee no one will have tasted but Eric, Mr. Allegro, and you, Ms. Cosi. Now Eric would like you two—mother and daughter—to put your heads together, master roaster and apprentice chef, and come up with a few dishes that would highlight the one-of-a-kind

Billionaire Blend that Mr. Allegro is sourcing right now. Blue sky, ladies; money is no object."

"Wow . . ." Joy's wide-eyed gaze appeared to drift away to the view of Paris stretched out below us, but I suspected her mind was already retreating into culinary dreamland, working on the problem.

I looked to Garth. "You have no other guidance?"

"A note of interest, perhaps, and one of advice."

Joy appeared to tune back in.

"First, the note of interest," he said. "The attendees of this dinner believe the best dishes have stories attached. Like the story behind Joy's connection to the restaurant where she works: Les Deux Perroquets—the two parrots."

"You know about that?" I asked in surprise.

He nodded. "Such memories make for memorable meals."

"And the advice?"

"The same Eric gives to his employees, especially in the mobile gaming division. In his parlance: all things being equal, the simplest solution is the best."

"That's pretty vague," I said.

"In these fast-moving times with complex problems, we must be nimble to succeed. We must be open to the unexpected, hone our problem-solving abilities to adapt and overcome."

"Sorry, but that seems pretty vague, too."

Garth smiled with strained patience. "That's because the specifics are up to *you*. You have your assignment. You have your deadline. Eric will expect your answer at dinner this evening."

With a snap of his fingers, the armed chauffeur was back in my life. "René will drive you to a place where you can prepare for dinner."

"What do we wear?" Joy asked.

"Eric has taken care of that. Just remember Occam's Razor, ladies."

"Occam's what?"

"It's a heuristic, Miss Allegro. There is an optimum solution to releasing the Gordian knot. We can waste valuable time attempting to untangle ourselves and possibly fail or we can cut through it with a single slice. And from what I understand, Miss Allegro," he tossed over his shoulder before heading off, "you keep your knives quite sharp . . ."

I froze at that—and it had nothing to do with the weather. Hendricks had just made a reference to a time in Joy's past when one of her very sharp knives had gotten her into terrible trouble.

Thankfully, the barb didn't register with Joy. She appeared distracted again.

But I wasn't.

While Joy began dreaming up gourmet delights, I began worrying about that big, fat folder the Bomb Squad discovered on Eric's smartphone, the one labeled *Clare Cosi*. And I couldn't help wondering what else from my past Eric Thorner planned to make use of in the future.

Forty-eight

∞∞∞∞∞∞∞∞∞∞∞∞∞∞∞∞∞∞∞

"**Ladies**, you look luminous . . ."

We felt mighty luminous, too, after spending hours at a day spa being exfoliated then primped, painted, and petted. Designer shoes and dresses arrived (French, of course, and speedily fitted to perfection), then Eric picked us up in a rented Bugatti and we were off—mother-daughter Cinderellas for one night.

The antique French car turned heads as René drove us through the Paris streets. For a good hour, we toured, sipping champagne as we circled the Eiffel Tower, rolled under the Arc de Triomphe, and passed over the city's graceful bridges, so beautifully lit with glowing *bateaux* bobbing along the dark waters like diamonds drifting on a black velvet pool.

Finally, we pulled up to the Place des Vosges, a palazzo-like structure across from a lovely tree-lined park. Our destination was a restored seventeenth-century town house that once belonged to the Duke of Chaulnes.

Joy literally squealed when she saw it. Housed inside was one of the most respected fine dining establishments in all of

Paris. The eatery had served royalty, heads of state, and at least one U.S. president. (And a dinner for two here would set mere mortals back a cool thousand bucks.)

When I saw the *name* of the restaurant, however, alarm bells sounded. L'Ambroisie—the food of the gods—was the French translation of Ambrosia, the very term Matt and I had chosen for the rarified Brazilian coffee, which was now all but extinct.

This can't be a coincidence, I thought.

Once again, it appeared Eric was planning a cunning chess move. I just prayed the result would not be an ugly scene—not involving my daughter, because I wouldn't stand for it.

Inside the restaurant, the décor was as grand as the palace of Versailles with crystal chandeliers, antique mirrors, and Louis XIV gilded consoles, yet the space itself was cozy with no more than forty seats.

Near the start of our meal, Eric waved over the sommelier and sent a bottle of wine to a nearby table of three formally dressed gentlemen—two trim and middle-aged; a third older and more heavily set. After dessert was served, the head waiter stopped by to whisper in Eric's ear.

"Oui, merci," Eric replied, then turned to us. "Would you ladies excuse me a moment?"

Joy and I watched as he moved to that table with a trio of gentlemen.

The men spoke to Eric in French, and he appeared to be as fluent as Joy and my ex-husband. To my surprise, he turned and casually pointed to our table.

Joy and I smiled politely at the nodding gentlemen.

"Pardonnez-moi," Eric said and came back to retrieve Joy.

With curiosity, I watched as Eric introduced her to the VIPs.

The heavyset older man with apple cheeks turned out to be a sixth-generation vintner from a renowned French family, and the two trim, middle-aged men were equally distinguished. One was France's Deputy Minister of Tourism and the other editor in chief of the *Marquess Guides*—the highly respected publications that Eric's company purchased to roll content into *App-itite*, his new mobile phone app for foodies.

The quiet dining room had become even quieter, and I realized Joy's mother wasn't the only one interested in hearing this conversation.

After the introductions, the Deputy Minister of Tourism asked Joy about her relationship to Les Deux Perroquets. With bubbly enthusiasm, my daughter told the story that Madame had conveyed to both of us many times—how she was related to Bettine, a young woman who'd scandalized her wealthy family back in the nineteenth century by running off to Rome with an Italian painter.

"When the young painter tragically died of influenza, Bettine returned to Paris," Joy explained in French, "but her family refused to take her back, so she began dancing at the Folies Bergère, where the owner of a nearby brasserie saw her, fell in love, and married her. Bettine kept two pet parrots, a gift from her young Italian lover. Respecting that love, which in its own twisty way led the woman of his dreams to him, the Frenchman renamed his Montmartre brasserie Les Deux Perroquets."

During the story, the three men nodded and began to smile and exchange pleased glances. Of course, I thought. What Frenchman wouldn't appreciate such a tale of found love? And what Frenchman wouldn't appreciate a beautiful young woman telling them the tale—especially one with a French heritage, who had a clear connection to the legend.

Joy herself appeared to have a grand time conveying Madame's family history—even if it had been scandalous at the time. Eric seemed pleased, too, and I caught him a few times observing me watching my daughter shine.

I admit, my Mother Hen radar was up. *There must be a strategic reason Eric is doing this, but what?*

Eric spoke again. "Joy is *also* the daughter of the man who sourced Ambrosia. Her beautiful mother, Clare, roasted it to perfection."

Eric gestured toward me, and the men shocked me by lightly applauding. (Later, Eric informed me these men had sampled my coffee at this very restaurant last fall—at fifty-five dollars for each rare, imported cup—and raved.)

I smiled in thanks and lifted my wineglass.

Finally, talk turned to the special blend Matt was sourcing, and I realized Eric was subtly pitching these VIPs on our Billionaire Blend. They asked him a few more questions and he turned once more to Joy.

"How would you use your parents' rare blend in your cooking, do you think, Joy?"

There it is . . .

Eric was asking my daughter for our solution to his assignment, which meant one or more of these men had the power to unlock the door to that Billionaire Potluck.

Forty-nine

~~~~~~

Joy understood immediately what was happening, and played her part to perfection, beginning with her inspiration from New York's Chinatown.

"A chef there had an interesting way of smoking duck with tea—and I've always wanted to try it. But I would use a Bresse chicken breast and smoke it using my parents' special coffee blend, infusing the succulent, French bird with the essences of earthy coffees sourced from the most remote regions on the planet."

"What then?" the vintner asked, eyes bright. "How would you serve it?"

"To start, shaved thin as a carpaccio with a dollop of crème fraîche, a drizzle of truffle oil, and a garnish of coffee caviar. I'd arrange the slices as petals, a blossoming flower of flavor on the plate."

The Deputy Minister of Tourism raised an eyebrow. "Did you say coffee caviar?"

"*Oui, monsieur . . .*" Joy briefly described a technique of molecular gastronomy, which allowed a chef to create tiny spheres of flavor from almost any liquid.

They asked her for more ideas, and she gave them—coffee and cream *lunette*, little, domed pasta circles with a filling of the same coffee-smoked Bresse breast shredded and tossed in French butter and black truffles. The delicate pillows would then be placed on a mascarpone-based cream sauce and finished with shavings of white truffles . . .

"Interesting use of Bresse chicken," the vintner said. "But you must promise not to follow your colleague's example and throw the poor birds back at the farmer!"

Everyone laughed, and Eric was now beaming.

My daughter and I had done what Garth suggested— created dishes around stories. I agreed with the Metis Man on that one: cuisine was lifted by the conversation around it, which made for memorable meals.

"What about dessert?" the editor of the *Marquess Guides* prompted. "What sweet would you make us, *mademoiselle*?"

"Coffee gelato, I think, made fresh from my parents' special blend. I'd use it as the center of a tiny bombe, layer that with crushed hazelnut praline and another layer of mascarpone gelato laced with Ugandan gold vanilla beans—my father told me about those," she proudly added.

"I'd create a thin espresso-infused sponge cake on the bottom layer and once the tiny layered ball was frozen, I'd finish the outside with a magic mocha shell using Chef Thomas Keller's famous method—Valrhona chocolate, cold-pressed coconut oil, and my parents' special coffee blend. I'd also want to emboss the chocolate with a design." She smiled politely at Eric. "For Mr. Thorner here, I might use a rose with thorns circling the bombe and paint it in using edible gold leaf."

A hush fell over the table as the group considered Joy's double reference to a bombe.

Touché, I thought. *If Garth can bring up Joy's explosive past, she can bring up Eric's . . .*

Luckily, Eric saw the humor. (We'd set him up for the

perfect punch line.) "It sounds absolutely delightful, Ms. Allegro," he declared. "As long as *your* bombe does not go off."

The table of men burst out laughing, and Joy glanced back at me.

Brava, I mouthed and lifted my glass again.

Finally, all three men glanced at each other. The vintner locked eyes with Eric. "I would very much like to taste this new coffee."

"I agree," said the Deputy Minister of Tourism. "And those dishes sound delightful, *mademoiselle*."

"I would like to taste them also," the vintner declared.

"So would I."

Joy turned to see who had spoken last. It was L'Ambroisie's own chef. Joy greeted him with a touch of awe, and he invited her to see his kitchen. With a silent glance of elation back at me, she followed him out of the dining room.

When Eric returned to our table, I leaned close.

"Merci," I whispered.

"No, Clare, thank you," he softly replied. "You and your daughter sealed the deal. On May first, I'll be bringing your coffee to my very first Billionaire's Potluck."

It was another elaborate setup, of course, another play by a young master player. I was grateful for the time spent with my daughter. Given the events of the past two weeks, however, I was now anxious to question Eric privately.

I tried to enjoy our coffee and dessert, but it wasn't easy.

I couldn't stop thinking of Madame and her worry for her old friend; of Nate, the earnest professor, sitting in jail; and of my own Mike Quinn with his dire warning.

More than ever, I needed to know . . .

Is Eric Thorner, the master strategist, also a mastermind of murder?

Fifty

~~~~~~~~~~~~~~~~~~~~~~~~~~~~~~~~~~~~~~

THE night had been a grand success and Eric was jubilant. After dropping Joy off at her apartment, Eric told his driver to take us "home," which turned out to be a charming town house on the Left Bank.

Eric's butler in Paris, an older man named Hervé, showed me to my room and quickly disappeared. My small suitcase was on the floor, my things unpacked.

I was about to change when I heard a light knocking at the door.

"Care for a nightcap?"

It was Eric, still in his formalwear. He shrugged, smiling like a schoolboy. "I'm still so juiced. I don't think I can sleep."

"It was exciting, wasn't it?"

"It was. Come on, let's talk in my room—"

"I would like to speak with you, Eric, but not in your bedroom—"

"Clare, it's a suite with a sitting area. Come . . ."

Now was my chance to question this man, really question him. With the amount of alcohol he'd consumed, I was fairly sure he wouldn't be able to lie without giving himself away, so I followed Eric down the hall.

True to his word, he fixed me a drink in a comfortable sitting area. If there was a bed, it was beyond one of the three closed doors off this space, which put me at ease.

A fire crackled in the hearth and Eric handed me a snifter of an obscenely delicious Armagnac. I had no doubt the vintage was rare and the price equally obscene.

"To the Billionaire Potluck," I said, tapping my glass to his.

"Where I'll debut the most expensive app ever marketed." Grinning, Eric set his snifter aside and leaned close. "I'll bet you never heard of the *I Am Rich* app?"

"You'd win that bet."

"It's real, Clare, or it was. The app cost a thousand bucks to download, but had no function at all. Eight people bought it. Some of them complained and it was taken off the market. The whole thing was crazy, but it got me thinking."

"About scamming people?"

"About an exclusive app for the superrich. A portal to purchase certain high end products that can't be put on the mass market because of their limited availability. My blue roses. THORN smartphones. The Billionaire Blend—"

"Advertising!" I cried. "That's why you wanted into the potluck."

He nodded. "The billionaire app is not something that can be sold in a magazine ad. But the potluck will involve importers, purveyors of specialty foods, vintners, people who will want to be included in the app. Billionaires who own hotels, casinos, and restaurants will hear about the app via that potluck dinner and they'll want it for themselves, for their managers, their chefs, and sommeliers. Once word gets out, the app becomes a Veblen good—the more expensive and exclusive it is, the more the wealthy and influential will covet it."

And the more Eric will profit. From the sale of the app, and from a percentage of cash he'll surely garner from each transaction.

"You made your fortune in mobile gaming. Are you going to give that up?"

"Game apps will have their day, become passé, and pass away," Eric replied "I want to grow something more permanent, create something my father would have understood and been proud of."

"You never speak about your parents."

"My dad was a sweet man. A big Santa Claus to his employees."

"He owned a chain of regional restaurants, right?"

"Big Billy's All-Nite Brunch. Twenty-four locations in the Midwest. The menu was comfort food—mac and cheese, meatloaf, roast chicken, spaghetti, twenty-four-hour breakfast." Eric drained his snifter. "Dad just wanted to make people happy."

I knew that Eric sold his father's regional restaurant chain for seed money to launch THORN, Inc. Now I wondered if that end to his family's legacy haunted him. Or was it something else? Guilt, perhaps . . .

"Before he was arrested, Nate Sumner told me the story of Eva's bullying, and her death—"

"Did Nate tell you how I changed the game after that poor girl's suicide? How I gave a million dollars to a nonprofit anti-bullying group?"

"He didn't."

"Of course not." Eric rose and began to pace. "I was devastated, Clare. It was like an ugly nightmare flashback . . ."

"Flashback?"

"With all my physical problems, I was bullied, too."

"You?"

"I suffered from Scheuermann's kyphosis. The older I got, the more twisted my spine became. The other kids called me Humpty-Dumpty because they were too ignorant to call me Quasimodo. The way my peers saw it, I was always falling off the wall and being put back together in the operating room. Even my sister joined the chorus."

"And your parents?"

"Dad did all he could. Spent a fortune on doctors—"

"And your mother?"

"When mother was sober, she looked at me like I was a freak. When she was drunk, she didn't see me at all. I hated it, Clare."

"Did you hate Nate Sumner for reminding you?"

Eric snorted. "Nate? No way. That poor old man was framed."

I blinked, astonished by his answer. "I agree. But who framed him?"

Eric poured another drink. "From that doubtful look on your face, you probably suspect me."

"You have to admit, it's ingenious. Framing Nate slows down Solar Flare, an organization that cost you money last year because of their protest against those *Pigeon Droppings* T-shirts. It also gets rid of Charley, who may have found out things you didn't want her to know . . ."

"Believe me, Clare, I had nothing to do with any of that. And I can prove to you that I didn't frame Nate in one sentence."

"Go for it."

"I'm paying my company's law firm to defend him."

FIFTY-ONE

~~~~~~

ERIC informed me that a few hours ago, a judge in New York City denied Nate Sumner bail. The old professor was stuck in Rikers, but Eric's lawyers were already crafting an appeal.

"If Nate is innocent, who's guilty in your eyes?" I asked.

"You forget, Clare. My car was supposed to be parked at the server farm when the bomb went off, not in front of your coffeehouse. My servers were the target. Grayson Braddock wanted to shut them down. I don't think he intended to kill Charley, but that's how it turned out."

"You don't think Braddock set the bomb himself, do you?"

"He was an Outback punk once upon a time, so I wouldn't put it past him. But Braddock is smarter now, so he no doubt hired someone."

"Someone who knew how easy it would be to frame Nate? Someone who had access to your schedule and could get into your car without suspicion?"

Eric frowned. "Yes. Which means Occam's Razor would be the wrong approach to take in this case."

"Run that by me again."

"Occam's Razor dictates that when you hear hoofbeats behind you, you should think horses, not zebras. But what if you're on the African veldt?"

"I get it. You're saying the police went for the obvious suspect when they grabbed Nate, because they thought they had physical evidence and a motive—"

"But I believe we're in Africa, Clare. The hoofbeats we hear are not horses, they're zebras. And the guilty party has a first name that's muddled those black-and-white stripes— *Gray* Braddock. I'm not going to let him get away with murder."

"Gray didn't do it without help. It looks like an inside job."

Eric shook his head. "The officers of my company are the only people with that kind of access. They've been with me from our start-up days. They're like family and I trust them."

"Garth Hendricks wasn't around when you were a start-up. How much do you trust the Metis Man?"

"Garth is my mentor, Clare. He became my mentor before we ever met."

"I don't understand."

"My life changed when I read his book. I used his principles to grow my company. I wouldn't be here now if it wasn't for Garth's teachings."

"That must be some book. What's the title?"

"*Puncturing the Donut: Thinking Outside the Corporate Pastry Box.*"

I laughed. "Garth Hendricks used to be a baker?"

"No, and that's not funny. The title is a business metaphor. Garth compares corporate cultures by postulating how different organizations might approach the problem of putting holes in donuts."

"You're kidding."

"I'm not. Garth showed how one company might create the hole before baking. Another company might cut a hole after frying, while a third company might use donut holes to make another product. The problem comes when a corporation builds their philosophy around manufacturing the hole—which, if you think about it, is the creation of nothing."

"But a very important nothing," I interjected. "You can't have a donut without the hole."

"Now you're thinking like Garth Hendricks."

I frowned. "I thought I was making a joke."

"Garth's philosophy is no joke," Eric shot back. "I used his basic tenets to make *Pigeon Droppings* a hit."

"When Braddock cornered me at the Source Club, he said you would never share that secret with me."

"'Why not? I have nothing to hide."

"Then tell me, Eric."

"In his book, Garth said that performance is nothing without performance art, and he was right. I launched THORN, Inc., with my college friends, and for a solid year we did the best work we'd ever done to make the best mobile game ever. We went on sale the same day as eleven hundred other apps, just one of the crowd. Sales were modest but steady, but it couldn't sustain our company for long. I soon realized the performance was over. Now it was time for *performance art*."

Eric poured his third Armagnac and rubbed his stiff neck.

"Back in those days, I ate a lot of meals at Dimmy's, an all-night diner in Bel Air. So did Judd Rogan, the director who made all those raunchy teen comedies ten years ago . . ."

I shrugged and shook my head.

"Anyway, I chatted up the waitress, found out Rogan called ahead to reserve the corner booth. Svetlana agreed to call me whenever that happened, and the stage was set."

"Stage?"

"When Judd Rogan showed up that night, the tables around his were filled with people playing *Pigeon Droppings* on their phones."

"Who were these people?"

"My staff. Me. Our friends. Even family. Once we hired actors. We put on that show three times before Rogan noticed. In the middle of the fourth act, he cornered Minnow, my chief programmer, and asked her what she was playing."

Eric paused. "Two days later, Rogan's agent called to ask if the director could put my app in his next movie. *Fake ID* was a huge hit for Judd Rogan, and because of the exposure, *Pigeon Droppings* became the fastest-selling app in mobile gaming history. All it took was a little street theater . . ."

"Street theater? More like a sting, It was trickery. You made Judd Rogan think he was buying into the hottest game app ever—"

"And he did, ultimately. No harm, no foul, as Garth would say."

Garth again. It was beginning to sound like the Metis Man was a bad influence.

"How long ago did you hire the Metis Man?"

"I know what you're thinking, Clare, but I trust Garth. Look elsewhere."

Eric's tone made me think that he had someone else in mind, but before I could press him, he groaned.

"What's the matter?"

"It's been a long day and my pain meds are winding down."

"I'm not surprised. You've been pacing since you started telling me your story."

"My shoulder is killing me and I sent my butler to bed. Could you help me off with this damn jacket?"

He turned and led me through a door, into a bedroom nearly as large as the sitting area. Eric lifted his arms while I unbuttoned the jacket and slipped it off, to reveal a crisp white linen shirt.

As I hung the jacket, I spied a blue velvet gift box on Eric's nightstand.

"Oops. You weren't supposed to see that until tomorrow. Might as well open it now."

"You have to stop giving me gifts—"

"It's not a gift. It's test marketing. I expect a report."

Inside I found a pair of black gloves. The Italian leather was supple, and they were my size. "They're lovely, and I thank you. But who test markets a pair of gloves?"

"You're the first. That's the only pair in existence right now."

"It's more than a pair of gloves, then?"

"It's a phone, Clare. Put on the left glove, place your thumb on your ear and speak into the little finger. Miss Phone will answer. It's already programmed and ready to use."

While he spoke, Eric moved stiffly to the dresser and popped a few pills, chasing them with the last of his Armagnac.

"Could you please help me with this shirt? I can't bend my arm enough to work the buttons."

That was obvious, so I took over.

Eric moved slowly as I pulled his arms free. Bare chested, I could see the bandages were gone, but an ugly scar remained.

I was about to back away when Eric suddenly shifted into high gear. Before I could stop him, he crushed me in his arms and kissed me.

"No, no, no . . . Eric, this can't happen . . ." I pushed until he released me, stepped back, and wiped my smeared lipstick with the back of my hand.

"You and I . . . we're *meant* to be together."

"Eric," I said evenly. "You know I love another man—"

"But I love you, Clare!"

"No, you don't—"

"I do, and it makes perfect sense. Garth says two things cause people to fall in love—intensity or propinquity. I fell for you when you looked into my eyes after that bomb went off and promised to take care of me. That was *intensity*—"

"More like infatuation, a passing fancy. You've had too much to drink tonight, Eric, that's all."

He seemed unsteady now that the painkillers were catching up to the Armagnac. Instead of arguing with me this time, he just shrugged, his energy drained.

I swung into Mother Hen mode, pulling down the blankets

and rolling him onto the bed, tugging off his shoes and socks. Eric didn't fight me, and he didn't get fresh—though I did draw the line at his request to help him off with his pants!

When he was snugly tucked, I grabbed the gloves and moved to the door. "Get some rest, I'll see you in the morning."

"For me it was intensity, Clare. For you it will be propinquity . . ."

I shook my head.

"We just need to spend more time together, you'll see!" he called before I left his room, went to mine, and locked the door behind me.

Fifty-two

〰〰〰〰〰〰〰〰〰〰〰〰〰〰〰〰

BACK in my room, I tried to call Mike Quinn—using my THORN phone, not the gloves, which I shoved into my coat pocket. Unfortunately Miss Phone gave me major attitude.

"Call cannot be completed as dialed," the digital vixen declared. "Please try again later . . ."

Funny how Matt Allegro had no trouble getting through five minutes later. The connection was lousy, but there was a good reason. Matt was calling on a satellite phone from Africa.

"I talked to Eric this afternoon," he said. "He's planning to fly you to Saint-Tropez. No doubt his final destination is a topless beach. Well, forget it, Clare. At this time of year it's cold and rainy. The weather's much warmer here in Uganda."

"Uganda!"

"You sold me on helping coffee farmers. Time to deliver. Get Eric down here."

"How?!"

"Easy. He'll go wherever you go, and I plan to take him places baby billionaires never go. This will not be 'glamping.' I'll e-mail you a list of things you should bring, and I'll tell you right now don't skimp on the aspirin, Pepto-Bismol, insect repellent—with DEET—and mosquito netting. Call me when you touch down in Tororo."

Matt had no trouble finding us at Tororo Airport—there was only one runway, and it was unpaved.

The town was unimpressive, too, resembling a suburban strip mall surrounded by dirt roads instead of concrete. Though areas of the Tororo District boasted panoramic views of Uganda's Mount Elgon, it took us four grueling hours to drive to the coffee growing region in the foothills.

During the long, bumpy ride, Matt told Eric that 90 percent of Uganda's coffee output was Robusta, easy to cultivate, but not prized due to its high acidity and bitterness.

"The small amount of Arabica produced is not held in high regard, either," Matt explained. "Farming standards are poor, and the beans aren't always picked at the optimum time, so the end product contains rotten cherries and under-developed beans. But what's really hurting quality and production is dry processing."

Matt told Eric that sun drying beans was labor intensive, because the beans have to be raked constantly, or they will develop molds that give the finished cup a metallic taste. Water processing was more efficient, but more expensive, too, requiring an investment the impoverished farmers didn't have.

The obvious question occurred to Eric. "If Ugandan coffees are unspectacular, why are we here?"

"Because on one small family farm in the foothills, something remarkable happened."

We finally arrived at a yellow wooden house clinging to the side of a hill, where Matt introduced us to the family matriarch. A cheerful woman with deep wrinkles, she served us roasted ground nuts—good old-fashioned peanuts, an important source of protein in this part of the world—along with boil-brewed cups of pan-roasted coffee.

Eric smacked his lips. "This coffee tastes like vanilla! Is it flavored?"

"Bite your tongue," my ex replied.

Matt explained that vanilla beans were Uganda's second biggest cash crop, and there were vanilla fields in the hills around us. Matt wasn't sure if it was cross-pollination or absorption of chemical properties through the roots, but the result of their proximity was a coffee with pronounced and pleasing vanilla notes.

After a lunch of *ebinyebwa* (a savory peanut and chicken stew that's native to the region), we toured the coffee fields and viewed the crude wooden drying platform. An ancient woman supervised a dozen children of various ages, who used long wooden poles to rake the coffee cherries drying in the sun.

"Where are all the men?" Eric asked.

"Most have jobs in the city," Matt replied. "Needless to say, they can't commute from Tororo so they're only home a few days each month. Their absence doesn't impact coffee production. In Uganda women and children do the farming."

"But these kids should be in school."

"There's a school down in the valley. But like I said, dry processing is labor intensive so they're needed here."

Eric nodded. "I propose we buy this season's harvest—the entire lot—at a fair market price. On top of that, I'll throw in a washing station. That way these kids can get an education."

"I'll make the deal," said Matt, hiding his delight.

I caught Matt's eye and smiled.

Good job, Allegro . . .

I'D been seat hopping during the entire flight to Thailand, trying to avoid sitting beside Eric, who couldn't keep his hands off me, much to Matt's amusement.

Eric continued the chase for hours, until he finally got bored and talked shop again. "What do you know about that coffee they mentioned in the movie *Bucket List*? Cat poop coffee, they called it."

"You're referring to Kopi Luwak," Matt said, frowning. "And it's an Asian palm civet, not a cat."

"You don't sound impressed."

"I don't want to pooh-pooh the whole Kopi Luwak phenomena, but there's a lot of fraud out there," Matt said. "Twenty years ago it was bogus Jamaican Blue Mountain and Kona. Today it's phony Kopi Luwak."

Matt explained that traditional methods were simple. Civets ate the largest, choicest coffee cherries for their juicy pulp. The bean went through the animal's digestive tract, where it fermented. Enzymes seeped into the beans, making the coffee milder, smoother, less acidic. The civets' excrement was then collected, the beans retrieved and roasted.

Bad changes came after Kopi Luwak was "discovered" in the 1980s, when old methods were replaced by intensive farming. Today, civets are fed a diet of coffee cherries and not much else, so they're far less discriminating and eat all the fruit, not just the choice ones. The natural selection process that occurred in the wild is bypassed, and so is quality.

"On top of that, fifty times more Kopi Luwak is sold than is actually *produced*, so most of the stuff available commercially is counterfeit," Matt concluded. "But if you're still interested in a not-so-crappy crap coffee, I say we go bigger. Much, much bigger."

FIFTY-THREE

~~~~~~~~~~~~~~~~~~~~~~~~

TWELVE hours later we arrived at an elephant refuge in the lush green hills of Northern Thailand. The sun blazed hot, but a jasmine-laced breeze off a nearby creek cooled the air.

Around a wicker table under a tall shade tree, we cupped Black Ivory while two dozen Thai elephants munched coffee cherries on the other side of a flimsy wooden fence.

"This stuff is preternatural," Eric gushed. "The smoothest coffee I ever drank. It's earthy, yet floral. And there are flavor notes I've never tasted . . ."

Matt informed us that the cup we'd just consumed would cost fifty U.S. dollars, and the roasted beans were priced at over five hundred dollars a pound.

"At the moment, Black Ivory's only available in high-priced resorts in Thailand, the Maldives, and in Abu Dhabi."

Cultivated on the same principles as Kopi Luwak, Black Ivory was considered to be superior because the beans passed through the elephant's digestive system at a slower rate, fermenting up to seventy hours. The enzymes broke down the coffee protein, making the finished cup sweeter and less acidic. Other ingredients in the elephant's stomach added interesting and unique flavor notes.

Black Ivory was prohibitively expensive because it took seventy-two pounds of raw coffee cherries to recover just *two* pounds of intact, digested beans. But we all agreed the final result was worth it.

"The best part of all is that these elephants are all rescue animals," Matt said. "Some of the profit from the sale of Black Ivory is used to protect at-risk elephants in captivity and in the wild. They'd love to expand this herd, save more at-risk elephants, and double the production capacity, but right now funds are scarce."

"Do they take donations?" Eric asked. "I'd sure love to help . . ."

OUR next trip took us from the elephant refuge to Thailand's Golden Triangle, where poppies were grown to make opium. In that area notorious for narco-trafficking and gang wars, a new kind of coffee trade—and a new kind of coffee *trader*—were flourishing.

Matt brought us to a tribe in the mountains who had taken complete control of their coffee business. They cultivated the fields, reaped the harvest, accepted orders by satellite phone or over the Internet. They roasted the coffee in a small facility on top of the mountain where it was picked, sealed the finished beans in valve-bags, and shipped them all over Asia.

It was the exact opposite of conditions in Uganda, where every step in the coffee production process was fraught with difficulties, and the middleman took most of the profit.

"The difference is infrastructure," Matt said. "Uganda's is primitive, here it's practically state-of-the-art. As communication grids improve across the world's coffee belt, this operation in Thailand could become the model for twenty-first-century coffee production."

* * *

AFTER stops in Jakarta and Hawaii, we moved to Central America, where we sampled cups from the *Cinturón de Oro*, the "Golden Belt" of El Salvador's coffee growing industry. There we discovered a remarkable bean growing on the slopes of the Ilamatepec volcano.

The Caribbean was next, with short stays in Haiti, and bordering Jamaica. Our final stop in this region was Costa Gravas.

Once racked by political strife that halted the nation's coffee production, the island country was now at peace, but still backward, even by the region's low standards.

Primitive or not, Costa Gravas was also one of the most beautiful islands in the blue-watered Caribbean. Eric was immediately smitten by this "paradise."

After a long hike, we stood on a promontory overlooking the ocean. Eric managed to slip his arm around my shoulders while I concentrated on the view.

"A man could set up an amazing life here, away from it all . . . if he had someone to share it with . . ."

Matt couldn't hide his "I told you so" grin.

I shrugged off Eric's arm and faced him. "This is hardly paradise. There's no Internet, and I doubt the average citizen ever saw a personal computer or a smartphone."

"It wouldn't take much to fix that," Matt added. "Thanks to satellite communications, Costa Gravas has cell phone access. Adding an Internet component shouldn't be too hard, and it would also be a necessary step before resuming the coffee trade."

I discovered how well the phones worked when Tucker interrupted me with a call.

"Hate to ruin your vacation, but preparations for this Appland party are getting brutal. You *do* remember we're scheduled to cater it?"

"Of course, Tuck. How can I help?"

"First of all, do you want guests to dip the Flourless Peanut Butter Cookies in your homemade Chocolate Reese's Nutella, or your Almond Joy Nutella?"

"Both."

Tuck sighed. "And what in the whole wide world are Nuts on Horseback?"

"It's my own invention. You've heard of Angels on Horseback, right? It's just oysters wrapped in bacon. Devils on Horseback replaces the oysters with dried fruit. Well, for Nuts on Horseback we're going to make bite-sized pieces of butternut squash, wrap them in bacon, and roast them with maple syrup."

"Oh, yum! Very tasty! Last question now . . . What in the world is Paleo Pizza?"

"No grains. It has a crust made of cauliflower."

"I don't live on that planet, CC. You better get back here and help us with this stuff."

I silently concurred. I wanted to attend that party because it was my best chance to get to know—and possibly interrogate—some of the employees in Eric's mobile gaming division.

"Tour's over," I announced when I hung up. "I have to get back to NYC."

Matt protested. "But what about South America?"

"We'll do it later," Eric replied. "I have business in Silicon Valley this week."

Eric shook Matt's hand. "It was a great coffee tour, Allegro, but digital duty calls."

Fifty-Four

My baristas were delighted that I was back. Nancy, Tuck, and Esther crowded around me as I handed out little souvenirs I bought for everyone. (While I was sure they were glad to see me, I had a sneaking suspicion they were so flummoxed by some of my catering instructions that they were simply relieved to have me take over.)

After fielding a few dozen questions, I headed upstairs to my second-floor office. When I opened the door, I was bowled over by a sickly sweet smell rising from a vase of red and white roses—dead roses.

I looked for a note while I called Tuck downstairs for answers.

"The flowers came while you were in Africa," Tuck explained. "Esther did what she could. She took good care of your kitties, and changed the water in the flower vase daily. But you were gone so long there was no hope of preserving them."

I finally located the note.

"The flowers are from Mike, but he only wrote one line:

'Roses white and red are best.' Why does that sound familiar?"

"It's from a Rudyard Kipling poem," Tuck replied. "I can look it up if you want."

"Thanks but I'll take it from here." I hung up and used my THORN phone to speed-dial Quinn in DC.

"This call cannot be completed as dialed . . ."

I screamed and tossed the smartphone on my desk. Using the landline, I tried again. *This time* I got right through, but reached an assistant who told me Mike Quinn was on a classified retreat with Homeland Security.

"Mr. Quinn's boss has an assistant who might be able to get a call through. Let me talk to Ms. Lacey's secretary—"

Ms. Lacey?! "Excuse me, did you misspeak? I thought you said *Ms.* Lacey?"

"Yes. Miss Katerina Lacey is Mr. Quinn's supervisor."

A woman? I sank into my chair. *Mike never once mentioned that Lacey—the boss who was always trying to lure him back to DC—was a woman!*

My shock was interrupted by a familiar voice. "Clare? Is that really you?"

"Yes, it's me! Oh, Mike, it's good to hear your voice. Why haven't you replied to my messages?"

"What messages?"

"I've been calling and calling, sending e-mails and texts—"

"I never got them. When I tried to reach you, I always got a message that said you were out of range . . ."

Oh, God. My THORN phone must have blocked all messages to and from Mike. That was the only explanation possible. Eric made sure I could never reach Mike for the entire trip, while he pulled his "propinquity" stunt.

Oh, I wanted to scream!

"I'm so, so sorry, Mike. There was a problem with my phone. If I can't get it fixed, I'm tossing it into the Hudson River and buying another."

"I've been missing you."

"Me too. I wish we were together, right now."

"Did you get my roses?"

I stared at the faded blossoms. "Yes, I did."

"And . . ."

"And—" I didn't want to do this over the phone, but I couldn't help myself. "Why didn't you ever tell me your boss was a woman?!"

A long pause followed. "It's irrelevant, Clare."

"No it is not! You should have told me."

"I didn't because I knew this was how you'd react—"

"But—"

"Calm down, all right. She's a battle-ax."

"I'm sure she's not."

He fell silent, and I took a deep breath, listening to my inner voice. *You and Mike are finally talking again. Don't blow this now . . .*

"Look, I'm sorry I sound suspicious. I know I have no right."

"You can say that again."

I closed my eyes, considering his point of view. "Let's not do this over the phone. Can you come to New York this weekend?"

"I'm sorry, Clare, but I can't. First you had to go away. Now I have to. After this conference, I'm flying to London for meetings with MI-6. Secured meetings—that means no computers, tablets, or smartphones. I'll be out of touch for several days."

"Is the 'battle-ax' going with you?"

"Yes."

"Why don't you hang her up in the Tower of London with the other medieval torture devices?"

Mike actually laughed, and I realized how much I missed that sound.

"You're obviously excited, Clare. I do love it when you're excited, but not about silly things like this."

"It's not silly—" I stopped myself, and smiled for the first time in a long while. "Listen, if you like me excited, *come home.* You'll see me more excited than you can handle."

"Can you hear me smiling?"

"I love you, Mike."

"I love you, sweetheart, and I promise I'll come back soon. Tell you what—I'll arrange a special dinner date. It'll be a surprise. Something to celebrate our reunion."

"I can hardly wait . . ."

When we finally ended the call, I felt much better, despite the fact that Mike had kept me in the dark about his boss. I understood his reasons—I was *trying* to, anyway.

The phone buzzed again. This time it was Nancy.

"Hey, boss! I have a question about this weird Paleo Pizza."

"I'll be right down."

Duty was calling for me, as well as Mike. It was time I focused on the party at Eric Thorner's mobile gaming division—aptly named *Appland*.

Fifty-five

⟨∾⟨∾⟨∾⟨∾⟨∾⟨∾⟨∾⟨∾⟨∾⟨∾⟨∾⟨∾⟨∾⟨∾

The East Coast headquarters of THORN, Inc., was officially open for business.

While Eric's staff oriented themselves to the new digs, my people prepared treats in the company kitchen for the opening-day celebration. Invited guests would arrive around noon, when my baristas were scheduled to roll out the snacks.

I was responsible for catering, and the recipes were my own. But there was more to do than serve up goodies. Tuck would be hosting an espresso-making demo, while Esther would give lessons on how to create latte art.

I was on the hook for a dessert performance, and was all set to fry up fresh, hot batches of my nonna's Italian donuts (as a little tribute to Eric and his love of the Metis Man's "out of the pastry box" philosophy). Despite my schedule, I refused to allow work to interfere with my *unofficial* duties.

I intended to finish what the late Charley Polaski had started. I would continue her investigation into Bianca Hyde's death and uncover the identity of Eric's car bomber—hopefully *without* ending up in the morgue.

Grayson Braddock had the strongest motive for setting the car bomb and framing Nate—but billionaires like Braddock were big-picture men. They wouldn't purchase their own groceries or drive their own cars, let alone plant an explosive device to blow a competitor sky-high.

Braddock would have used an accomplice, most likely a mole inside THORN, Inc., to provide inside information about Eric's whereabouts, to access restricted areas like the server farm, and to plant the bomb.

So how does a coffeehouse manager uncover a corporate spy turned assassin? Okay, that's one I haven't figured out yet.

By the time I arrived at Eric's shiny new office building, housed in what was once an old toy factory, the sidewalk was crowded by gawkers watching animated light sculptures of flying dragons projected onto the company's twelve-story glass façade.

With the exception of THORN's high-tech display, this quiet, tree-lined Manhattan neighborhood of modest, low-rise structures (once tenement buildings and small factories) looked nothing like what it had become—part of the second largest technological hub in the world, a little Silicon Alley to California's legendary Silicon Valley.

Google, Mashable, and Bluewolf, Inc., all had offices here in Chelsea, and Tumblr was just down the block. These companies were attracted by the district's charm, and the availability of old buildings with high ceilings and plenty of natural light.

Ironically, during the twentieth century, this little area had been the center of America's toy industry—and in my view, nothing had changed much in the twenty-first. Apps, e-games, digital devices, and social media sites were the toys of our time.

I pushed through the gawking crowd, then THORN, Inc.'s glass doors. After clearing security, I noticed Esther in front of the company logo.

"Hi, boss. Isn't this a cool place?"

"How's it going so far?"

She shrugged. "Everything's copacetic inside the castle—"

"Castle?"

"You'll see. Oh, and there's a woman with Ashleigh Banfield glasses and a T-shirt looking for you."

I scanned the people around us. "*All* of these women are wearing horn-rims and tees. How will I recognize her?"

"This one is Eric's sister."

I wondered if there was another Thorner sister, because Esther's description didn't come close to matching the evil glamour queen I'd argued with at the Source Club. Either way, it didn't matter. Since Eden was near the top of my to-be-interviewed list, I headed upstairs.

Stepping off the escalator, my jaw dropped. The entire second-floor gallery was taken up by a full-sized replica of a medieval castle topped by a sawtooth battlement.

I recognized Eric's sister as she approached me through the arched portcullis.

Esther's description had been on target. Eden Thorner had swapped her contacts and slinky dress for chunky glasses, snug denims, and a form-fitting white tee emblazoned with the word *Milady*. She offered me her hand, and a (surprisingly) welcoming smile.

"It's nice to have a second chance to meet you, Ms. Cosi. Please allow me to apologize for our first encounter—"

"No need to apologize."

"Yes, there *is*, Ms. Cosi. You have to understand, I was frantic with worry that night. First someone tried to murder my kid brother, and then he decides to check himself out of the hospital *against* his doctors' orders." She shook her head. "When I saw him dining at the Source Club, I thought he'd risked his health, possibly his life, simply to indulge another one of his reckless infatuations."

"You thought I was some kind of gold digger?"

"Yes, frankly. I'd never seen you before, and I had no idea Eric had important business with you. I feel terrible. I behaved like a monster, Clare, because I thought *you* were a monster."

"Let's forget the whole incident and start over, okay?" I smiled (guardedly). I still wasn't sure if this woman was friend or foe—to me, anyway. She seemed protective of her brother, so I doubted very much she was helping Grayson Braddock sabotage him . . . *Or was she? Could Eden have a motive to double-cross her brother? How forthcoming would she be if directly questioned?*

I cleared my throat to find out: "I take it Eric's had some problems with his past . . . infatuations?"

"My brother's a genius in some things, but not all things."

"'All things' being women?" *Bianca Hyde came to mind, but I thought it best not to mention her—yet.*

"It's understandable, my brother's naiveté, given what he went through growing up. While his peers were attending school, learning to drive, and going out on dates, Eric was stuck in hospitals and rehab facilities."

"It must have been difficult for him."

"His computer was his only friend. I guess it paid off, but Eric can be gullible where women are concerned."

"Where is Eric, anyway?"

"He flew back to the Silicon Valley offices. Eric was away so long he has to play catch-up."

"Oh, too bad." *Okay, I was fibbing.* I was incredibly relieved Eric wasn't going to be here. I wanted to question his people without the boss hovering. (I also hoped someone here could figure out how to *unblock* Mike Quinn's calls on my THORN phone!)

"I didn't know this was going to be a theme party," I said, still studying Eden. "I do love the décor."

"We're rolling out a sword and sorcery game app in June, so we decided that should be the theme. Just be thankful it isn't *Pigeon Droppings*."

Oh, Lord, what a thought. "My Italian grandmother thought bird droppings were lucky," I confessed, "but I'd hate for anyone to wonder if that dollop of white in their espresso macchiato was something other than steamed milk."

We both had a laugh.

"Pardon me, Milady."

The youth interrupting us was tall enough to be a center on the Knicks basketball team. Lean and gangly, he self-consciously swiped at straight black bangs, then tugged at an oversized black tee with *Slayer* spelled out in fiery letters.

"It's party time, boss. Everyone's waiting for the hostess."

"Tell them I'll be right there, Darren."

"Yes, Milady." Darren bowed deeply before departing. "Your wish is my command."

" 'Milady,' huh? That's an interesting title."

"I know, it's a little childish. Darren's the one who gave it to me. He has a romantic streak—and he's obsessed with sword and sorcery games." She shrugged. "You have to admit, it's more impressive than 'Senior Projects Manager.' And 'House Mother' just sounds pathetic."

"Hear ye! Hear ye! Let's party!" an amplified voice proclaimed.

"That's my cue, Ms. Cosi. I'd better go."

"Can we speak again after the party?" I asked "I may need help with a project."

"Of course, Ms. Cosi," Eden replied. "Anything I can do to help."

"Please, call me Clare."

"Only if you call me Eden—*and* give me first dibs on those freshly made Italian donuts on your menu."

I watched Eden go, realizing that Eric had been right about one thing: I did find her likeable.

Fifty-six

〜〜〜〜〜〜〜〜〜〜〜〜〜〜〜〜

The castle's courtyard was convincingly medieval, with a faux-stone floor and a "keep" where our food and drinks were served, buffet style.

Everything else was right out of downtown Tokyo.

High-definition computer monitors had been mounted along the foam castle walls, displaying big-screen versions of the game apps developed by THORN, Inc.

Pigeon Droppings was represented, side by side with its 2.0 and 3.0 upgrades. *Plague Me* was another gross-out game ("Cure patient zero before you catch the plague"); *Spaghetti Bender* and *Bear Trap* were strategy games ("Smarter than wildlife, or are you *game*?").

I was more comfortable with the foodie apps. *App-itite* in all of its international permutations, and *U R What U Eat* were both impressive. *Count Calorie* also conveyed vast amounts of useful information, though I certainly wasn't the demographic for a calorie-counting app with a vampire mascot and the tagline *This Doesn't Suck*.

I did very much like the Jackson Pollock–sized wall canvas

for finger painting—with light. Using just their digits, staffers were able to create doodles and drawings on the wall via a projection device the size of a clock radio. Like many of Thorner's apps and devices, *Handpainted* was voice activated. All the painter had to do was request the color he or she wanted.

Meanwhile in the center of the courtyard, Eric's staff had activated something they called a Spectrum Digitizer. The device, about the size of a small refrigerator, projected holographic sculptures all around it. And when two young men called up the *Dojo* program, I knew I was witnessing the future of gaming and entertainment.

In a burst of floating color, a full-sized 3-D ninja materialized and crouched down in a fighting stance, waiting for action. The two human players began battling the holographic ninja, leaping, ducking, punching, and kicking at the warrior of light, while a mechanical voice kept score using words like *Strike! Dodge! Wound! Miss!*

At the side of the courtyard, a line of standing consoles displayed other inventions. One held a full-sized holographic computer keyboard—a projection in midair meant to serve as an accessory to Eric's advanced THORN phones. As I tested it, sensors picked up the movements of air molecules around my fingers, deciphering and processing each keystroke.

I was air typing a test text message to Esther when I noticed a pair of lurkers intensely watching me. In their twenties, they looked so much alike they had to be brothers—or sisters. With oversized *Slayer* tees and matching unisex haircuts, it was tough to determine gender. A quick Adam's apple check revealed they were likely a brother and sister. They whispered to each other and disappeared.

My skin prickled, and I listened more closely to the conversations around me.

This was supposed to be a party, yet the tech staff seemed stressed about their projects. The event sounded less like a fun get-together and more like a group debate in the basement of a college computer lab.

"Look at that! The image *still* pixelates in the third quadrant!"

"Play testing revealed some issues."

"Issues? It's buggy!"

"The Go-Board rejected my design document. I hate educational games."

"So tweak the refresh rate—or adjust your meds!"

Over the arguments, I heard a familiar voice and spotted Garth Hendricks in the crowd.

The Metis Man had gone totally native for today's celebration—Native American. A buckskin jerkin encased his torso, and brown, leather pants covered his legs. His feet sported moccasin boots with Navajo designs, and his pierced ear displayed a tiny dangling dream catcher.

He was holding court with a cluster of teenagers—boys, mostly, but a few girls, too. With oohs and aahs, the group watched a series of videos showing amateur rockets launching from fields, backyards, school playgrounds, and parking lots.

When the Metis Man noticed me, he turned things over to Eden's intern, Darren the Giant.

"Who are those kids?" I asked.

"Our Junior Rocketeers," Garth proclaimed like a proud father. "Each one designed and built a rocket that's reached a thousand feet into the air and returned to Earth with its payload—a single egg—intact."

"That's impressive."

"Thank you. And I've heard impressive things about you—and your daughter. Paris was a great success. Eric was very pleased with your performance."

"Eric was the performer. I was just trying to help."

"Are you having fun helping us today?"

"I'm technically working, and so is everyone else, it seems. Eric's staff is clearly obsessed with their work."

"I take responsibility for that!" Garth beamed as he said it. "The real goal of management should be to make *meaning,* not money. Tasks should be presented as existential challenges to engage the employee's imagination."

"Oh?"

"People working toward a meaningful goal will not stop. THORN's technical staff puts in twelve-hour days, and they come in on weekends, too, because their only goal in life is to meet the challenge, solve the problem. *This* is the new workplace model!"

I considered the building we were standing in and thought about the workers in the toy factories of the previous century. They worked ridiculously long hours, too, but in those days it wasn't called "the new workplace model." It was called a sweatshop.

Hearing shouts of warning, I looked up to see a pair of young women sliding down a spiral chute through a rabbit hole in the ceiling. A few people scattered so they could land on their feet.

"Eric told me I'd see sliding boards here, but I thought it was a metaphor."

"When work is fun, we *want* to do it," Garth declared, "seven days a week, if we can . . ."

So it's a "fun" sweatshop.

"Eric's people do work hard, but we help them make it *feel* like play."

"I see . . ." *No time for a personal life, but that's okay, you have a sliding board.*

Putting Metis Man's philosophies aside, I began to wonder which one of these hard workers would benefit most if Eric were out of the picture. And if he *were* out of the picture, then who could do Eric's job? The Metis Man? Garth Hendricks could lead a company, but he wasn't a programmer.

Eric's sister Eden shouldered leadership responsibilities, but they were organizational. Did she have the technical knowledge to effectively steer a digital company?

At a dead end, I simply asked Garth. His reply . . .

"Minnow could do it. She's Eric in distaff."

"Minnow?"

"Wilhelmina Tork. She's close to Eric, one of the original founders of the company. And Minnow already heads the Game Development Division, which was Thorner's old job. Now that he's a corporate officer, Eric can't do everything, so before we moved East, he promoted Ms. Tork."

I scanned the crowd. "Where can I find Minnow?"

"In her office on the tenth floor."

"She's not attending the party?"

"Minnow is not a party person." He lowered his voice. "A high IQ combined with anger issues."

"I have a barista with a mild case of the same, but I love her dearly."

The Metis Man nodded approvingly. "Understanding goes a long way in this world. Understanding inspires tolerance, and an open mind is a creative mind."

Applause interrupted him. "I'd better get back to my kids."

"First, could you point the way to the elevators?" I asked. "Or should I just climb the sliding board?"

Fifty-seven

꩜꩜꩜꩜꩜꩜꩜꩜꩜꩜꩜꩜꩜꩜꩜꩜꩜꩜꩜꩜꩜꩜꩜

The elevator opened and once again I came face-to-face with the Unisex Twins.

The pair perked up when they saw me. "Oh, hi!" they chirped in (yes) unison.

"Hello."

They exited the elevator, flanking me the way my cats do when they're hungry. Two pairs of big, brown eyes gazed at me expectantly. I eased past them, into the elevator.

"Bye," I said.

"See you later!" they peeped, waving to me as the elevator closed.

Okay, that was creepy.

I turned my attention to the layout of the tenth floor, a huge open space filled with natural light. Crossing the restored old planks, I passed a dozen workstations with state-of-the-art computers. The only "office" on this floor was more of a large cubicle, situated in a corner beside the massive window.

As I approached, I heard the tapping of keys. The view

overlooking Madison Square Park was spectacular, but the woman behind the desk only had eyes for the data dancing across four huge LED screens.

I knocked on the partition.

She whirled in her chair and appeared startled at the sight of me. Slowly she slid her chunky, black glasses down. Her blue violet eyes were as vibrant as Madame's and they were staring 3-D daggers at me.

"What do you want?"

"Sorry. I'm looking for Wilhelmina Tork?"

"Minnow."

"Yes, I'm looking for Minnow."

She sighed with annoyance. "My *name* is Minnow."

"Hello," I said, stepping inside. "I'm Clare—"

"I know who you are."

Uninvited, I sat down. "Then you know I'm a friend of Eric's."

Her frown deepened and her eyes dropped to a desk littered with little toys and figurines. I recognized Jack Skellington from *The Nightmare Before Christmas,* and an array of resin dragons, but the rest of the characters (Anime? Comic book? Video game?) eluded me—with one exception. I recognized a plastic *Alice in Wonderland,* dressed in iconic Disney garb, but there was no White Rabbit, no Cheshire Cat, and *this* Alice grinned like a psychopath and clutched a bloody knife.

"Garth tells me you were with Eric's company from the beginning. I also heard you've been promoted."

She looked up then, and I realized that hidden behind the heavy, black eyewear, Minnow was striking. With a triangular face and delicate features, her pale, flawless skin made for a stunning contrast to her raven black hair—a tangled, frizzy riot that could have doubled as a wig for Gilda Radner's Roseanne Roseannadanna (an ancient, cultural reference for Minnow's generation—although they *could* Google it).

Frowning, Minnow reached for a bone gray disposable cup

from Driftwood Coffee and smugly waved my competitor's logo in front of me like it was Kryptonite and I was Superman (at last, a reference both our generations would get).

Taking a long gulp, she drained the contents.

"You could get a refill at the party," I suggested. "We're serving an Almond Joy Latte with homemade Coconut-Chocolate-Almond Syrup. There's a Reese's Cup Latte, too; we make it with our own Chocolate–Peanut Butter Nutella. And if you prefer dairy-free—"

"I only drink lattes from Driftwood Coffee," she sniffed.

"How about something to relax you?" *(You look like you can use it.)* "I can pour you a very pretty Cloudy Dream or how about a Hazelnut Orgasm?"

"What are they?"

"Pousse-cafés—delicious layered drinks with tasty liqueurs, the kind usually served with after-dinner coffee."

She actually look tempted for a moment but then shook her head and tugged at the hem of her baggy tee. "I'm very busy, Clare. Could you please get down to business?"

"I understand THORN, Inc., is rolling out a new game in June—"

"At E3."

"ET?"

"E-*Three*, Clare. The Electronic Entertainment Expo. It's the annual industry showcase where new digital games and devices are introduced."

"And your THORN app is going head-to-head with Grayson Braddock's rollout of a similar game, right?"

Minnow smiled. "Kind of."

I blinked. "Could you please elaborate?"

She shrugged. "Two years ago, Eric picked up an advanced reading copy of *Dragon Whisperer* at Book Expo. As soon as he read it, he knew the novel would be hot. Eric's a genius about things like that."

Wow, a first. Minnow had briefly shed her disdainful tone when she spoke about Eric.

"I know the book," I said. Practically overnight, *Dragon Whisperer* had made dragons more popular than sexy vampires, walking zombies, comic book superheroes, and boy-wonder wizards.

"Yes, but there was a massive problem. Grayson Braddock controlled the licensing for *Dragon Whisperer* through his publishing division. Eric had us develop the game before he secured the rights to the dragons, characters, and storylines. He was sure Braddock would be thrilled with our prototype and instantly grant our request for rights. But when the idea was presented to Braddock, the Aussie shut us down."

From what I knew already, the conclusion seemed clear. "After Braddock saw what you developed, he decided he could create a game on his own, and keep all the profits?"

Minnow nodded. "But he can't. Braddock doesn't have the platform to launch an app game; he's never done it before."

"What if he hired Donny Chu?"

"Donny has the skill to build a game, but sell it?" Minnow shook her head. "You need a genius like Eric for that."

There's that word again. Minnow was clearly impressed with her boss.

"We have *Pigeon Droppings*," Minnow continued. "Which means we own a chunk of the market already, and we can use that popular and established game to launch a new one. You see? Get it now?"

"Yes. And I assume, because Braddock wouldn't sell Eric the gaming rights, Eric changed *Dragon Whisperer* to *Slayer*, and used generic dragons and heroes to get around Braddock's copyright?"

"That's right," Minnow replied—this time with a tad less attitude. "We're going to beat Braddock, too. I think even he knows it. Better yet, my teams are creating residual and satellite apps using the same designs, the same programs. A *Slayer Training Manual* app. A *Field Guide to Dragons* app. We'll be selling add-ons and extras before Braddock even gets his lame-o *Dragon Whisperer* app off the ground. Before you know it, Eric will have the movie rights sold to *our* dragon characters—"

The phone on Minnow's desk rattled. Instead of lifting the receiver, she punched a button. "This is Minnow."

"Garth here," a disembodied voice said. "Is Clare Cosi with you?"

"Yes, unfortunately."

"Clare," Garth continued, "the Junior Rocketeers are setting up for your demonstration."

"I'll be right down."

"Oh, Minnow," Garth added. "I just wanted to tell you the light sculpture program on the Spectrum Digitizer is beautiful. You should come down and see it."

"I've seen enough of it! I installed the Digitizer myself and fine-tuned the program all night. The ninja ain't beautiful, Garth. He's still too herky-jerky."

I rose. "I'd like to speak with you again, Minnow, if that's possible."

The girl swung her chair away from me.

"Sure," she said, facing her four computer monitors. "But next time, make an appointment."

Fifty-eight

∿∿∿∿∿∿∿∿∿∿∿∿∿∿∿∿

WAITING for the busy elevators took several minutes, but I absolutely refused to ride the sliding board to the second floor. When I finally arrived, the setup for my Italian donut demonstration was well under way.

The scent of hot oil from the portable deep fryer filled the second-floor gallery, attracting an eager crowd.

"Hey, boss, glad you're here," Esther said, handing me an apron. "Casey and Sunshine would like a word with you."

"Did you just say K.C. and Sunshine?"

"Our parents' favorite band," Casey said.

Esther gestured to the Unisex Twins, who gaped at me with wide grins.

"Hello again," they warbled.

"Hello back," I said.

"We were wondering if you could come here tomorrow, Ms. Cosi?" Casey asked.

"Early," Sunshine added. "Very early, before anyone else comes in. That way—"

"The office is empty," Casey said, jumping in. "We could grab a conference room before the other teams get in—"

"And really get a head start on our work," Sunshine finished with a giggle.

"Our work? Our work on what?" I asked, my skin prickling again.

The pair glanced at each other, then at me. They seemed unsure how to answer.

"Boss?" Esther tapped an imaginary wristwatch. "It's time."

"Look," I told Casey and Sunshine, "I'll talk to you after the demonstration, and you can tell me all about this 'work' that we're supposed to do together, okay?"

"Great!" Casey cheeped, smiling again. "Can't wait—"

"To talk later—"

"Byeee."

"Listening to those two is like watching a tennis tournament." Esther rubbed her neck. "I think I got whiplash."

I slipped behind the fryer and checked the temperature with a candy thermometer. "Where's the dough?"

"Tuck went to the refrigerator to get it."

The oil was the perfect temperature. Beside the portable fryer, a metal table had been set up to hold the dough, the frying net, the powdered sugar, and plenty of paper serving plates.

While we waited for Tuck, I ran the talk through my head. I'd start by mentioning the many culinary cultures that enjoy fried dough sweetened with powdered sugar, honey, or glazes—Croatia's *krofne*, for example, or Germany's Berliner. The Italians traditionally make a heavy filled donut called a zeppole, but my nonna's recipe box provided me with a unique treat—a sweet version of a savory fried dough, which more closely resembled the hot, fresh beignets of New Orleans's French Quarter.

"Here I come," Tuck cried, parting the crowd.

He carried a covered tray laden with yeasted dough.

"I hope the dough didn't get warm," I said.

"It's chilled, CC," Tuck replied. "Cold enough to give me freezer burn."

"Let me take that before you drop it, Broadway Boy," Esther said, snatching the tray.

As Tuck moved closer, his right leg touched the metal table leg. The bright, white yellow explosion shocked us all. Sparks flew and an impossibly loud crackle ripped the air. Repelled by the electric charge, Tuck flew backward, sailing ten feet before he crashed to the ground. One of the wide-screen monitors fell over and shorted out, creating more sparks.

People screamed and backed off, but some rushed forward to help. I was there first.

"Tucker!" I screamed.

"Don't touch the table, it's electrified," I heard Metis Man warn.

Crumpled on the floor, my barista looked like a broken toy. The fallen LED monitor crackled beside him.

I smelled smoke over the stench of ozone, and realized Tuck's pant leg was smoldering. I ripped off my apron and smothered the blaze, afraid to use water in case there were more live wires around.

Esther joined me, tears streaming down her cheeks. "Come on, Tuck," she whispered as we turned him on his back.

"Talk to me," I begged.

But Tucker Burton wasn't moving—and he wasn't breathing.

Fifty-nine

~~~~~~

Esther and I spent three harrowing hours at the Beth Israel Medical Center waiting room without hearing a word about Tucker's condition.

In the minutes after the accident, Garth Hendricks and I performed CPR. Miracle of miracles, Tuck responded. His eyes fluttered and he seemed to be breathing by the time the paramedics loaded him into the ambulance.

Esther and I followed in a cab. We reached out to Punch, Tuck's significant other. Now the compact, muscular man sobbed on Esther's shoulders, praying for Tuck in English and Spanish.

I was about ready to smash through the glass partition and take a nurse hostage when someone called my name.

It was Dr. Hosseni, an East Indian man with a thick mustache and a confident demeanor. He didn't wait to deliver the good news.

"Mr. Burton will be fine."

"Oh thank you God! *Madre de Dios*!" Punch cried.

"Ditto," Esther said.

"He was very lucky it was his leg that touched the electrified table," the doctor explained. "The charge ran from his calf to his foot. Had Mr. Burton touched that cart with his hands, the charge would have run up his arms and into his heart, stopping it. Your friend was very nearly electrocuted."

"When can we see him, Doctor?" I asked.

"Now is fine. You may go through that door, and the nurse will guide you to Mr. Burton."

Esther, Punch, and I followed the woman to Tucker's bedside. Frankly, I expected the worst: intravenous tubes sticking out of every arm, an oxygen mask, beeping medical devices, and a near-comatose Tucker.

Instead my assistant manager was wide awake and sitting up! He greeted us with a big grin and open arms.

Punch leapt onto the bed and clung to Tuck. When they finally broke their embrace it was Esther's and my turn for hugs. Tuck reassured us that he felt fine and expected to be discharged in the morning.

"Some minor burns, and I twisted my leg. But none of that matters. I'm just happy to be alive."

Tuck showed Punch the bandages on his calf.

"*Madre de Dios!*" his partner cried.

"Relax," Tuck said, patting Punch's hand. "I've had worse things happen on stage. When I was in an all-male version of *Macbeth* at the East Hampton's Summer Stock Theater, a spear carrier set me on fire!"

The relief I felt was mixed with anger. "I don't care what you say, Tuck. This is serious!"

"Don't get your voltage up, CC, I'm fine."

"Only because of dumb luck. You touched that cart with your leg. But if you had touched it with your hands, you would have been killed. Someone is responsible for putting you here—and I'm going to find out who!"

* * *

AFTER leaving Tuck's hospital room, I went right back to THORN, Inc. As I approached Eden Thorner's office, she motioned me forward, holding a wireless phone to her ear.

When her brother had converted this old toy factory, he'd removed a section of the roof so the top-floor executives would have natural light. But on this winter evening, the light was gone early, the moonless sky above sooty gray. Now the room's only illumination came from unnatural light—computer terminals, workstation lamps, blinking gadgets.

Tuck's near-death experience had set me on edge; the eerie lighting only made it worse.

Eden directed me to a chair and sank into her own. After ending her call, she rubbed tired eyes and met mine.

"I had to beg OSHA not to shut our office down for six months while they conduct a federal inspection for workplace safety. Fortunately I know the director. We shot wolves together in Wyoming."

"You shot wolves!"

"With tranquilizer guns. We were *tagging* the wolves, Clare. Putting Eric's GPS chips on them helps the Wyoming Wildlife Preservation Society track migration patterns—"

Oh, that's right. Eric had mentioned something about Eden tagging wolves. But he hadn't mentioned his *GPS chips*—and that's when I knew: The Metis Man had found me and Joy in Montmartre, seemingly by magic. But it wasn't magic. Eric's GPS chips were installed in his THORN phones; I was sure of it, which meant he could track anyone with his phones, practically anywhere.

"Anyway," Eden continued. "I assume Dr. Hosseni gave you the good news."

"You know Dr. Hosseni?"

"He's my personal physician. I wanted your barista to have the very best care. The doctor tells me Mr. Burton will be up and around in a day or two."

"I'm very glad about that. Tuck's more than an employee; he's my best friend."

"Well, your best friend is about to receive a *very* generous compensation check, unless he wants to sue us—in which case all bets are off."

"I doubt Tuck will sue anyone. He's just happy to be alive." I leaned forward in my chair. "So how did this happen?"

"A freak accident. The power cable to the Spectrum Digitizer, if you know what that is?"

"The holographic projector . . ." *The device Minnow told Garth she worked on all night.*

"The high-voltage wire to the projector was frayed, defective," Eden explained. "Somehow it made contact with the metal table." *The table I was supposed to work from during my demonstration!*

"You saw the result, Clare."

Yes, someone I love almost died in my place. "I need a favor, Eden. It concerns Charley Polaski—"

"The private investigator?"

I blinked in surprise. "You knew the truth about Charley?"

"Of course. Charley came to me early on. She was investigating the death of Bianca Hyde, and she asked me to do a meta-search of our database to find any files referencing the actress."

"What did you find?"

"Not me." Eden shook her head. "That's not my function here. I asked my intern to do the work, Darren Engle."

"Is he here?"

"Sure." Eden used the phone to summon the giant.

Darren arrived in under a minute.

"Darren, do you remember the search you did for Charley Polaski?"

His head bobbed. "Sure. I copied and stored the results."

"Call them up on my terminal. You know the password."

Darren sat behind Eden's desk and worked the keyboard.

A huge LED screen sprang to life. It took Darren just seconds to retrieve the files.

"Yeah, I remember," Darren said. "There was one huge file called *Witch/Bitch* filled with nothing but pictures of Bianca Hyde. Tabloid photos, scans from entertainment magazines, stuff like that."

The photos began to appear in a slideshow format. They kept on rolling by the whole time we spoke.

"This looks wrong," Eden whispered. "Like something a stalker might do."

"Who collected these images?" I asked.

Darren faced me. "The data was stored in Wilhelmina Tork's computer, Ms. Cosi."

Minnow? "Why would she have these files?"

"No authorized reason," Eden said. "However . . ."

"Go on."

"Well, the truth is that Minnow has had a serious crush on Eric for years, ever since college. It's totally unrequited on Eric's part. He knows about it, and he's very kind to her, but he's told me privately that he can't see her as more than a platonic friend—"

"Wait," I cried. "Go back to that last photo and freeze it."

Darren tapped keys. The image showed Bianca Hyde in a pink, string bikini, arm in arm with another starlet. What interested me about the picture was the background. The photo was taken in front of a yacht christened *Made in the Shade.*

"That's Grayson Braddock's yacht!"

It was Eden's turn to be shocked. She looked closer at the photo. "Oh my God. What is this?! Is it just a coincidence? Or was Bianca spying on Eric for Braddock?"

Darren checked the date stamp and told us the photo was taken about six months before Bianca met Eric. I asked Darren to print a copy for me. When he left the room to retrieve it, I turned to Eden and lowered my voice.

"Did you know that Charley Polaski was working with her

ex-husband, Joe? Apparently she was sending him important notes."

Eden did a double take. "I didn't know. How do you know?"

"Joe Polaski paid me a couple of visits. Unfortunately, the police think Joe may be involved in the bombing so he went underground."

When Darren came back, I thanked him for the photo and stuffed it in my bag. "Quick favor," I added. "Can you unblock someone on my THORN phone?"

Darren and Eden exchanged glances.

"Didn't you ask Miss Phone to unblock?" Darren asked. "It should be very simple."

"On this particular issue, Miss Phone has become Miss Attitude."

"That's weird," said Darren. "I wonder why."

Ask the billionaire genius, I thought.

"Give me your phone and the numbers you want unblocked, and I'll program the fix via computer interface."

"Thanks," I said, and handed everything over.

A few minutes later, I was good to go, THORN phone back in hand, incriminating photo in my bag.

"One last thing," I said. "Is Minnow in the building now?"

Eden rose and called up the security log. "Yes, she is."

I rose. "Then I'm out of here."

As I crossed the hall, I ran through various scenarios in my mind. One thing I did know. I had to reel this little fish in, and by the time I'd pressed the elevator button I had a plan.

Now all you have to do is get out of Appland alive . . .

It's a funny feeling to be waiting for an elevator in a building with someone who may want you dead. My hairs prickled as I watched the digital numbers count up the floors. Suddenly a hand gripped my shoulder!

I screamed.

"Sorry, Ms. Cosi, we didn't—"

"Mean to scare you."

Oh, good heavens. It's just Casey and Sunshine.

I took a breath. "What is it you two want?"

"To show you our barista app. Eric told us to work with you—"

"Yes," Sunshine continued. "He sent us a memo. It's a really cool app. Eric told us—"

"That you know how to make so many drinks you can really add to the archives—"

"So, do you want to see it now?" asked a grinning Sunshine.

"We're happy to give you a demo," Casey added. "Come with us . . ."

The elevator arrived and I jumped inside, eager to escape this "fun" house.

"Later!" I called as the doors shut.

Right now I have a Minnow to catch . . .

Sixty

~~~~~~

For the first time in her life, Esther Best was dressed for success—and it made her thoroughly miserable. In the bedroom of my duplex above the Village Blend, Esther stared at her reflection in my full-length mirror and shuddered.

"Do I have to go out in public like this?!"

"If you want to catch the person who nearly fried Tuck, *yes*," I said.

"I look so normal I could be my sister!" Esther cried.

In the pinstriped suit and button-down blouse, she looked ready to officiate a will or manage a hedge fund. In truth, she was going undercover.

"Don't forget the shoes!" Tucker waved the patent leather pumps. "Heels define the woman. Four inches is optimum in business settings. Any taller and you're a showgirl. Any shorter and you've got the 'mommy look.' You don't want to look frumpy."

"Call me frumpy again and you'll see stars!"

Tuck winked. "As long as Channing Tatum is one of them."

Esther frowned at her hair—what she could see of it,

anyway. The flamboyant half beehive had been tamed down and tied back into a neat little bun with a gray, velvet scrunchy.

Nancy stepped up. "I should preserve this moment." Before Esther could duck, she snapped a phone picture.

Esther glared. "Post that on Facebook and I'll break your thumbs."

"What's the matter? Don't you need a professional photo for the next Barista Latte Pouring Competition?"

"In this outfit? I look like an espresso idiot! Delete it!"

"No."

"Then say good-bye to working thumbs." Now Esther turned to Tuck and pointed at her shoes. "I can't walk in these, Broadway Boy! I need my Keds."

"Stop whining," Tuck said, covering his ears, "or I'll forward Nancy's photo to your Boris."

"Enough!" I clapped my hands. Two days had passed since Tucker's near-fatal mishap, and my floppy-haired barista was still pallid and walking with a slight limp. I was out of patience. It was time to nail the person responsible. "Okay, kiddies, the cab's waiting downstairs for Esther and me. Everyone else, back to work!"

On the cab ride over to Chelsea, I reviewed my plan to tap on Minnow's aquarium and see where the little fish swam.

I knew from yesterday's surveillance that Wilhelmina Tork took her morning lattes at Driftwood Coffee and hung out at a table for about an hour before reporting for duty at Appland.

Today, a disguised Esther would be waiting for her.

While Esther observed, I would phone Minnow with alarming news. If the girl hung up and followed her normal routine, then Minnow was likely guilt-free. But if Minnow panicked and took off to meet with her accomplice (Joe Polaski's "they"), then Esther would follow, keeping in touch with me by smartphone until we hooked up.

It was a desperate plan, but with luck I would either learn

the identity of Minnow's accomplice, or eliminate the girl from the suspect list.

I waited in Madison Square Park for Esther's call. It came on schedule.

"The Minnow has landed," she reported.

"Time for my call," I replied. I placed Esther on hold and rang Minnow (it was nice of Eric to provide the directory to his entire organization in my THORN phone). She answered on the first ring.

"What?"

"Minnow? This is Clare Cosi."

"I *know*. Never heard of *caller ID*? What do you want?"

"To give you a heads-up. Lieutenant DeFasio of the Bomb Squad thinks you were involved in the death of Charley Polaski—"

"Are you mental?" Minnow cried.

"The police have evidence, and it looks convincing—"

"What evidence?!"

"Got to go," I said, ending the call.

I quickly took Esther off hold. "Well?"

"Oh God," Esther said in a whisper.

"What's happening?! Did Minnow spot you?"

"No, it's this awful Driftwood espresso. The crema is like dish soap. And you should see what passes for latte art. The oak leaf on their maple latte looks like poison ivy—"

"Focus, Esther, you're undercover!"

"Sorry, boss . . . Yes, Minnow is acting somewhat frantic. She's holding the phone. She's sending a text . . . She's checking her screen . . . Nothing yet . . . Wait! Looks like she got a reply, and now she's flying—like a bat out of Brooklyn."

"Stay close to Minnow and stay on the line," I commanded.

Esther sighed in relief. "Anything to avoid drinking this swill."

Fifteen minutes later, Minnow climbed the stairs of the

20th Street entrance to the High Line, an elevated freight train bridge over Manhattan's West Side that had been transformed into New York City's most unique public park. The High Line ran from 14th Street and the Meatpacking District, right up to 30th Street, to end just four avenue blocks away from Penn Station.

"Where are you, boss?" Esther asked.

"Just down the street. I can see the High Line's concrete pillars."

A blast of January cold buffeted me and I missed Esther's reply. "Say again?"

"This is bad, boss, in so many ways."

"What's the problem?"

"First, these heels are killing me. Who wears shoes like this, masochists?"

"Esther!"

"Second, this section of the High Line is very narrow and practically deserted. There are no bushes or trees, and nothing to hide behind. If I follow her, then try to loiter until she meets her secret friend, Minnow is going to spot me a block away—literally."

"Is she walking uptown, or downtown?"

"Down."

"Maybe we caught a break," I said. "Dante moved into that high-rise building near the Meatpacking District, right? Do you think he has a view of the High Line?"

"I wouldn't know," Esther huffed. "The jerk hasn't invited me over yet."

"Let's go find out."

DANTE Silva was my nighttime barista and my late-shift superstar rolled up in one charming, tattooed ball. He could pull a killer espresso, and his cool, laid-back artist persona, coupled with his warm smiles, drew lots of coeds from NYU and Parsons School for Design.

He followed in a distinguished tradition of the Village Blend's struggling artists: barista by night, painter by day—although that was usually *midday*. Dante was plenty peeved when we rousted him out of bed before noon, then dragged him up to his building's frozen rooftop.

"Best I can do," Dante said, blowing into his hands to warm them. "I don't have a view of the High Line from my apartment, or much of anything, so I come up here to the roof when I want to paint."

It was even windier up here than it was on the street, and railings were nonexistent. Thankfully no one had a fear of heights.

Dante led us across the silver-painted tar to the very edge of the building. Unsteady on her heels, Esther stumbled once and nearly brought down some resident's satellite dish.

The view was spectacular, but the High Line was a half block away, so Dante handed Esther his Nikon SLR camera with a giant telephoto lens, and kept a pair of opera glasses for himself. He gave me the big guns, a pair of German-made binoculars his grandfather "got in the war."

"Told you this was a great spot. You can see blocks of the High Line from up here," Dante said.

"I can practically read lips, too," I replied as I gazed through the powerful lenses.

"That's nothing," said Esther. "With this lens, I can see molecules!"

The High Line was practically deserted, and for a tense minute I thought Minnow had slipped the net. Then I spied her, huddling on a bench overlooking 16th Street. She was near the stairs to the street, but no accomplice was in sight.

Esther and Dante homed in on her, too. Together we watched and waited.

"Someone's coming up the stairs," I said, followed by an "Oh, Lord."

In a vintage Cossack coat and Russian fur hat, the Metis

Man was easy to spot. I watched Minnow wave Garth Hendricks over, and the Metis Man sat down beside her.

"Where did he get that outfit, Nicholas and Alexandra's Pre-Revolutionary Czarist Boutique?" ragged Esther.

"Isn't that on Fifth Avenue between Tiffany and Fen?" Dante asked.

"He looks like he just stepped out of *Anna Karenina,*" Esther cracked.

"Nah," said Dante. "More like *War and Peace.*"

Down below us, Garth and Minnow were arguing. Minnow rose to leave, but Garth pulled her back down for a finger-wagging lecture. Soon they were practically shouting. Though I was too far away to hear, I could guess what was happening: the bad guys were having a falling-out.

"Actually," I said, "this whole mess is starting to look more like *Crime and Punishment.*"

Sixty-one

~~~~~~

THAT night, I sat on the edge of my bed, considering my next step.

How can I break this news to Eric? How can I tell him that two of the people he trusts most in the world are murderers?

To me, it made perfect sense. The Metis Man was head of the Junior Rocketeers. If he could teach kids how to build rockets, he was perfectly capable of constructing the bomb that killed Charley.

But why?

That's what Eric would ask, and I had an answer.

Minnow was in love with Eric and insanely jealous over his affair with Bianca—that's why she kept those digital images of the actress in the *Witch/Bitch* folder. She must have killed Bianca in a fit of jealousy.

The LAPD had reviewed hotel surveillance tapes. But they had been looking for Eric and other past boyfriends of Bianca. If Minnow had disguised herself enough, she could have gotten away clean. And it appeared she did—until Charley started investigating.

At some point Minnow had sought out Garth, the company's Big Brother, and confessed to the crime. Then Garth found out about Charley's private investigation (on behalf of Bianca's family), and he became the Fixer and eliminated the problem along with the PI.

It made absolute sense; but it was still only a theory. How was I going to prove it?

I didn't know. Not yet. But Eric had to hear it anyway, and I had to tell him, face-to-face.

That meant I had to get Eric over to the Village Blend on some phony pretext—and it had better be a good one, too. Or he'd get the wrong idea about our "romantic prospects."

None of the coffee Matt sourced had arrived yet, so inviting him for a tasting of his Billionaire Blend was out of the question.

I *could* bake up something special and invite him over for a taste. But Matt's "Lovin' from the oven" phrase warned me away from that ploy, too.

Then I saw Nate Sumner's book, lying on the dresser. He'd handed it to me before he was arrested, making me promise to give it to Eric.

Perfect! I'll tell Eric about the book and ask him to stop over and pick it up.

As I reached into my bag for my THORN phone, I picked up the book and checked to see if Nate had autographed it.

Spilling the purse, I jumped to my feet.

There was no signature, but Nate had left a message. He'd scribbled an e-mail address inside the front cover—for the missing Joe Polaski, Charley's ex-husband! Under it, Nate had scrawled that now-familiar stanza—

"Roses white and red are best."

The poetic words were the same ones Nate had blurted out when the Feds arrested him. At the time, I thought he was merely reacting to the blue roses that I'd placed on the table. But now I knew Nate meant it as a warning, just as Mike had: *Stay away from Eric Thorner!*

In my heart, I didn't believe Eric was a murderer. But . . . what if Eric *already knew* about Minnow and his Metis Man? What if Eric was protecting Minnow because of her value to the company?

Could Metis Man have cleaned up the mess and played the Fixer with Eric's consent?

It was a real tangle, but Joe Polaski was my Occam's Razor.

He claimed he could provide the information I needed to cut to the truth—information his ex-wife had uncovered while she was *under*cover as Eric's driver—and finally I had a way to reach him.

I retrieved the THORN phone from the debris on the floor. While Java and Frothy played "mouse" with my lipstick tube, I composed an e-mail and sent it off.

Fifteen mouse-chasing minutes later, I received a reply.

Meet U on High Line @ 1:00 AM. Will leave maintenance gate on S side of 18 St. unlocked. Come alone. JP

The High Line again. Where I had just seen Minnow conspiring with Metis Man.

Come alone, huh? We'll see about that.

I had the cab drop Matt and me off in front of the Fulton Houses, a block and a half away from the High Line. I figured we could sneak up on anyone who might be waiting there to ambush us. Matt was dubious.

He also groused about the cold. "My blood is thin, Clare. I've just spent weeks in the tropics."

"So have I, thanks to you, and you don't hear me complaining," I shot back, suppressing a shiver.

"Well, I am glad I'm here. The last thing I want you to do is meet this nut alone."

"He did tell me to come alone, and he might bolt when he sees you."

"He might," Matt conceded, "but where can he go? The High Line is closed and locked tight. Once we're up there, the only way out is through the unlocked gate where we came in, so if we block it, he's stuck."

I considered Matt's reasoning, and took it to its logical extreme.

"Joe might be thinking the same thing, only he's figuring to block the exit so we're the ones who are stuck."

Matt's response was to stop dead in his tracks.

"What? Don't tell me you're checking out!"

"I'm not," Matt said, pointing. "But somebody else did."

On the street under the High Line, I saw police cars and uniforms. They surrounded a covered figure sprawled in the middle of the street. We tried to get closer but the cops stopped us at their crime scene perimeter.

"You can't go any farther. There's an accident investigation."

"What happened?" Matt asked.

"Some guy fell off the High Line."

More uniformed officers lingered nearby. One of them was Sergeant Emmanuel Franco, Joy's boyfriend (at least I hoped he still was).

Franco was about to approach when he noticed I was with Matt and stopped dead.

The two men shared an unhappy history, and now was not the time to relive it, so while Matt grilled the cops, I flashed Franco a finger phone and silently lip-synced "Call me!"

"Let's go," Matt said a moment later. "The cops won't tell me a thing, but I have a very bad feeling the corpse under that blanket is your pal Joe Polaski."

I shivered again, but not from the cold. I had the same bad feeling.

Sixty-two

∽∽∽∽∽∽∽∽∽∽∽∽∽∽∽∽∽∽

Instead of calling me, Franco arrived on my doorstep after his shift ended. He'd shed his uniform in favor of distressed jeans and a muscle-hugging sweater. I hung up his jacket.

"I hope I didn't wake you," he said.

I shook my head. "I couldn't sleep if I wanted to. I needed to talk to a cop tonight, and you fit the bill."

"You could have called Mike."

"That's another subject entirely." *A thorny subject.*

Mike and I had been missing each other for weeks. My world coffee tour; his Justice Department conference (with a *female* boss); missed messages, misunderstandings. We had a lot of ground to make up—at least I hoped and prayed we could. Clearly, one of us had to get on a train, and it wasn't going to be me. Not tonight, anyway.

"*You* were at the crime scene, Franco. What can you tell me?"

"About the face diver on 19th Street?"

"Yes, what was his name?"

"Joseph Polaski, age fifty-seven. He was wanted for questioning—"

"For the car bombing in front of this coffeehouse?"

"That's right. How did you know?"

"Did the investigating officers find anything on the body? Papers? A computer flash drive?"

"They found a wallet, a couple of credit cards, and twenty bucks."

"Do you really think he took a 'face dive' or did somebody push him?"

"Pending toxicology or a suicide note, my guess would be the latter. It's tough to kill yourself by hopping over the High Line's rail. A three-story fall is no guarantee of success. Joe managed to land on his head, and what a mess. You should have seen—"

"Stop. I don't want to have nightmares." I chewed my lower lip. "Look, I want to tell you a story, Manny. A long story. Should I make coffee?"

"Oh, yeah. I miss your coffee. And could I have some of those Crunchy Almond Biscotti, maybe?"

"Of course."

"And a few of those glazed Pumpkin Muffins? And maybe a French Apple Cake Square while you're at it?" He shrugged. "I missed my donut break."

OVER coffee and a plate of pastries, I told Franco everything that happened to me since Eric's car blew up. He listened without once interrupting, letting it all come out in a tumble of free association. When I finished, I took a breath.

"So what's your opinion?"

"Well, I'm kind of prejudiced, seeing as Mike Quinn is my old boss, but—and it's a Jennifer Lopez–sized 'butt'—this rich guy Eric Thorner sounds extremely hinky."

"Hinky."

"It's clear Eric is a player, a master manipulator. Sociopaths are like that."

I considered the charge, but . . . "Eric doesn't seem like a sociopath to me. If anything, he feels too much, becomes infatuated too quickly. He needs a mother's love."

"So does Norman Bates."

"Look, if Eric is guilty of murder, why is he paying for lawyers to defend Nate Sumner? Nate was framed for the car bombing. The crime appeared to be solved with a nice, neat bow—"

"Not so neat if Joe Polaski had evidence to the contrary. Hiring lawyers for Nate, a beloved figure in the city, makes Eric *appear* innocent, doesn't it? So there's public goodwill toward Eric. At the same time, he gains the confidence of Nate and is able to pump him for information about Joe—a liability that needed to be eliminated."

"And tonight he was, that much is clear. Joe is dead, and I feel terrible—and responsible. Joe was supposed to meet me on the High Line. I lured him out of hiding."

"Aw, don't go blaming yourself, Coffee Lady. He's the one who came looking for you. Twice. Whoever chucked Joe over the side is to blame. Not you."

"Yes, but *who* exactly chucked him over the side? Do the detectives have any leads?"

"They're reviewing security camera footage, but whatever happened on the High Line is going to stay a mystery. The cameras go off when the park closes." He paused and met my eyes. "You're still in business with this guy, Eric, right?"

"Right."

"If you can find hard evidence, Clare—anything incriminating about Thorner or his people—you be sure to let me know, okay?"

"I wish I could find something, other than theories." Despite three cups of my Wake Up the Night blend, I yawned.

"I'd better go," Franco said, rising.

He put on his jacket, but paused at the door. "Hey, by the way, thanks for talking to your daughter."

"She called you?"

"Oh, yeah. Joy and I had a *long* chat, nearly all night long . . ."

"About what?"

"About *everything*," he said, and the smile of love on his face told me (nearly) everything I needed to know. "I'm sure she'll text you about the details. See you around, Coffee Lady."

Sixty-three

~~~~~~~~~~~~~~~~~~~~~~~~~~~~~~~~~~~~

I was groggy and sticky-eyed when my alarm clock sounded. All night, I'd tossed and turned, heartsick over the ugly truth—Eric Thorner was very likely an accessory to murder, and I had been his dupe, inadvertently leading him to the one man who could prove it.

Reluctantly I rose and fed my hungry beasts. Then I settled my furry girls on their favorite window stoop, dressed, and headed downstairs to help open the shop.

Tuck had arrived before me and was already filling the pastry case with our bakery delivery.

"Good moooorn-ing," he warbled, still on a survival high from his near-death experience.

"Need coffee," I moaned.

Tuck sat me on a stool at the counter and pulled me a double.

"It's so bright and cheerful today!" he chirped, unlocking the front door. "I just know something marvelous is going to happen."

I muttered into my cup.

"Oh, my goodness! Something marvelous is happening right now. A limo just pulled up to the curb!"

Oh, God, not Eric. Not now!

I was still getting used to the idea that Thorner was a criminal, but I hadn't worked out how to prove it. Not yet!

Fortunately, our first customer of the day wasn't the Boy Billionaire from Silicon Valley—it was that Big Billionaire from Down Under, the one who'd confronted me at the Source Club.

"Hello there, darlin'. Charming place."

Pausing in our doorway, Grayson Braddock struck an impressive pose. His hand-tooled leather duster was custom cut to his huge shoulders. With a confident flourish, he removed a pair of designer sunglasses, loosened his cashmere scarf, and swept the wide-brimmed Outback hat off his shaved head. Then he swaggered across our wood-plank floor and took over the stool beside me like he owned it (or was about to).

I glanced at Tuck. He read my mind. *For this, I'm going to need a triple.*

"You're up early," I said as Tucker began the pull on our new Slayer.

"Naw, darlin', I *just* got back from Sydney. It's about dinnertime there."

"I see. Well, what would you like, Mr. Braddock?"

"*You*, darlin', can call me Gray." He flashed a toothy grin.

"Only if you drop that *darlin'* stuff and call me Clare."

"Deal—and you choose for me, Clare, you're the coffee expert."

I had Tuck pull a *doppio* for Braddock, as well. He served us both, along with a plate of warm Blueberry Blondies.

Braddock sipped the espresso.

"Oh, my," he said. Then he blinked, as if startled, and I knew the amazing notes the Slayer was able to pull from Matt's beans—the bright citrus, spicy cinnamon, and earthy chocolate—were dancing on the man's tongue. "Crikey, that's damn tasty!"

"Glad you like it, but I presume you didn't rush here straight from the airport just for coffee."

Gray drained his demitasse and smiled down at me. "I'm here to extend an invitation. I'd like you to fly to Miami tomorrow and be my guest at the South Beach Wine and Food Festival."

"South Beach, Florida!" Tuck cried.

I shot Tuck a stern look. "I'm sorry, Gray, but—"

"Come on, Clare. Don't be a wet blankie. There's nothing wrong with mixing business and pleasure."

"What *business* do you and I have?"

Gray leaned close. "I have information for Eric Thorner—valuable, game-changing information that your little friend *needs* to hear."

"Why would you want to help Eric?"

"I didn't say I wanted to help the kid. I'm saying that Thorner needs this information to make an important decision. He and I have too much bad blood between us. He won't listen if it's coming from me, but I know he'll listen to you."

I took a long, hard look at Grayson Braddock. If he were truly guilty of murder or conspiracy to commit murder, it would have been *insane* for him to show up here with an invitation like that. A guilty man would have stayed put in Australia—at least until the investigations were over. Still, the idea of having to "be his guest" to hear some kind of secret information reeked of an ulterior motive.

"Why don't you tell me now?" I challenged.

"The truth?"

"Please."

"This is an old-fashioned horse trade, Clare. My good buddy Chef Harvey asked me to invite you. He's still embarrassed about that Ambrosia incident at the Source Club; he's eager to repair his reputation with you, and, well . . . I'd like to have your company, too. Give it to me, and I'll give you the information."

"What *sort* of information is this? Give me a hint, at least."

"Let's just say that something serious is happening inside Eric's company and he needs to know about it for his own good—and the good of his company."

That gave me pause. Braddock talked like he knew what I knew. Was it possible he had proof of Minnow and the Metis Man's conspiracy?

"Honestly, Clare, I'm not peddling a load of codswallop. You can trust me. Bring a chaperone if you like, bring two or three, bring a whole party!"

"I'll come, I'll come!" Tuck cried, literally jumping up and down. "Oh, my God, South Beach! Can I bring my boyfriend?"

"Sure, the more, the merrier!" Gray proclaimed. "I'll have my secretary send over tickets. You'll fly first class, stay in my hotel. Say yes and you'll be in sunny Miami by noon tomorrow."

Tuck implored me with his eyes. "It sounds *marvelous*, CC, please, please, *pleeeease?*"

"I'll consider it. *No promises.* First I have a phone call to make."

"Good enough, Clare. Here's my card—call that number and the plane tickets will be waiting for you. Hope to see you ladies under the palm trees!"

B RADDOCK was hardly out the door before I hit the speed dial for Matt.

"How would you like to go to South Beach?"

"With you? Tempting, but I can't, Clare. I'm meeting with coffee brokers today, and then Eric and I are flying to Brazil."

"Brazil? Why? It's not harvest season, is it?"

"It's a good time to grab coffee cuttings. We're going to Terra Perfeita to snatch a few Ambrosia plants."

"Is that wise? The Brazilian government locked down that plantation with the DEA because of its connection to drug dealing. Aren't you going after forbidden fruit, so to speak?"

"Don't worry, I have a plan."

I groaned inwardly. In Matt-speak "don't worry" and "I have a plan" were red flags.

"Eric wants to cultivate Ambrosia on the island of Costa Gravas," Matt explained. "The kid learns fast. It's a brilliant idea. Far more lucrative than blue roses. He might end up growing the finest single-origin coffee in the world, if he stays in it for the long haul."

The world deserved another chance to experience Ambrosia. But the world might not get it if Eric Thorner was involved.

"Listen, Matt, I have something to tell you."

Without dropping Franco's name, I recounted my conversation with the young officer. By the end of the discussion, I'd so convinced myself that Eric was involved in murder that I tried to dissuade Matt from making the trip to South America with him. When I'd finished my pitch, I waited for Matt's "I told you so" lecture.

It never came.

"You're off track," Matt said. "Way off track. I've spent time with Eric, and so have you. He's not a killer and we both know it."

"Have *you* been blinded by dollar signs?"

"What's that supposed to mean?"

"It means we've switched positions. Now that I think Eric's hinky, *you* think he's swell."

"I don't think he's a murderer, that's all. And speaking of murder, tell me more about this information Grayson Braddock promised you, and why you have to go to Florida to get it."

"Grayson called it an 'old-fashioned horse trade.' My company for his intelligence, which is ridiculous. Braddock's surrounded by a flock of willing women. Why me?"

"You really don't understand men, do you Clare? It's obvious—to me anyway. Braddock and Thorner are in competition—for *everything*. Braddock wants you because Eric had you—"

"How many times do I have to tell you! Eric Thorner and I never—"

"I know that! But Braddock doesn't."

I groaned—outwardly this time.

"You're a big girl, Clare. You can handle Braddock—"

"You actually *want* me to go to South Beach?"

"As long as Tuck and Punch are your chaperones, you'll be okay. Just stay close to them and find out what Braddock knows. I'll keep an eye on Eric, and one of us is sure to find out something."

"I'm not convinced."

"Then think about this: Joe Polaski died last night because he had information about Eric. Six hours later, Braddock shows up on our door claiming he has information about Eric."

"Now you're saying Braddock killed Joe Polaski and grabbed his evidence?"

"More likely someone working for him did the dirty work . . ."

I closed my eyes, defeated. "You're right, Matt. I have to go."

There was no more debating. If Grayson Braddock had gained possession of Joe's evidence, I had to go to South Beach and find out—and learn exactly *what* that evidence was. Otherwise Joe Polaski died for nothing.

SIXTY-FOUR

〜〜〜〜〜〜〜〜〜〜〜〜〜〜〜〜〜〜〜〜

GRAYSON Braddock was as good as his word (so far, anyway). Tuck, Punch, and I flew out of the New York cold and into Florida's tropical sun. By noon the next day we were standing on the sidewalk in front of Miami International Airport.

Braddock had a car waiting to meet us so we could avoid the crush at the taxi stand.

"So this is how the other half lives," Tuck purred as he settled into the air-conditioned passenger compartment.

"The other half?" Punch said. "More like the other one percent."

"Dial back *El Revolución*, Fidel Castro," Tuck replied. "It's our lifestyle now! Well, for the rest of the weekend, anyway."

As the limousine took off for South Beach, we passed the poor unfortunates forced to jockey for a taxi. My eyes went wide when I spied a familiar face in the crowd.

"Is that Minnow?"

"The little fish you were trying to catch?" Tuck craned his

neck, but it was too late. Minnow—if it was Minnow—was already out of sight.

ADJOINING suites had been reserved for us at the Ocean Meridian, a pretty, pastel pink jewel in Grayson Braddock's chain of tropical luxury hotels.

We'd just checked in when I spotted Braddock in the hotel bar. In golf togs, another pair of designer sunglasses on his head, and a cold beer in hand, he held noisy court with a group of middle-aged men dressed for eighteen holes.

I sent Tucker upstairs with my luggage and headed to the retro ocean-themed bar, where I immediately confronted Braddock beside a neon-lit aquarium where lovely mermaids and strapping mermen gracefully swam.

"Okay, I'm here," I said, ignoring the living wallpaper. "When are you and I going to talk?"

"Crikey, darlin', you just arrived! You're in Florida now, not Manhattan. Ease up on the throttle." He paused and leaned close. "Get yourself comfortable, Clare, and I'll pick you up in an hour. We'll visit Chef Harvey at the festival. On the way, we'll talk."

OF course, we didn't talk. Not about Eric. Not about anything. He insisted there were too many amazing things we simply *couldn't miss* eating and drinking under the Wine and Food Festival's massive circus tent.

His eyes were masked by yet another pair of sunglasses. These looked space-age, something akin to Google Glass, and he hid behind them, taking a series of eyewear phone calls as he plied me with gourmet samples prepared especially for the VIP foodies in attendance.

Tasmanian Shrimp Glazed with Ginger and Garlic; Mini Croque Monsieur with Smoked Salmon and Caviar; Pan-Seared *Wagyu* Steak on Rosemary Ciabatta; Roasted Lobster and Gruyère

Croquettes; Pancetta-Wrapped Smoked Cherries; and Sea Scallops with Seaweed Butter—a dish as fresh and tangy as the salty ocean breezes—all accompanied by sample-sized portions of delectably dry, sweet, fruity, and buttery red and white wines.

When we finally found Chef Harvey, he hurried out from behind his booth to greet us.

"Clare Cosi, how good of you to come," he said, pumping my hand. "You must try my take on America's obsession with 'surf and turf.' Mine features *yuzu*-braised lamb and tarragon prawns."

When I emerged from my food trance, Chef Harvey invited me to a party held in his honor aboard Grayson Braddock's yacht, *Made in the Shade*. I was wary, but he absolutely insisted I come.

"Can I bring my friends?" I asked, pointing out Punch and Tuck.

"Of course, but make sure you bring yourself!" Chef Harvey replied.

"What happened to Braddock?" I asked Tuck a moment later. "He disappeared on us."

Punch and Tuck scanned the tent.

"I don't see him," Punch said. "And Braddock is hard to miss with those space-age shades."

Tuck agreed. "Did you notice? He's worn a different pair every time we've seen him. I wonder how many shades he has?"

Punch and Tuck exchanged glances. Knowing Gray Braddock's womanizing ways, the pair blurted out the same answer: "Fifty!"

"Wait here," I told my chortling chaperones. "I'll see if I can locate Gray, the billionaire with fifty shades." They burst out laughing again; I rolled my eyes. "I'll come back for you."

After negotiating the large crowd, I finally reached the exit. Blinking against the sun, I wished I'd remembered to pack my own shades!

As my vision cleared, one of the people-moving carts breezed past me. In the back row, between a pair of Bermuda shorts—clad retirees, I saw Wilhelmina Tork in jeans and a shapeless tee.

"Minnow!" I yelled.

If she heard me, the girl didn't react, and the cart went by too fast for me to chase it down.

What is Minnow doing in South Beach? I wondered. *She sure didn't strike me as a foodie. Does she have business with Braddock? Is she part of the mystery Gray used to lure me down here?*

Before I jumped to too many wrong conclusions, I had to make certain I'd actually seen Minnow, and not some look-alike. Fortunately, I knew who to ask.

BACK in the privacy of my hotel suite, I placed a call to Eric's sister, Eden Thorner.

"I need your help," I said. "Do you know where Wilhelmina Tork is?"

"She's working at home today, sick with a winter flu."

"Well, I'm in South Beach, and I need to know if Minnow is down here, too."

"What would she be doing in—"

"Look, Eden, I know your THORN phones have GPS tracking chips in them. You're a company officer. If you have access to the tracking, *please* check to see if Minnow's phone is in Florida!"

"All right, Clare, calm down. I'll call up the tracking." A minute passed. "No, Clare. The GPS chip in Minnow's phone shows that she's right here in New York. Darren Engle lives in the same building. He feeds her fish when she's in California so he has an extra key to her place. I can have him check on her if you like."

"That's a relief, thanks," I said. But it wasn't entirely. *Am I that paranoid?* I was either going crazy or the stress of this case was truly getting to me.

"Clare, what's going on?"

"I can't explain now. I'll tell you all about it when I get back. You'll just have to trust me, okay?"

I hung up before Eden had a chance to turn Quiz Master.

I was suddenly exhausted. *It couldn't have anything to do with the wine I'd consumed, right?*

The yacht party started at eight this evening, still a few hours away, so I decided to take a nap. Getting into bed, I heard the muffled voices of Tuck and Punch laughing and talking in the adjacent suite.

I wanted Mike, but he was far away now, in so many ways.

Eyes welling up, I reached for my THORN phone and sent him a text, just three words—

I MISS YOU.

I waited. And waited. But nothing came back, and I drifted off, letting the big, feather pillow catch my tears.

Sixty-Five

~~~~~~~~~~~~~~~~~~~~~~~~~~~~~~~~~~~~~~~

"CLARE, this is your programmed alert. You have received a text message from Michael Quinn. Clare, this is your programmed alert . . ."

I yawned, blinked, and reached for the phone to shut off the uber-annoying fembot voice. Finally, I saw the screen.

MISS YOU 2.

"Oh, Mike . . ."

I wanted to write back, tell him where I was and why, but I was already running late.

Within the hour, I was showered and dressed and went looking for Tuck and Punch, but they weren't in their suite. Down in the lobby, the chauffeur from the airport approached me.

"Have you seen my two friends?" I asked him.

"Mr. Burton and Mr. Santiago have already left for the party, Ms. Cosi. Shall we go?"

It was such a short drive to Gray's yacht that I could have walked. As I crossed the gangplank, I realized two things: the party was already in full swing, and I was overdressed.

Lights blazed and music blared aboard the 150-foot mega-yacht. And the sundeck on top was crowded with men in beachwear and sweet young things in string bikinis and platform flip-flops.

In my tasteful sundress and wedged sandals, I might as well have worn a nun's habit.

Oh, Lord. What kind of party is this?

When Chef Harvey invited me, I assumed I was attending an elegant function with food industry professionals. The loud music, half-dressed girls, and half-drunk "dudes" had me ready to turn around then and there, but Grayson spotted me and called out from the deck. In a polo shirt and shorts, he waved me forward with one hand (a cocktail occupied the other).

Well, Clare, you came this far, I thought. *There are plenty of people around. And you do still have two chaperones, speaking of which—*

"Where are my friends?" I asked the moment I stepped aboard.

"Dunno," Grayson replied. "Probably in the salon with Chef Harvey. That's where you'll find the bundy and champers."

"Excuse me?"

"The booze, darlin'!" He grinned. "You Yanks need to learn the King's English."

When I first encountered Gray at the hotel bar, he was drinking beer. At the festival, he'd switched to wine. Now he thrust his glass under my nose; I smelled juniper berries and tonic water.

I considered the billionaire's inebriated condition and concluded it might actually *help* my cause. In vino veritas, and Gray had already had plenty of vino.

"Want me to skull it?" he asked, shaking the glass until the ice clinked.

"Sorry, I don't speak Aussie."

Grayson drained the glass, presumably to demonstrate a "skull."

"Ready to find your friends now?"

"Yes, please."

He took my arm. "Follow me."

We entered the big ship's interior, made a couple of turns, and walked down a short staircase.

More steps and more doors, and we arrived in a long, carpeted, empty corridor with cabins on either side. It was quiet down here. *Too quiet.* And we were completely alone.

"Where are we going? Where are Tuck and Punch?"

"Truth, Clare? Your friends are across town, at a big cosplay bash."

"What!"

"My assistant texted them earlier about the change in plans. They think you're there, too, in costume, but you're not—because I wanted us to have some privacy."

"This is *not* what I agreed to—"

"Ah, but it's what's you *wanted*, isn't it? You've been trying to get me alone 'to talk' since you got to South Beach."

He tugged my arm, but I dug in, refusing to go any farther with the man. "That's it, Gray. I'm out of patience. Tell me why I'm here, right now, or I'm leaving."

The deck lurched under my sandals, and I realized the ship was casting off—a nanosecond later I found myself fighting off a giant, bald, Australian octopus!

"I think you're awesome, girlie! Crazy wicked—"

"Stop it!"

"And that hard-to-get act's a corker. I've been waiting for this moment all day—"

"Get your drunken hands off me!"

Braddock released me all right, so he could tear off his polo shirt. "Time for a lesson in *Gray's Anatomy*!"

I took off down the corridor. Gray misunderstood my intentions.

"Lookin' for a private bedroom, darlin'? Try the door on your right."

What I wanted was an *exit*, so I opened the door on my *left*—and stopped cold.

The room was hung with red velvet curtains. A medieval stock loomed beside a whipping post complete with handcuffs, and mirrors lined the ceiling.

Holy cow! I slammed the door.

"Not your speed?" Gray called. "No worries, darlin'! Try a door on your right, *your right!*"

I lunged for a door on my *left*, and gasped again.

The décor was more mundane, but in the middle of a posh, leather couch I found Minnow locked in an embrace with an inebriated Donny Chu—the young programmer I saw having dinner with Braddock at the Source Club. Donny had worked for THORN, Inc., but was now helping Braddock launch his mobile gaming division.

I sputtered, staring.

This was the proof. Clear as day. Minnow was the traitor in Eric's organization.

She must have left her phone in New York to fool Eden and Eric and everyone!

Hearing the shirtless billionaire approach, I continued down the hall. There was some kind of commotion in Minnow's cabin, but I kept running.

I found a flight of steps and climbed them. A moment later, I burst onto an open lower deck, startling partygoers.

Made in the Shade was just getting under way. The yacht was about fifty yards from shore, and I knew all those hours swimming laps at the Y were about to pay off.

I kicked off my sandals and approached the ship's rail.

Minnow burst onto the deck a few seconds before Grayson, with Donny Chu close behind.

I climbed over the rail, took a deep breath, and dived. It was a big drop, but no higher than the diving board at the Y. I cut through the surface and came up again, blowing water.

"Girl overboard!" a woman yelled.

"Clare!" Minnow shouted.

Then I heard Donny Chu. "Minnow, where are you going? Don't do it!"

A body splashed into the water nearby. *It's Minnow,* I realized. *She's coming after me!*

The girl broke the surface right beside me. As I took off swimming, I heard Braddock's voice from the deck above—"Forget about Minnow, Donny. There are a lot more fish in the sea!"

I kicked my legs and pumped my arms, but it was no use. The spiteful girl was splashing after me, and she was getting closer!

Minnow killed Bianca Hyde and blew up Charley Polaski, I thought in terror. *And now she's going to drown me!*

Then everything went black.

Sixty-six

〜〜〜〜〜〜〜〜〜〜〜〜〜〜〜

I felt the tide lapping at my bare feet, and I opened my eyes.
I lay flat on my back on the beach, soaking wet, staring up at
Wilhelmina Tork silhouetted by a tropical moon.

I tried to speak but choked instead. Minnow removed her
hands so I could roll over and empty my stomach. At some
point during the retching, I realized Minnow had administered CPR.

"Did you just *save* my life?" I gasped between breaths

Minnow nodded. "I learned CPR in the Girl Scouts."

I propped myself on my elbows, my back sticky with sand.
"Me too."

She smiled at me, a genuine smile. "I'm glad you're okay,
Clare. You really freaked me out."

"So you didn't try to drown me?"

"Of course not! Some bikini bimbo on the top deck threw
you a life saver and it smacked your head. You were knocked
out cold, so I hauled your butt ashore."

"What were you doing aboard Braddock's yacht? Eden
thinks you're in New York."

Minnow hugged her knees and told me everything.

That scheme Esther and I had rigged to entrap her at Driftwood Coffee had spooked her enough to start looking into Charley's death herself. She'd asked the Metis Man to help her, but her request only angered him. Soon Minnow came to the same conclusion I did—Braddock had a mole in Eric's company.

To flush the traitor out, Minnow went undercover; she contacted Donny Chu and *pretended* she was ready to defect, to leave Eric's company for Braddock's.

While I waltzed around the Wine and Food Festival with Gray, Minnow had spent the day with Donny, and she managed to get the skinny on Braddock's mobile gaming division.

"They've got nothing!" Minnow declared. "Braddock realized early that there was no competing with THORN, Inc., so he switched tactics. Instead of trying to fight Eric, Braddock decided to buy Eric's company right out from under him—by poaching the talent."

I nodded, familiar with that scenario in my own business.

Minnow explained how Braddock figured he could have it all: hot properties to exploit through his publishing division, and the talent to make the games people would buy.

"Donny kept saying how I was the jewel in the crown and that Gray would pay me millions. Then he got drunk and got fresh. I tried to fight Donny off, but he was just too big. When you opened the door and distracted him, I got away."

"What about the *Witch/Bitch* file?" I asked. "Darren found hundreds of pictures of Bianca Hyde in your archives—"

"For *Enchantress,* a mobile app game Eric asked me to develop." Minnow shook her head. "That was back when *he* was enchanted with Bianca. When she died, Eric killed the game, too. Six months of work down the crapper."

We sat in silence for a bit. A couple of guys passed us, saw Minnow's slicked wet T-shirt, and wolf whistled.

"And the mole?"

"There is no mole, Clare."

But someone killed Charley, I thought, *and Bianca, too.*

Minnow said the Metis Man became angry when she asked for his help. *Could he be guilty?*

And then there was Anton.

Eric Thorner's manservant said he "would do anything" to protect his man. What about murder? First Bianca, then Charley.

Or maybe Eric had killed Bianca himself, and Anton stepped in, eliminating Charley to protect "his man."

I outlined those scenarios to Minnow.

"Eric's not a killer," she said firmly. "I know him, Clare. I love him—"

"You love him?"

Minnow lowered her eyes. "Since college," she whispered. "Since the day we met . . ."

"Have you ever told him?"

"Of course not. You've seen the kind of women he dates: starlets and models. They're beautiful and glamorous. When he looks at me, all Eric sees is the little tomboy friend he met when I was a freshman and he was a junior."

Minnow shook the sand from her hair. It was still wet, and she slicked it back. With her wild mop tamed, Wilhelmina Tork was stunning. Another wolf whistle confirmed that she had a body to match her face, one she always hid behind baggy, comfortable clothes.

"What do we do now?" Minnow asked.

"I'll give Eric a call. He has a plane. I'm sure he'll pick us up. Then you can tell him everything."

It was a good plan. When I reached Eric, he had just taken off. There was only one problem. He was on his way to São Paulo with Matt.

If we wanted to hitch a ride home, we'd have to go by way of Brazil.

Sixty-seven

～～～～～～～～～～～～～～～～～～～～

Once again, I was aboard Thorner's private jet.

Waking up after a full night of sleep, I left the Gulf-stream's master bedroom to find Minnow already up and huddled with Eric over coffee and muffins at a corner table. No doubt she was continuing to fill her boss in on Braddock's grand plan to undermine Eric's mobile gaming division.

Rather than interrupt, I poured morning coffee for myself and joined Matt. Like Eric, he'd spent the night in one of the plane's half-dozen giant recliner chairs.

"When are we landing?" I asked.

"São Paulo—Guarulhos International is only about an hour away now. Brazil, here we come."

"Great," I muttered. A four-day detour to South America certainly wasn't on my schedule. All I'd wanted was a ride back to my coffeehouse.

"What's eating you?"

"I should have hopped a commercial flight back to New York. I don't know why Eric insisted I join Minnow. She knows much more than I do. She was the one spying on

Braddock and Donny Chu. All I did was avoid an ugly lesson in *Gray's Anatomy*."

Matt shot me a look. "You know why Eric wanted you aboard: 'propinquity and intensity.' That's his philosophy on romance, isn't it? He still thinks if you spend enough time with him, you'll fall in love."

"Well, he's got to get over it."

Matt smirked. "I don't know, Clare, play your cards right and you could be the most famous cougar since Demi Moore."

"What if I don't want to play cards *or* be a cougar?"

"Consider your options before you try to survive on a flat-foot's salary."

"Let's not go there. I'll only get cranky."

"Don't you mean crank*ier*?"

"Give me a break. A mere eight hours ago, I was fending off an Australian octopus and nearly drowned after a beaning by a nearsighted beach bimbo."

"Sounds like *intensity* to me. Too bad for Thorner he wasn't there to save you instead of Minnow."

I glanced at wide-eyed Wilhelmina Tork—the only completely contented passenger aboard this aircraft. She was basking in Eric's undivided attention. It didn't matter what they were talking about, Minnow was just happy to be with the man she adored.

"It's a tragedy," I whispered. "Eric wants me, but I'm in love with Mike. Meanwhile Minnow is obsessed with Eric, and has been for years."

"Yeah, sure." Matt rolled his eyes. "It's a recipe for misery."

"Your tone is heartless."

"You expect me to shed tears over a boy billionaire's love life?"

"What about poor Minnow? Oh, Matt, she's the perfect girl for him, if only he could see it. She can be difficult on the surface, but down deep she's so brave and beautiful. She reminds me of our daughter. I *wish* there was something we could do."

Matt glanced at Minnow and fell silent for a minute. "You know what?"

"What?"

A devious little smile crossed his face. "Eric Thorner's not the only guy on this flying RV who can grant your wishes." He pulled out his smartphone. "Maybe we can do something . . ."

THAT afternoon, the four of us piled into a rented Land Rover and headed out of the city and into the Brazilian countryside. Our destination: Terra Perfeita, the notorious "forbidden" coffee plantation.

I admit, I was a little nervous as we pulled up to the farm's chained front gate. The plantation had been put on lockdown by the government for its recent role in assisting traffickers of *oxidado* (aka Brazilian crack)—and I wasn't sure how Matt planned to get us in.

After shutting off the engine (and the air conditioning), Matt warned me, Minnow, and Eric to *stay put* in the vehicle. He got out and approached two of the four police officers guarding the farm's entrance with fairly serious-looking automatic weapons. For a good fifteen minutes, Matt spoke to them (in fluent Brazilian Portuguese).

I rolled down my window. It was summer in this hemisphere, and the afternoon sun baked the dusty dirt road, but the cool breeze flowing down from the green hills brought relief, and a riot of fragrances. I closed my eyes, inhaling blossoming flowers and ripening pineapples, bananas, mangoes, and the exotic local jabuticaba.

"What are they talking about?" Eric whispered.

"I'm sure they're haggling over the price of admission," I said.

Minnow's eyes widened. "A bribe?"

I nodded. "They might be speaking Portuguese, but discussions of money are universal."

Matt was all smiles when he finally climbed back in the Land Rover. "We have the plantation to ourselves for the rest of the day."

"What did that big guard say to you?" Eric asked.

"He warned me about the drug gangs. They're still prowling the area."

"Drug gangs!" Minnow cried. "But this is the middle of nowhere!"

"Punks from São Paulo and Rio sometimes take over abandoned farms, where they set up *oxidado* labs," Matt told her. "The gangs go unchallenged because rural cops aren't equipped to deal with them."

The officers removed heavy chains from the front gate and motioned us through.

"Welcome to Terra Perfeita," Matt declared, "coffee's Garden of Eden . . ."

He glanced at me and I nodded. (I certainly hoped it would be.)

After bypassing the large plantation house, we headed into the coffee fields, clouds of dust rising in the Rover's wake.

"The best plots are up that hill." He pointed. "We can unpack our picnic then scout for plants. After lunch, we'll head back—"

Sudden gunshots exploded behind us, long bursts of automatic weapons fire followed by a flurry of individual shots.

Matt swerved off the dirt road, into a shallow valley. He drove along the bottom of a bumpy gulch until we reached a small stone building, where he cut the engine. In the distance, more shots rang out, followed by an explosion. Smoke filled the sky in the direction of the front gate and big, main house.

"Grab the food and blankets, get into that little stone building, and stay there!" Matt shouted. "I'll find out what's happening."

Matt disappeared into the thick brush as we emptied the Rover of its supplies and scrambled into the darkened hut. Huddled beside a rustic fieldstone hearth, we listened while the shooting continued.

"Maybe we should have brought our own security," Minnow moaned.

"You remember what Matt said at the hotel," I whispered. "Security would have made you a flashy target for kidnappers. Better we look like clueless American tourists than a billionaire and his entourage."

After another bout of yelling and gunfire, things got ominously quiet.

Minutes passed before Matt burst through the stone hut's wooden door. He was panting and his khaki vest was covered with blood.

"Oh, my God. You're shot!" I cried.

"No, no . . . this isn't my blood. I'm okay. But the two policemen I spoke with aren't. They're dead. The drug dealers have taken over the plantation's big, main house and they're blocking the road. We're not getting out of here in the Land Rover."

Minnow whimpered. Eric paled.

Matt reached into his pocket and held out a gun. "Take this, Eric. I pulled it off one of the dead officers."

"What the hell!" Eric cried but Matt thrust the weapon into his hand.

"I know this area and I can get us out of here alive," Matt promised. "You just have to do what I say."

Eric and Minnow nodded.

"Now listen carefully: I'll divert the gang away from this building and ditch the Rover. Then I'll double around on foot and slip past the roadblock. The hike to town will take me a couple of hours, but with luck I'll hitch a ride, and when I come back it will be with a SWAT team."

"What do we do in the meantime?" Eric asked, one arm around a now-sobbing Minnow.

"Stay put. This little farmhouse is boarded up and hidden. The gang is using the big, main house. They're not going to bother with this little hut—unless you make noise or show your faces. And *do not* use any phones or electronic devices. These drug gangs use scanners to keep tabs on the movement of police. If they see your signal, they will seek you out. Remember, kidnapping and extortion are big business down here."

Before Matt could leave, I jumped up and threw my arms around my ex. "You're not going alone, Matteo! You're the father of my daughter and I'm going with you! Better we die together than spend our lives apart."

I kissed Matt *hard*, and he kissed me back. When we broke the lip lock, I clung desperately to my ex. Eric appeared devastated.

"Sit tight," Matt said. "Wait it out till morning. You have a blanket, food, water, wine . . . you're all set."

As we turned to leave, Eric gripped Matt's arm. "I appreciate the risk you're taking to get us out of here safely. Thank you."

"I'll do everything I can," Matt vowed.

With that, my ex took my hand and we slipped through the door. A few moments later, we were in the Rover again, driving away from the farmhouse and toward the drug dealers.

"CARE for another drink, Matteo? Clare?"

The man asking was Jorge, the man in charge of the Brazilian police officers who were supposedly "killed" by drug dealers in the firefight.

Of course, nobody was killed.

What they were, however, was happily paid off (with a relatively small sum in U.S. dollars). For that "performance fee," the rest of Jorge's pals agreed to remain back at the plantation, shooting off guns every hour or so to make Eric and Minnow believe they were surrounded by deadly gangsters.

I yawned and stretched on my poolside lounge chair, smiling my thanks to Jorge. "No more alcohol or I'll pass out. I'm going for another dip; then I'll dress for the restaurant."

I was treading blue water when Matt appeared. He sat down on the edge of the pool. I swam up to him.

"How do you think they're doing?" I asked.

Matt shrugged. "We'll find out in the morning. Right now we have another problem. This little hotel is short on space. We'll have to share a room."

I slicked back my wet hair. "Nice try."

"I mean it, there's only one bed in this whole joint."

"Listen, Allegro, this cupid setup is for one couple, not two. If there's only one bed, then you take it. I'm fine on an inflatable pool raft."

My ex frowned, defeated. "Fine. You'll get your own room."

"Don't sulk, Matt, it'll give you wrinkles."

THE next morning we pulled up to the farm's little stone house and peeked through two loose boards in a front window. Minnow and Eric were under a blanket beside the hearth, wrapped in each other's arms.

"Nice job," I whispered in Matt's ear.

"Thanks, but I have to credit my mother for this one."

"Madame is a real player, I'll grant you that. But I didn't know you called her for advice."

"Didn't have to. I'm her son. I grew up with her sayings."

"What?" I cocked my head. "Love comes from 'propinquity with intensity'? She said that?"

"No." He smiled. "'Turn up the right heat at the right time and you can brew up almost anything.'"

Sixty-eight

∾∾∾∾∾∾∾∾∾∾∾∾∾∾∾∾∾∾∾

On the plane trip home that evening, Matt spoke excitedly to Eric about the Ambrosia cuttings he'd bagged from Terra Perfeita, but the billionaire was only half listening. It was clear he was more interested in refocusing his attention on his newly discovered passion—for Wilhelmina Tork.

The next morning, when the two emerged from the privacy of the bedroom area, I made fresh coffee.

"We should be back in New York in another hour," Matt declared, checking his watch.

"And back to work," Minnow added with a beaming grin for Eric. "I'd better check my in-box."

When Wilhelmina pulled her THORN, Inc., smartphone out of her backpack, I did a double take.

"Minnow, did you have that phone with you in Florida?" I asked.

"Of course."

"You didn't leave another phone in your Manhattan apartment?"

"This is my *only* phone," Minnow replied. "Thank goodness it's waterproof and shockproof, because I jumped off Braddock's yacht with it in my pocket!"

Waterproof! Shockproof!

Rocked by the double shocks, I fell into one of the plane's recliners.

My *first* shock: Eric's sister, Eden Thorner, was a liar!

When I'd called from Florida, Eden assured me Minnow was in New York. But why lie?

"Oh, my God!" Minnow cried.

"What?"

"It's Darren . . . Darren Engle. My alerts for THORN, Inc., sent me to the news story. They found his body in *my* apartment with his head bashed in. They say there was no forced entry. He was murdered by multiple blows to the head from *my* dragon slayer resin statue. *I'm* wanted for questioning!"

TWO hours later, we were back on the ground and Eric was driving Minnow straight to his lawyers' downtown offices.

The billionaire was bringing an army of high-priced suits to One Police Plaza to help untangle the web that had ensnared his brand-new beloved.

My goal was the same: to free Minnow of any charges and throw a net over the true guilty party. But I had no patience for untangling. I was going to cut straight through this mess, and I couldn't do that picking apart legal threads at police headquarters.

My destination was the West Village—and not my Village Blend, even though (regardless of the early hour), I really needed one of Matt's double espressotinis.

What I needed even more was face time with my favorite NYPD Bomb Squad commander, Dennis "the Menace" DeFasio.